TUNKASHILA

OTHER BOOKS BY GERALD HAUSMAN

Turtle Island Alphabet
Ghost Walk
The Gift of the Gila Monster
Turtle Dream
The Sun Horse

TUNKASHILA

*From the Birth of Turtle Island to the
Blood of Wounded Knee*

GERALD HAUSMAN

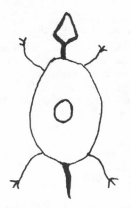

ST. MARTIN'S PRESS
NEW YORK

Design by Janet Tingey

Map: *Tribal Settings, 1600–1900*

Library of Congress Cataloging-in-Publication Data

Hausman, Gerald.
    Tunkashila : from the birth of Turtle Island to the
blood of Wounded Knee / Gerald Hausman.
        p.   cm.
    ISBN 0-312-09928-2
    1. Indians of North America—Religion and mythol-
ogy—Fiction. I. Title.
PS3558.A76T86   1993
813'.54—dc20   93-25936
                                                        CIP

For Robert Weil,
who asked for blue corn

Contents

PART TWO
MYTHS OF LOVE, LOSS, AND LEAVING

PART THREE
MYTHS OF POWER

PART FOUR
MYTHS OF WAR

PART FIVE
MYTHS OF TWO WORLDS

Acknowledgments

SPECIAL thanks to Laura Ware, Ricia Mainhardt, Roger Zelazny, Jay DeGroat, Mariah Fox, and Sid Hausman.

In addition, I would like to thank Lotus Light for permission to reprint "The Song of the River Mother" and "The Story of the Messenger," which have appeared previously in *The Sun Horse: Native Visions of the New World.*

A Sioux medicine man once stopped in a field of grass to talk to a stone. Addressing it reverently, he called it Tunkashila, *which means "grandfather." "Oh, Grandfather, tell me how the world began." And the stone spoke.*

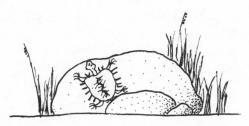

Author's Note

T U N K A S H I L A, as the epigraph suggests, is the history of the world as told by a stone. It has been said that the little bears resemblance to the large: microcosm, macrocosm, which is why, in this case, a simple stone, a chip off the shoulder of a mountain, should rightly tell the tale of the beginning, middle, and end of the world. In Native American mythology, this little stone harkens back, and bears witness to, the creation of the earth. It is, in this sense, a part of the stream of time; a part of the source of all things; a participant in the pageant of all life.

Yet our fabled stone is not the only one who speaks of the events of greatness here. We have in *Tunkashila* many narrators, each vying for the right to tell his or her part of the tale. These are the Holy People of creation, the first animals, the first two-leggeds. In the beginning, no distinction was made between the two: Men and animals were one. But, as time went on and life grew more complex, the two no longer merged but became distinct and separate. Their voices in *Tunkashila* retain the oral quality of the spoken tradition while also remaining true to the legend of their characters. It is fitting, then, that Owl, for instance, should speak in secret, muffled tones, woven from the shadows of the night, and that Deer should speak in leaps and bounds. Such metric considerations are a part of each narrator's personality and manner of speech.

Introduction
Tunkashila, the Grandfather Spirit

H E Siberian land bridge as the symbol of the Native American entrance into North America is shrouded in mystery and misunderstanding, for the bridge brought suffering rather than deliverance. What shrouds it as a symbol is our failure to comprehend its meaning. In the centuries that came after its crossing, we find a history marked with blood spoor. As the rocks and canyon walls attest in petroglyphic art, the first natives of North America stepped upon the earth not tentatively but gently. They walked, as the Navajos say, in beauty.

And their world was rhythmical rather than conceptual. Their art was neither private nor exclusive; it was an act of being, of living, of placing one's feet upon the earth in beauty. It was a simple ritual function, and whether seen as word, emblem, or deed, it had the unique virtue of seeming innocent, unburdened, clean, wholly personal, fully tribal.

In the Native American storytelling tradition, which is one of the finest and most intrinsic of tribal arts, it has often been said that all utterances are sacred. Speech is cyclic, flowing into and from a region of power that is transhuman but that is actualized on the human plane by the magic of words. The storyteller becomes his own listener, hearing not only his words but his mind listening, searching for the right expression or thought. A good storyteller hears with his heart as well as his ear.

We have come now to a time when many of us—Indian and non-Indian alike—would like to revive the sacred utterances of the human heart, to record and pass on the word, to nurture it, to cast a holy circle around it, so that the word might once again stand as the honorable spoken testimony of the life lived, the story told, the bond sealed.

Working with Native American texts, translating them, not literally but culturally, I have often wondered at the precise definition of the word *translator*. In Latin, it means "one who carries across," literally, one who bridges the gap in understanding, one who makes the figurative crossing ferryable. To translate *Tunkashila*, I listened to hundreds of stories from all parts of this country and went through myriad printed documents, speeches, and turn-of-the-century tales. Some of these, I carried in my mind for years, while others, read or heard only recently, have begged to be written down.

My mother collected certain of the stories in this book while traveling through the West during the 1930s. I still have her journals written in her elegant calligraphic hand. The most recent legends came to me through informal storytelling gatherings with Native American friends, primarily in the Southwest, where I have lived for the past twenty-some years.

There are nearly seventy tales (including the subtales: stories within stories) of this kind in *Tunkashila*, told by narrators of such varying tribes as Creek, Navajo, Tsimshian, Choctaw, Iroquois, Pascagoula, Lakota, Blackfeet, Tewa, Tiwa and Towa Pueblo, Hopi and Zuni, Apache, Crow, Roanoke, Chesapeake, Powahatan, and Seminole. The narrators of the stories are animals as often as deities and Earth Surface People. At one time, as many of my Native American friends have emphasized, there was no difference between such beings; they were all as one. They came out of the earth and sky together; they lived communally, not separately; they were the sharers of the first breath of life.

Over the years, I have begun to see a palpable similarity in the stories that I have been collecting. And it seems to me that the tales have begun to take on a singular voice, that of a universal conscience. *Tunkashila* is a book of beginnings, a book of changes, a song of myths made when the world was young. The tension of *Tunkashila* grows out of the human imagination as it seeks to define man's place in the ancient cosmogony. Here, then, is the ceremonial story of the earth, the natural mother of all earthly beings.

Tunkashila is a large drama in small parts. The scenes are built upon the *terra cognita* of Turtle Island. Hundreds of tribal myths are woven together, along with characters who are common to all tribes: the trickster, the chief, the warrior, the shaman, and the lover. The genealogy of the gods may differ, but the elements of which they are representative—earth, air, water, and fire—remain constant. How these forces commingle with mortal beings is the mythic story of humankind. Whether Greek, Roman, or American Indian, the personages of power operate under the same conciliatory relationship, with love, hate, and forgiveness as the guiding principles of their lives. The story of man is charged with blood fire and madness, but, in the end, it resides in harmony, the disparate forces propitiated through ceremonial song, dance, and prayer.

The mythic world of Native America has a supreme deity—Earth-Maker, Great Mystery—synonymous with the name God. Alongside him are First Man, First Woman, First Animal People, First Earth Surface People. Each American Indian tribe had, in some form, a legend of the Great Flood and a supernatural being who summoned the events of change. This is usually Old Man Coyote. As the builder of the canoe, the bringer of fire, the giver of tobacco, Old Man Coyote is the universal creator, destroyer, rebuilder. He is devil and messiah, and it is partly through him that we learn why the world is the way it is—a place of uncommon things, unequally measured and frequently misappropriated. Balance comes about, as the myths plaintively show, through divine intervention and through human interaction with the deities. Together, the two raise the world to a fourth level of existence, the plane upon which we now live. What, you may ask, is the matrix, the mortar that holds the disparate parts, the many raised voices of *Tunkashila*, together? The answer may be found in an Onondaga myth: "It is thought," the narrator says, "that all things on earth, which are here present, can change, or exchange, their bodies." And yet the essential life-forms of Native American mythology are elders, the grandfather spirits of each earthly entity; this is the concept embodied in the very word *tunkashila*. Thus every mountain has an elder mountain to which it refers; each stone may be said to have derived from an elder mountain's original presence.

As the Iroquois legend informs: "Winter is the Old Man of the Woods, who taps the trees with his war club on the coldest nights. Spring is the Young Man of the Woods, whose face is full of sun. Together these elders share two different worlds, yet there is reciprocity between them; they move reciprocally in and out of one another's presence, and they share the same earthly abode, the great woods."

It is the sense of sharing various godlike attributes that holds the many voices of *Tunkashila* together. Through them we understand, more painfully today than ever before, that the world is harder to keep than to make.

Tunkashila travels through the veils of mythical time as one narrator after another tells his or her version of the creation. The stories of origin come to an end, however, when the tales of war and enmity begin. These are the warrior myths: man against animal, man against woman, man against man, man against spirit, and man against monster. These are the apocryphal tales, which show that human understanding has utterly failed to grasp the consequences of warfare. As my Navajo friend Jay DeGroat once said, "The days of war and pillage for the Navajo were like the days of darkness for us; there was our tragic flaw. According to my father, there was a great chief who knew this, and warned; but he was not listened to by The People; and thus came our downfall as an independent nation. . . . " Many tribes, in retrospect, have said the same: Black Elk said it on his high hill of wisdom at the end of his life; Wovoka, foreseeing cataclysm and praying for the millennium, wished only for peace.

Tunkashila closes with the coming of the first white man, which changes forever the tribal life of Native America. Life ends tragically as the "ungreening" of the earth becomes a backdrop for the wars between the Native Americans and their white invaders. It happens that the old ways are praised in story and song just as the new ways have come to eradicate them. We see a whirling night of chaos emerging out of the blood tide of battle, and the people speak of how they have been abandoned by their own deities, very nearly extinguished, as a result.

The last tales weave together a series of turn-of-the-century myths: the appearance among the people of a messiah, a man with wounded palms, a Native American version of the story of Jesus Christ. There are also several versions of the "white brother/sister" tale, the legend that the Hopis call *Pahana*—two races, white and red, coming together as one, in peace.

The American Indian prophets, Sitting Bull, Wovoka, and Black Elk, appear in the final chapters of the book. What these divine messengers seem to be saying is that the world is one, if only we might see it that way; if only we might lay down our arms and learn again to be brothers and sisters. In the end, though they knew the old world order was fading, the people prayed to see the light of the millennium. In *The Prayer of Black Elk,* the prophet says: "Great Maker, pity us, your two-legged children, for we have suffered much, and will do so again. . . . I know in my heart that the heavens and all below them, earth and her creatures, all change, and we, part of creation's great hoop, must also suffer change. We are not bodies only, but like bird people, winged spirits, as well, able to travel, as I have many times, to the cloud world and beyond. . . . Give us your sacred sight, oh Grandfather."

Thus ends the dream of greatness, which Black Elk called "a beautiful dream." And so, too, ends the book of beginnings, the grandfathers of life turned to myth.

GERALD HAUSMAN
Tesuque, New Mexico

PART ONE

MYTHS OF CREATION

BOOK 1

The Creation

IN WHICH THE MAKER PUTS THE ROUND EARTH
IN THE CENTERING PLACE OF THE UNIVERSE

H A V E come to tell the story of changes, bodies and beings, mortal and immortal, who make up this world and to tell how the world itself came to be. I measure my words against those of the deities; I honor the earth, our mother; the sun, our father; their children; and all holy people that make up the world.

This song I sing is the story of creation, the tale of what happened from the world's beginning to our own days, the time that is now. Before the rutted trail that curved out of the north country from whence the people came on ice sleds long, long ago; before the deerskin legging, the silver concho, the turquoise stone. Before the long rows of male and female corn bending in the sun; the cowrie shell and the wampum belt; the mountain chant, the happiness chant, the night chant, the dawn chant. Before the two-legged people, the animal people, the insect people. When all creatures spoke the same way and words were not needed but voices were raised; before the syllables of song that told this story; back beyond memory, mind, and meaning.

Before the sea was, or earth or heaven, nature was all alike, a shapelessness, and this chaos, so called, stretched to the four quarters of the universe and was immeasurable: an emptiness so great that it was beyond the comprehension of any mortal being. However, they

5

say the Maker was one with the vastness of the universe; he was a part of it, as no mortal could ever or would ever wish to be.

So, what was there was abstract and without form: the emptiness, the whirling void, the thought of the Maker—nothing else. They say that from the Maker's thought and heart was created a lump of earth, which was brought out of his being, placed upon four strands of deerskin—from these thongs he drew from the pattern of things to come—and so he put the round earth in the centering place of the universe, the place wherein he, and he alone, might dwell.

That done, he considered what was and what was yet to be.

As yet, there was no sea reaching along a fringe of shore, nor balanced air that might be breathed; no sun, moon, stars, or heavenly bodies of any kind. There was only the earth, pinioned to the four corners of the universe by the deer-hide bonds of the Maker. But they say that this earth, though shapeless, was of fine conception and that the Maker drew out of himself the gray mist of beginnings, which he warmed with his breath until it caught fire. Then he blew upon it again, creating a vapor of flame that rose up into a fiery sheet that lapped the earth.

This was followed, they say, by a tumult of rain that collected in pools and made the great sea, the ocean, which formed a gathering place in the void, filled it, so that the earth now had something to embrace it, hold it in place. Then the Maker cut the deer-hide bonds, let the earth go free. He saw his creation hold firm yet float in the empty void.

There was now a contention of forces—heat and light against cold and dark; wet at war with dry; soft at odds with hard. And there came about the earth a whirling, an eddying of raw power, a tempest of damaging things. Clearly, the earth and the great sea were not at peace. So the Maker reached within himself once more and drew out the first sacred seeds: Holy People, a tribe of stars. These he placed in a cloud of his own warm mist breath and bid them not shine but merely glow until such time as they might come to know the earth, for they were the primal part of his design, the first breathing deities.

Then he placed three seeds in the great sea: Beaver, the builder; Turtle, the mother; Water Beetle, the swimmer. These were the first people: Two were guardians of water and earth; and one of water only. And as soon as they touched the water, they grew into themselves and knew the meaning of life.

Now the Maker, great though he is, did not take it upon himself to shape the world as if it were a clay pot upon which he would inscribe his own designs. No, the Maker, having thought the creation through, having coaxed it into being, warming it, seeding it, understood the need to withdraw from his creation so that things might happen of their own will, their own accord. Time passed, as it always will, and, as the Maker withdrew, his seeds—star people and water people, creatures of heaven and earth—came out of their dreamless dream and lived.

Time is the grass that grows out of eternity. And time's grass grew, and in the growing, a calm came over creation. The star people lived in this calm and took counsel from it. Thus, it was, in the grass-rooted calm, that a star person, a woman, whose duty it was to watch over the first sacred star tree planted in the Maker's mist, fell asleep, forgot the tree, let it die. And the chief of the star people, finding the star tree dead and the guardian asleep, tore the sacred tree out by the roots, making a great hole in the cloud cover that was the star people's earth. Through this first sacramental tear in creation's field, the star chief threw first the star tree, then the dreaming star tree's guardian, who, falling, came awake.

As she spun through the sky, dropping down to the great sea, Turtle, the water mother, looked up and saw her. Turtle quickly told Water Beetle what was happening, and Water Beetle went to the bottom of the sea, brought up mud in her hands, and patted it on Turtle's back. Beaver came along and helped, and soon the mud on Turtle's back grew into a pretty little island. And all the while, the star tree's guardian and the sacred tree fell through space, wheeling through the empty sky.

The island grew, becoming Turtle Island, the land we live on now. So when the star tree's guardian and her tree touched down upon it, she was saved from drowning. A branch of the sacred tree, though seemingly dead, came alive in the rich earth brought up from the bottom of the great sea; and now the star tree's guardian cared for it as if it were her own child. It grew, flowered, its roots penetrating deep into Turtle Island. And this, the people say, is how the world was born.

The Four Worlds

IN the beginning, there was a green age of goodness, a time cherished for its beauty, its free will. No law or punishment was called for: Fearfulness was unknown because our bright world was still unmade, unblessed. The beings of creation, while Holy People, were struggling in the darkness for the way, the ways, the manner in which to live in divine harmony with all of life. The first people were Coyote, the trickster; Turkey, the seed planter; Badger, the earth digger; Beaver, the builder; Turtle, the mother; Locust, the bow shooter; Wolf, the wanderer; Water Beetle, the swimmer; and Ant, the worker.

Now the first world was dark red. There was no sun, moon, or stars, and the people wandered with a blood-dark cloud hanging over their heads, bearing down on their thoughts. Eventually, though, they sought and found a hole in the eastern clouds, and so they traveled into the second world, which had a dark blue storm cloud hanging over the top of it. This cloud world flickered with crackling blue light. It was here that the people discovered they had feelings; but as they shuffled in the shadows under the writhing blue light, a dark mood came over them, a restlessness, which sent them to a hole in the clouds, this one off to the south.

Now the next cloud world was a smoky yellow, and through the rags of mustard-colored mist the people walked along fearfully, and a strange madness came over them. So the third world was blemished by mistrust and madness, and from this, Coyote, the trickster, made his bid for power by stealing Water Monster's babies and running

8

off with them. Coyote's theft caused Water Monster to unleash a flood.

Now the people migrated to the west, seeking higher ground. And so it was that they told Coyote to return Water Monster's babies, which he did, and this delivered the people to the fourth and final world. This fourth world was brighter and warmer than the earlier ones, and the people called it the Place of Dawning because the sky was as white as the dawn. However, there was no sunshine, as we know it, and the people were still struggling with their feelings, trying to find ways to express them. It was difficult and strange, and they were difficult and strange people.

Old Grandmother Ant led them to a crossing place, a spot where two rivers met in the middle, and here the people made their first camp. Yet a fight broke out among them. Old Grandmother Ant then advised the men and the women to make separate camps. But after a while, the women grew thin and their crops failed, and they were unable to find any game. They grew lonely for the men, who had plenty of game and good crops on the other side of the river. They yearned for them and so sought to please themselves in the loneliness of their lodges, using odd bits of bark, stone, and cactus. Soon after this, the women became pregnant; and that is how monsters, the first of their kind, were born into the world.

It would take too long to tell how widespread that evil was, and yet the story of evil incarnate, the tale of the wicked Shapeshifter, came about at that time. First Man saw him and tried to stop him, saying, "I create good with my right hand, evil with my left hand. I am filled with evil, yet there is a time to employ it, a time to withhold it. What thoughtless person would use evil for his own and not the people's gain?" This question has never been answered. But First Man did his best to tell the tale, as you shall see.

The Story of Shapeshifter

OF THE DARKNESS INHERENT IN THE ONE KNOWN AS
SHAPESHIFTER AND HOW FIRST MAN TURNS
EVIL INTO GOOD

IT was I, First Man, whom Shapeshifter resented the most, for I was the leader of the people, the one they looked up to. From the first, I saw his shifting ways, his need to alter his presence. You may ask what he looked like, and I would be hard-pressed to tell, for he changed shape as often as the air changes direction. One time, he looked like Wolf, the wanderer. Another time, he assumed the shape of Hawk, the wind walker. There was darkness where his face should have been, and his eyes were embered barbs of light that glittered on and off when he expressed anger. Often enough, I saw nothing of him, for he passed like smoke.

Once, I saw him come out of the pinewood, cross before our camp, where someone, an ant person, spoke roughly to him. There were many ant people sitting around the fire for warmth—red, yellow, brown, and black ant people. And he fell upon them in a reckless fury, rending heads from necks, shearing throats, cracking skulls, snapping limbs, scattering them like broken sticks.

And when I called to him, all I saw were his pointed ears vanishing in the night. He had a temper, that one. Then, when we came to the crossing place where the women and the men had set up separate camps, Shapeshifter, who had taken on the form of Coyote, his friend, slept with any woman he chose. Sometimes, Coyote joined him and together they would have the same woman, sharing her like a roast of meat.

You may ask why I—since I was the one responsible—did not

capture and banish him. Yet, I ask you this: How might you banish a shadow, a bit of fluff, a pinch of dust? He might, if he wished— and occasionally did—assume the shape of a man, but rarely. Usually, he had wolf ears, pointed red eyes, a long, dark mouth full of evil teeth.

He had sway over most of the people, and I was losing my power to him. The others were under threat of his rages, his insane attacks, and when they went to meet him, he was not there, for he had already changed into some new thing: a gust of wind, a beard of grass, a pebble of frost.

Then a giant was born of one of the women. It resembled the cactus she slept with at night, yet the thing grew huge in size. In fourteen days, it was larger than any tree: Cactus Giant, rumpled green, gnarled of face, hair of many-needled nastiness, feet of horn. And when he bled, if he bled, which was not often, blood the color of spit came out of his wound, poisonous to the touch. His deep-set eyes had no pupils; only white orbs buried in fatty layers of dark green corpselike skin.

Yet the first time I saw this violent thing uproot our camp and knew from whence it came, I thought of the one person who might overpower him, and who, in the turning of his will from evil to good, might yet prove to be our most valuable friend. I was thinking, of course, of Shapeshifter. So when Cactus Giant had gone to seek other ways of wreaking havoc, I consulted the isolate camp fire of Shapeshifter and found he had assumed the form of a dung beetle, sitting on a pile of petrified dung. When he saw I paid no attention to him, he changed into a pool of thickening blood, bubbling at my feet.

"Listen to me, Shapeshifter," I said, "I don't care what shape you are, so long as you listen to what I have to say."

He changed then into a large furred ear that dangled out in space, listening, I supposed.

"All right then," I began, "I've a favor to ask of you, and, perhaps, a truce to make. It's come to my attention that you and Coyote got out of hand because of something I did."

The furred ear changed abruptly into a fanged mouth with graying teeth. The hairy lips were smiling most agreeably.

"If my guess is correct, Coyote has brought evil upon us because he's displeased with the name I gave him. I will, therefore, change his name to First Angry. I've also given him the responsibility for childbirth and the bringing in of rain. Both of these things he likes very much, so he's promised to behave himself from now on. Now we come to you, Shapeshifter. You're no prankster, but you are a wielder of evil. Yet, in comparison to Cactus Giant, you're a person of virtue, a friend to all."

Suddenly, Shapeshifter altered his appearance: The grinning fangs melted on the night wind and the two-legged person he once was rose up before me. He was a middle-sized man with well-greased shoulder-length hair and a nicely formed body. He wore a deerskin breechclout, with nothing on his upper body.

I did not indicate to him that I detected any change in his appearance, but went on talking plainly, as before.

"My offer to you, Shapeshifter, is this: I want you to kill Cactus Giant and any other monsters that still roam the land. If you will do this, I'll make you Guardian of the Game, and it will be your job to watch the game animals upon which we now depend for our living."

I did not have to speak further, for the man he once was stood up and said, "Consider it done. I shall be known as Guardian of the Game!"

"You must kill Cactus Giant first," I reminded.

He said that he would, and he did try his best to subdue that unruly one. And because Cactus Giant could not see what attacked him seemingly from all directions at once, he ended up an ugly puddle of bubbling ooze, but Shapeshifter could never completely vanquish him. Cactus Giant kept coming back, growing out of the soiled sand into yet another humped and prickly creature. It was then I understood that this monster might always be with us, for what it represented, an ill-gotten child, was the offspring of evil doing. And it happened that the women understood this and mended their ways, so that, in time, Old Grandmother Ant told me to bring the women together with the men. It was her wish that they might live together as one. I did this thing as she requested, thus bringing harmony into our lives, even though the monsters of indiscretion still roamed and threatened the land. At least Shapeshifter was no longer our enemy; he had become our guardian.

The Meeting of the Gods

N O W it seemed that the world—with the sparkling birth dew still upon it—was ever in danger of destruction. Evil was a thing that could not be gotten rid of, something that kept coming back to insinuate itself into the lives of the people. Evil, it appeared, propagated evil. And though Coyote was somewhat tamed and Shapeshifter was doing good, the cactus giants (there were many of these, not merely a few), stone giants, gray giants, and white giants filled the land with evil. The stench of their corpses would not go away even after they had died, and the land was marred with the spill of blood, which, wherever it ran, turned black and purple, and made the badlands, which are there to this day.

So now the Holy People, who watched over the earth, got together on top of the tallest mountain, which was called the Mountain Around Which Moving Was Done, and spoke of these things, and Mother Earth said, "I stopped the ant people from fighting, but they still continue; they like to do it very much."

Big Thunder said, "They won't be tamed; fighting is their way."

Mother Earth replied, "The worst of them have been burned away. The ones left are good; they want only to build their lodges."

"Look at the land!" Blue Wind lamented. "Yes," added Little Rainbow, "scarred black with burnings. Nothing can grow."

"Give the earth time; it will sprout anew," Mother Earth promised.

Now Sun Father listened to what the Holy People said, but it was up to him to consider what ought to be done to ensure the good world made by the Maker. What rules, he wondered, might bind harmony to this sundered soil? What might be done to stop the wicked giants from destroying what was good? He thought deeply on this and then decided that the only way to protect the earth from the havoc brought on by the people's misconduct was to create a terrible disaster, one that would end bad ways once and for all.

He turned, therefore, to the dark blue deities, the wind people, and told them to blow without cessation. He spoke to the cloud people, telling them to lie low over the land, to wrap the giants in chains of fog and masks of mist. He told Water Monster to let loose the gates of her great water cave and flood the land, drown the people, cleanse the earth. He put aside his lightning sticks, charged with fire; better, he thought, to drown the world by flooding water.

The Flood

HOW THE GREAT FLOOD IS PROPHESIED BY SMALL
SPOTTED FROG AND HOW THE ONE NAMED LISTENER
SAVES HIMSELF AND THE WORLD OF MAN
BY LISTENING

IN the cave of Water Monster, the stone gates were lifted, and the winds swept across the land, making eerie sounds, combing the hair on all of the trees, loosening the soil, sending up skirling devils of dust. South Wind cut through the sky with blue vengeance; North Wind roared black breath down the corridors of canyons; West Wind screamed a yellow song along the precipices; and East Wind, white as ice, tore the corn crops from their roots, leaving them fringed with frost. And then the wind people went back to the caves of the four directions, singing the chants of things to come. But the stone gates of Water Monster stayed open, leaking water.

Now, the earth people went along, as before, picking up the pieces of their world, doing what they had always done. Those who fished went out to fish; those who hunted went out to hunt; those who worked the soil turned again to the battered earth. And it happened that two fisher people sat by a camp fire on the edge of a great swamp, near the place where Water Monster lived. Water Monster's dominion stretched far and wide, a dark, watery bog quaking with small wriggling things.

She herself was a witch, a slick and sodden hag whose skin was well oiled with slime. She spent her days working water spells, her nights asleep in a damp, drooly cave. Yet while she slept, her legless tribe—plaited snakes and whiskered fish that crept on land—went about doing her bidding, scattering the seeds of the coming flood. The frog people also worked for her, singing the night away, chanting

15

the doom to come, calling storm clouds to bring down a murderous rain.

However, Small Spotted Frog did not sing with the rest. Somehow, he took pity on the world. Out of the croaking darkness, his singular song was heard rising above the rest, and it had a hopeful ring, for he told the earth people how they might prepare for what would come.

Two people sat by the edge of the swamp: One was called Honors Himself; the other was Listener. They sat before a small sourwood fire, the only friendly thing in that huge, grawking swamp. "I don't like frogs," Honors Himself said to Listener, and he glowered into the moss-soaked night, listening to the high, shrill piping that rose above the dismal choir.

"I'm going to see why he sings those high notes," Listener said, and he left the warm fire and waded out into the water lilies. He found Small Spotted Frog, brought him to the fireside, and asked him, "Little one, why do you raise your voice so high on such a night?"

Small Spotted Frog answered, "I speak the prophecy." But no sooner had he said this than Honors Himself got up from his place by the fire and picked Small Spotted Frog up by the collar of his coat and pitched him headlong into the fire.

"That was an evil thing," Listener said, reaching into the coals and helping Small Spotted Frog out of the tangled blossoms of flame. Then he put him back on the log where the three of them were sitting. But, straight away, Honors Himself took Small Spotted Frog again, this time by the front of his coat, and tossed him violently back into the flames. And once again, he was rescued by Listener. Four times in all, Small Spotted Frog was thrown into and pulled out of the fire; yet the tongues of flame didn't wrinkle his skin, for Mother Earth had daubed him with spots that wouldn't burn.

However, after the fourth time Small Spotted Frog came out of the fire, he spoke plainly to Listener. "The prophecy I speak is true; the water will come and flood the land. Prepare, prepare." Honors Himself sneered, returned to the village, and thought no more of it. But Listener stayed in the swamp and every night he spoke again to Small Spotted Frog, who told him all that he knew. "How shall I prepare?" Listener asked.

"In the time to come," Small Spotted Frog said, "the water will cover the land. You must make a strong raft and tie it with hickory rope to the tallest water oak in the swamp. When the water comes, you'll float into the sky; yet the rope will hold the raft so you'll not float away into the Forever."

Listener heard Small Spotted Frog, and he began to make preparations for building the raft, but whenever Honors Himself came around, he scoffed at Listener's work, making fun of what he was doing. "Listener's got no sense," he reported to his other friends back in the village, and all of them laughed and made fun of Listener.

Now when the log raft was finished, Small Spotted Frog came to see it. "Put bunches of grass between the cracks of the logs," he advised, "so the beaver people won't eat off all the bark." Listener did this, and later on, when the raft seemed complete and the rope was braided and secured to the water oak, Small Spotted Frog said that the work was good. Then he told Listener, "Soon the water will come; now you must build a fireplace of mud and stone and keep the watch fire always burning." Listener did this, and soon the swamp's long black fingers began to spread out onto the land.

The swamp swelled, filling the riverbeds until they ran over the earth in rivers of black; and still they ran on, changing dry for wet, inundating all but the highest ground. And the water rose higher still, coming all the way to the village, covering the lodges in a murky tide. But the people were content to fish from the roofs of their lodges, spearing and eating raw mud suckers, ignoring the rising water. At last, the flood covered their roofs, and the people tried to swim to higher ground, but there was nowhere for them to go. The land was drowning in the deepest water the world had ever known. And the unlistening people, intent on their ignorant ways, were drowned. But even so, Listener sat on his raft. The bird people, who held on to the tops of the trees, asked him how high the water was going to go. He told them he did not know.

The flood kept rising until it covered all but the dome of the sky, where there was one bright arc of light. There, Listener's raft was anchored, weaving in the fast-floating current. Far below in the darkening tide, fish were flying through the silent columns of hickories and oaks; dead corn rows were now home to the curve-backed eel; alligators toppled roof peaks with huge sluggish tails; whisker-faced sea cows floated over corncribs stocked with golden ears of corn.

And as the floodwaters continued to rise, the bird people cleverly found a way to hook their claws onto the underpinning of the sky. Their tails dipped in the great flood and were wetted in a such a way as to make their tail markings run together: Hawk's tail was thus stippled in brown and white bars; Cardinal's ran red to the tip; Turkey's was foam and froth to the end. And long after their tails dried off, the bird people kept these tail-tipped reminders of the floodwaters, and they remain that way to this day. In time, the flood began to recede, leaking through a tiny hole in the earth. Then Small Spotted Frog appeared alongside Listener's log raft and told him that the earth was going to bubble and boil before it grew firm again. "Stay on the raft for four days after the flood goes away," he warned, then he hopped into the water and went away.

Now when the water went down, the earth was still wet and muddy, and the only people around were the bird people and Listener. After four days, Listener started to look for some other people, but he couldn't find any. Walking in the dark mud of the new world, he saw that his were the first tracks, and suddenly a great and inconsolable loneliness came over him, for he thought that the flood had taken all things, or nearly all, and those whom water, by chance, had spared, starvation would slowly conquer.

Listener and Mosquito Woman

OF LISTENER, THE LAST MAN ON EARTH, AND OF HIS
MARRIAGE TO MOSQUITO WOMAN, WHO BRINGS
CHILDREN INTO THE NEW WORLD

LISTENER studied the desolate earth, the ruined land. As far as he could see, the trees were bent by the burdensome floodwaters. The tides of mud had crushed the green hills and plastered them with brown glaze. Where once the level plain had been, there was now the vast mirror of an inland lake. Even the cloud-piercing peaks were shrouded in swamp weed, runnels of swamp water spilling down their steep sides.

Seeing that the world was all desolation, emptiness, and silence, Listener sat down on a sunken tree and, head in hands, blocked the painful vision from his eyes. However, as he covered his eyes, he heard a whining sound, high-pitched, droning, at his ear. It seemed to come from everywhere, and at the same time from nowhere. There was no way, therefore, to tell what was making the noise, so Listener, already burdened with bad thoughts, put it out of mind.

That first night in the new world, Listener made a fire and crouched before it, watching the flames, as if they might be able to deliver him from the terrible emptiness that enveloped him. Beyond the comfort of the fire, the stars glittered in pools upon the plain. The night was like infinity, a thing of no beginning and no end; and Listener, in the heart of this immensity, felt a hollowness well within him. Then he heard the voice of Small Spotted Frog, who appeared in front of him.

"The world," Listener told his only friend, "is not the world that I once knew." He stared across the starlit plain to the stranded,

19

broken trees encrusted with slick mud. "Don't be troubled," Small Spotted Frog told him. "Soon someone will come; you'll not be alone for long."

"There's no one left for me," Listener said morosely.

"Someone will come," Small Spotted Frog said again, and he swam off into the great night of starry water. Soon after he had gone, though, Listener again heard the droning noise that had persisted in plaguing him that day. It grew in volume, whining steadily. "Who's there?" he called, but there was no answer, only the infernal whining noise that persisted at his ear.

"Oh, my husband," the noise sang.

"Where are you?" he asked.

"Here," the noise whined.

Then he felt something light on his arm; in the dying firelight, Listener saw an insect person with a very long nose, skinny bowlegs, and large wings.

"Are you my wife?" he asked uncertainly.

"Once," the insect person replied, "I was just like you, but the flood changed all of that. Now I'm Mosquito Woman, an insect person who's always hungry for blood."

"Why do you say that you are my wife?"

"Because now that I've tasted your blood, I have a great craving for it."

Listener didn't really desire a mosquito wife. He felt that mosquitoes were vain and ill-mannered, but he was desperate for company. And yet he wondered why he had come so far, only to end up with a woman who would whine endlessly in his ear and, when he slept, drink the blood out of his body. However, his loneliness reminded him that he was too much alone. And at that moment, his heart grew round with grief, and he felt that a mosquito wife was perhaps better than no wife at all. "All right," he offered, "if you're so hungry, you may have some of my blood."

That night, Mosquito Woman drank her fill. But Listener had nothing to eat, and he went to bed hungry. She slept in the inner fold of his ear, whining as the stars wheeled in the heavens. Listener foolishly tried to sleep but could not, for the noise she made kept him awake, and, because of his name, he had no choice but to listen. "Wife, can't you stop that noise?" he pleaded.

"Only if you kill me," she whined in his ear.

In the morning, however, she was there cooking his breakfast for him: a large trout she had hooked with her nose. Listener was pleased with this, for though he had not slept, he was now, at least, being fed. Perhaps, he thought, his wife could please him in other ways, as well.

The morning of the second day, Listener was again fed a fine fat trout that was caught on the end of his wife's long nose. He ate hungrily and, after eating, felt well fed. But later on when he asked his wife to braid his hair, he saw the reflection of his face in a puddle of water. "Wife," he said, "can this be me? I look so pale and weak."

"It is you, husband," she said, and went on with her braiding.

The morning of the fourth day that Listener and Mosquito Woman had lived as husband and wife, he was given his usual meal of fish, and he ate like a starved man, polishing off all of the bones as well as the eyes and the head. But again, as his wife braided his hair in the early-morning light, Listener noticed his reflection in a puddle. What he saw was not himself but a famished and frail version of what he had once been. "Wife," Listener complained, "there is something wrong with me."

"Do you feel ill, husband?"

Falling forward, Listener sank to his knees. His eyes fluttered as if he was asleep or in a trance, yet his mind was quite clear, and he saw a glowing all around him. He watched without moving as his wife put her long nose into the water to catch another fish for him. The water stirred and then became violent. An enormous fish crashed to the surface and swallowed Mosquito Woman whole.

Listener, though weakened from the blood his wife had drained out of him, used his remaining strength to crawl to the edge of the water. There he saw the great trout that had swallowed his wife.

The trout hung suspended in the still water, a giant, silver fish, gleaming in the clear prism of the lake. His hand shot out, and he caught the trout by the gills. He dragged it on the muddy bank, where it flopped furiously for its life. "Fish," Listener said angrily, "you've taken my wife from me, therefore I must take your life from you—"

"No," the fish gasped. "Husband, don't you see? It is I, your wife!"

And as Listener looked on in amazement, the silver trout changed into a glimmering woman, more beautiful than any he had ever seen. Her skin was soft as if dusted with apple pollen; her hair hung down like fresh rain. And as he looked at her, he felt the awful weariness come away from his limbs, and he sat up and rubbed his eyes. "This is a dream," he murmured, "it can't be real."

"No, husband," she said, "it is real, and I am yours as long as the grass shall grow."

And that was how Listener, the last man on earth, married a mosquito who was eaten by a trout who changed into a lovely two-legged woman who then became the first woman to bear children in the new world.

Sun Father and Mother Earth

IN WHICH SUN FATHER MAKES LOVE TO MOTHER
EARTH AND HOW THEIR CHILDREN RIGHT-HANDED
SUN AND MOON WATER BOY COME INTO THE WORLD

SUN Father had been studying Mother Earth from the house of the sun. Parting the clouds at his door, he watched as the floodwaters bubbled about her, forming a whitecap of foam around the top of her head. What is she doing down there? he wondered. But he liked looking at her naked back, her shoulders shining, the streaming of her long hair in the sunlight, the roundness of her buttocks when she bent over. Was she playing, naked, in the floodwaters, he wondered, or just washing her hair?

So, throwing a blue blanket on his turquoise horse, he rode down out of the clouds, with a sunbeam for a bridle and a rainbow for reins. He rode down out of the sky, a blue light about his face. Out of the sky he came, a corona of sun pollen all around his turquoise horse.

Mother Earth raised her head from the water where she was washing her hair, which fell to her knees, and she saw him sitting there on his mount, the golden air burning in his wake.

Ah, he thought, she is more lovely this way. He thought of a ripe peach.

She shaded her eyes from the brilliance of his gaze, shyly covering her breasts with her long black hair. He dismounted slowly, gracefully. Four sun dogs guarded the turquoise horse and, not far off, four colored bears of the four directions stood watch. These were a blue bear of the south, a jet bear of the north, a coral bear of the west, and a pearl bear of the east.

23

"What do you want of me?" Mother Earth asked, straightening her coverlet of blue-black hair.

He enjoyed her beauty for a long time without answering.

"It is that time," he said.

And although she was covered in the strands of her own glistening hair, his words suddenly uncovered her. They made her naked before the gaze of his eyes. Then all of the distance between them vanished. He cast a noon-colored blanket of blue fire onto the grass, and she went to it and waited there for him.

He came to her side, then spoke softly to her.

"The waters have cleansed the land," he said sadly, "and still the people have not learned their lesson. I know that you've hidden some of them inside this mountain of yours; I also know that the women are still having sex in the unnatural way."

"This is true," Mother Earth said, "What do you intend to do?"

"I would ask you the same."

In the distance, far from where they sat on that blanket of noontime blessing, the lakes of fire gleamed topaz. Far out across the hammock lands, the giant shadows of evil birds fled across the landscape. And farther still, in the trembling distance, the grotesque figures of stone giants lumbered about with their stone axes on their shoulders, their heads cocked to one side as they belched disrespectfully at the heavens.

"More monster birds and stone giants," Mother Earth lamented. Then she added, "I thought that if I just saved a few of the women . . ."

"Those creatures out there plaguing the land are the offspring of evildoing," he said darkly.

He stared out at the staggering size of the stone giants off in the distance; they were equal in proportion, he thought, to the women's misconduct. "There is but one thing to do; I will place myself in you, give you my seed. It is time."

She assented then and he came to her. She opened herself to him— the blue of his skin meeting the brown of hers. And they met in the middle of themselves, delighted in the satisfaction they gave each other, the world of sky procreating with the world of earth. And when they reached the fullness of their joy together, four rainbow people appeared, watchfully, over them, casting a misty arc that was a bond between the two worlds.

In four hours, she was with child; in four more, she was at the water's edge cleansing herself when, in the fullness of his lust, he met her again, went after her in the water. He caught her as she buckled under him. They wrestled, sported in the pleasure of liquid love. And he took her then at the water's edge, thrusting himself eagerly. Clutching the sand, she made faint cries and drew him in as deeply as he wanted to go. He took his power and magnified it with hers; and over them again, the rainbow people, coursing across the worlds of water, air, fire, and earth, appeared.

In four more hours, she was with twins, which, four days from that time, were born on the sacred mountain called the Mountain Around Which Moving Was Done.

"I name our offspring the Twin Brothers of Light," Sun Father declared to Mother Earth, and she assented happily because she had borne the twins well and she loved her husband.

"The first boy shall be known as Right-Handed Sun, for he was conceived in the sun that caresses the earth, as I came to you the first time, from the right."

"What will we call the second son?"

"The second one shall be known as Moon Water Boy, for he was conceived in the water that is drawn by the moon, as I came to you the second time, from the left."

Then Mother Earth said, "As I faced your black bear guardian of the north, so shall Right-Handed Sun have the full power of the north in him. He'll be bold, strong, the warrior son who will kill the stone giants and the other monsters that roam the land. This son shall bring long-lasting peace to the people."

Sun Father smiled pleasurably; he was proud to have sired such a great son as this one was destined to be, for he knew that Mother Earth's prophecy was correct. As he listened now to the far-off thunder of the stone giants' axes grinding down the mountains, he knew that the monsters' days were not long in number.

"And what of Moon Water Boy?" Sun Father inquired. Of this son, he wasn't so certain or so proud.

"As I faced the blue bear of the south, so Moon Water Boy should have the gentle power of the south in him. He'll move from the left, the heart side, and his voice and manner will be gentle and kind. His way will be full of praise for all things that live, and he will show his brave brother how to be more moderate."

"It is good," Sun Father said, "one the warrior, one the seer." And he climbed upon his turquoise horse, which reared up, fiery hooves of blue pawing the air. As the sun dogs and bear guardians joined the procession and came to the side of the great blue horse, Sun Father took the rainbow reins in his hand, touched them but once, and the horse surged into the sky, heading for the thunderheads that were the front gate of the house of the sun.

BOOK 2

The Story of the Sun's Son

The Story of the Death of the Monsters and the
Shaping of the Earth

The Story of Bear Woman

The Story of the Sun's Son

HOW RIGHT-HANDED SUN VISITS SUN FATHER IN
THE HOUSE OF THE SUN AND HOW THE FAMINE
ON EARTH IS ENDED

H E house of the sun sat upon the shoulder of a thundercloud, high in the sky; mortared with white fire, roofed in sheets of shining light. Here was a radiance not meant for mortal eyes. The house of the sun was beyond the dreams of men. However, this did not prevent the Sun's son, Right-Handed Sun, from possessing dreams of the unattainable.

His troubled sleep was visited by fleeting phantoms, magnificent birds, gray giants made of stone, the fabled doorways of his father's house. In his dreams, he saw the four doorways leading into the house: Wind's door, blinding blue; Bear's door, night-blackened; Lightning's door, gold-bolted; Snake's door, dawn-whitened. Of these apocryphal doors, the boy dreamed idle dreams, never passing through the magic portals, never hearing his father's celestial voice, only seeing the magnificence of the mighty carved doors shielding his eyes from the holy glare within.

The years had passed, the boys had grown from children to young men, and yet neither brother had ever seen his father, though their mother often told stories about him. Right-Handed Sun dreamed of his father every night. Once his mother told him of the time Sun Father went out hunting for his elder sister. Her name was Night Sun. She was lost in the great pathway of the stars, trying to find her way home, so Sun Father went searching for her. He met the scorpion, whose diamond-pointed stinger was aimed at his heart, and he bent it back so that it turned away from the earth.

On his wanderings, searching for Night Sun in the waterfalls of stars, Sun Father saw the Great Bear. This was the one who once, long ago, was startled by men down on earth. Pierced through the heart by their arrows, Great Bear fled into the sky, became the star bear we see at night. And now each fall, he splashes the autumn trees with bear's blood, turning them red, gold, and bronze.

So it was that Sun Father finally discovered his lost sister, famished, dazed from her long walk. She had gone off into the star deserts, grown thin from lack of food. Now she was so meager, he vowed to build up her strength, which he does, fattening her to fullness every month, until she looks round and fat. But then, when she sees herself, her surprise is so great, she runs off again, and he must go chasing after her. Thus the whole cycle is repeated, as it is today: the growing and thinning of Night Sun, the moon.

Right-Handed Sun loved to hear these stories about his father because they fed his dreams, and his dreams were eaglelike in their prodigious hunger. They say that sooner or later, all things come to those who dream, not to those who have no dreams, who live in darkness, unlit by desire. And one day it happened that Right-Handed Sun found a ladder that led up into the sky. Climbing it, he passed beyond the last rung, which emptied into the vastness of vaulting blue. There he hung, suspended like a dragonfly, wondering what next to do.

Father Hawk came by then, angling on a red-shouldered wing, and told him, "You've always been good to our kind. Take one of my feathers. See where it leads you." So he took one of Father Hawk's blood dark wing feathers, and the feather carried him across the sky, which then turned to clear ice. His feet skimmed over the icy blue, his heels casting sparks of frost in his wake.

And so, he made it over the iced lake of noon. And then he came upon a craggy cliff wall that extended to the top of the tallest thunderheads, and he attached himself to the cliff rock, climbing hand over hand. In time, he came to a shelf of stone that couldn't be traversed—it hung out over his head, preventing him from going farther. Right-Handed Sun made his camp there for the night, hooked by his own will to the sheer and unforgiving stone.

By dawn, his frozen breath fell like a sprinkling of snow upon his shirt. His eyes, snow-blind, saw nothing; his hands clawed; his tongue prayed for deliverance. It was then that South Wind came by, whistling up a storm. "You've always paid homage to the wind people," South Wind said to the boy. "Take my shirttail in your hands. I'll pull you up the cliffside." And he did, while the fringes of his tail wind whipped the boy's face and the pitch of his voice ascended in shrilling waves of rolling air that tumbled stones from their perches, making a stone rain that lasted for months on earth.

At last, with Father Hawk's feather still in hand, Right-Handed Sun was delivered by South Wind to the four doors of the house of the sun. And there he stood, eyes slitted—first, from the morning frost and then from the glitter of noon, sun pummeling off the burnished doors of foil-gleaming light. He had dreamed of this moment since he was a child. Now he was actually there, at the altar of the doors, the threshold of his father's house. He shook shamefully in fear. What was he to do now he was there? Doubt filled his heart, swamping him in self-pity; he wept.

Then he saw a small, crooked worm, hunching, inching toward the great doors of the sun. "Where are you going, little one?" he asked.

"I'm the honored guest of the sun," Little Worm said.

"You?" Right-Handed Sun said incredulously.

Little Worm stopped his laborious hundred-hipped crawl and looked up at his interlocutor. "Be in nothing so moderate as self-praise," Little Worm said, "that is what I always say. But I also say, never underestimate your own worth. What you see before you is a lowly worm, and you would think, What can such a one be doing before the lofty house of the sun? Yet I am expected, even desired, at this august house. You see, it is I who puts the magic into the hoofbeat of Sun Father's horses. Yes, little, lowly, lopsided I."

Right-Handed Sun stared at Little Worm, amazed.

"Cousin, tell me how you do this?"

He answered, "At the appropriate time of year, I go to the Mountain Where Flint Is Kept, gather up all the sacred flints, take them here, and store them in the hooves of the horses of the sun. Then they can gallop through the gemstone trails of the night without losing their footing."

"Cousin, how can you do such a thing? It would take you forever to crawl to the Mountain Where Flint Is Kept."

"You look," Little Worm said critically, "but you hardly see."

Right-Handed Sun nodded. "You're right, I cannot see."

"Look again," Little Worm told him.

Right-Handed Sun looked through the slits of his eyes; what he saw—a beautiful butterfly—danced in the air on flowered wings. "Remember, one is not always what one appears," Little Worm called out. And then Wind's door opened, and Butterfly, dazzling in soft cotton clothing, floated through the blue portals. Then the great door closed.

Once again, Right-Handed Sun was alone and partially blind. He stood before the burnished doors. At Snake's door, he tried to think of the word for Great Serpent, but he couldn't remember it, so the mighty door remained closed. At Bear's door, he tried to remember the word for Bear Guardian, but it slipped from his mind, and the door stayed shut. At Lightning's door, he struggled with the word for *zigzag*, but it just wouldn't come to him, and the door never opened. Then he came back to Wind's door, and remembering that South Wind had carried him aloft and brought him there, he sang the Wind's song, adding all the praiseworthy words he knew for the virtues of the winds. And Wind's door, magically, opened and he was swept through the portals into the great hall of the house of the sun. The hall was decorated with exfoliating sunbeams; they were all over the mica-schist mirrored walls, the engraved floor gleaming of sunstruck brick.

"Who comes here?" spoke a resounding voice that made the heavily carved timbered ceiling rumble and shake.

Although Right-Handed Sun had never heard his father's voice, he knew that this was his father who spoke to him. "It is I," he replied, "your son." Now, as it was the end of the day, Sun Father was in the hall of darkness, veiled in black light. "Come here where I can see if you are truly my son," the voice ordered, and Right-Handed Sun responded, moving out of the main hall, gilded with the light of the sun, and into the darkened chamber.

"What is wrong with your eyes?" Sun Father questioned.

"I am sun-blind," said the boy.

"You will soon be able to see again. I've hung the sun in my medicine bag in the east wing of the house. Here it is already night; the darkness should soothe you."

Sun Father walked around the boy, measuring him with his eye. He is handsome enough to be my son, he thought, but I think he is much too shy. I shall test the boy's heart, then I will know if his disposition is brave or cowardly.

Suddenly, without warning, Sun Father threw a bolt of black lightning at the boy's head, but Right-Handed Sun, being a warrior, felt it coming and ducked. The black bolt thundered behind him, sending up a column of snakelike smoke.

"Well done," Sun Father said, and once more he fired a saffron bolt that shrieked past the boy's ear, then another of turquoise that crackled, and finally one of fire coral that struck him full in the chest, knocking him backward. Yet he was unhurt because he had tucked Father Hawk's sacred feather over his heart, and it had repelled the dangerous bolt, thrown it back on the hurler himself, who whistled as it beveled the air at his ear.

Right-Handed Sun got to his feet. "If you wish to prove or punish me further, I am ready for your next attack," he said, "but I tell you that it is I, Right-Handed Sun, your own son, who speaks before you now."

"You do seem to be my son," Sun Father mused, "and yet . . ."

I must give you a test of the mind, not just of the body, Sun Father said to himself, as he circled the boy, wonderingly; then, if it is really who I think it is, I will give him a father's true welcome.

"Who," Sun Father asked, "stole the voice of Talking God?"

"The one called First Angry."

"And who is the one with the evil name, who was later given a good one?"

"The person you speak of was first called Shapeshifter, but after he performed good deeds, he was known as Guardian of the Game."

"And which name does he prefer now?"

"The second one."

"And do you come from the left or the right?"

"I come from the right; my brother from the left."

"And for what reason?"

"From before our birth. I don't know; it is our nature."

There followed a long, unyielding silence during which Right-

Handed Sun could hear his father's feet moving lightly, rhythmically across the floor. Presently, the boy felt a strong hand on his shoulder. "You have proven to me that you are mine. Welcome, my son, to the house of the sun."

Then Sun Father took the boy's hand in his and led him through the many doors and along the many corridors until the two of them reached the rear portal of the night that led out into a great dark corral. Reaching into the medicine pouch that hung about his neck, Sun Father took out a tiny eagle feather, a bit of down fluff; and this he brushed upon his son's eyelids four times. The boy blinked his eyes and could see well again.

"What is in the corral of the north?" Sun Father asked.

Right-Handed Sun looked and saw the horse that his father rode only at night. Jet mane swept back on long, sleek neck, the horse's fine coat agleam with grains of mica.

"This is Nightway," Sun Father said.

"May I ride him, Father?"

"What you want, my son, is dangerous; you ask for power beyond your strength and years. What you ask to ride is the most powerful horse of all. I myself am frightened sometimes to see the earth so far below when I ride upon his broad back. Nightway will whirl as the stars whirl, and when he throws his head, the stars rain down like nuggets of white and gold. He may outrun a comet, leap the tail of a shooting star, break his hooves on the backbone of the great bull whose lowered horns try to gouge you. He may dance by the wicked scorpion, dodge the paw of the blood-speckled bear. However, I promise you he'll never tire of galloping—not when hell smoke comes out of his nostrils, not when his flinty hooves turn to ash on the upper circle of the rainbow bridge that leads back to earth. Beware, my son, I don't want to give you the gift of death. I am proved, therefore, a father by my father's fear."

His warning ended, but no caution was taken by the overeager son, who saw himself riding grandly down to earth on his father's fabulous mount. And so, into his excited hands, Sun Father gravely gave over the reins of jet. He stroked Nightway's silken neck. "Take him back to earth with you," he whispered into Nightway's ear. "Take him through the north and through the night until you come to the dawn land of earth."

The last thing the boy said to his father was about the drought that had followed the flood on earth. "All of our game animals have died," he said. "There is no food left anywhere."

Sun Father said, "The animals are being killed by the giants and the other monsters; these you must kill yourself. The food I give now will take care of the people, but you must make it back to earth to tell them I have done this."

Sun Father opened the gate of the corral that was near the east of the house of the sun. Right-Handed Sun heard muffled thunder, and suddenly out of the east door, there poured a mighty river of animals, all the ones that had been killed by the stone giants and monsters. These were their spirits, a cataract of hooves and horns, heads and tails—deer, buffalo, antelope, and sheep—a river of horns flowing off the edge of the cliff, pouring down the heavens, a ghostly herd of phantom shapes.

"There, it is done," Sun Father said. "You and your people will have food to live. Now see to it that you make it to earth." He touched Nightway's flank, and the great horse sprang off into the starry abyss.

Right-Handed Sun had no time to wave good-bye to his father, for Nightway took the bridle made of forged meteors in his teeth, bit down, and pulled the hapless boy to the back of his thrusting head. The reins slipped out of the boy's hand, and as he listed to one side of the heavy-necked horse, he lost all control. Now Nightway felt the full run of his freedom; his legs leapt wide to the rhythm of his hooves as they rang on the moonlit cobbles of the stars. In reckless abandon, the surging horse took the midnight sky; his smoke-plumed nostrils flared, tail flashed, parting the star grass as his hooves of flint tore up the velvet road of darkness.

Far now from his father's house, the frantic boy tried to grasp the flapping, flinging, jetted reins. If only I might seize them, he thought, then all might not be lost—but if I can't . . .

And the hooves danced sparks and the long mane drank the darkness and made a song as it flew. Far below, Right-Handed Sun saw the dawn-flushed land, and he grew pale, his knees knocking against the soaked plates of the massive runaway horse. His hair burned at his ears as he and the horse fell through the vapor-trailing night into the spreading rose-tinted dawn. Now the jeweled stars splintered off, arcing and spinning, and night was indeed dying as they fell, the stars themselves expiring. The morning was coming on as fast as they were falling—the rosy dawn expunging the night-frozen stars—and below, the day reddened; the moon's crescent went pale; sky and earth were suffused in the stain of the wild blood-rose morning. And still they plummeted out of control.

Now as the dawn was amply aglow, the shadows of night all but gone, Nightway cut through the peach-colored clouds, pawing, breaking free, still falling. Then Right-Handed Sun made one last try to take the reins, and reaching out, he managed somehow to catch one, then two. Holding both, he reined as hard as he could, not the little pull of a mortal but the goodly grip of a god. And he felt, as a result, the double buck of the braking horse as they went into a sidelong lurch that crashed horse and rider into the white-walled meadow of the sudden cloud bank.

The great horse turned to the left, skidding against peaks and pinnacles, mounds and mountains, crags of shaggy cloud mist; and then to the right, plowing through the peach-blown desert dawn, making a splendor of thunder as up came the massive sweat-runneled neck and down came the hammered skull into the shattering cloud plane. Everywhere the pink clover, born of clouds, spotted the sky in raggy shreds. And the fantastic horse came plunging down, parting the graveled dawn as—finally, momentously—it churned upon the solid earth, its hooves drumming the molten morning, the dust rising up in golden fountain sprays. The ridden horse at last bowed to the unthrown rider. And so, seeing them safely home, Sun Father smiled from on high.

The Story of the Death of the Monsters and the Shaping of the Earth

OF THE FIRST MONSTER SLAYER AND WARRIOR RIGHT-
HANDED SUN, WHO, WITH HIS BROTHER, MOON WATER
BOY, MAKES THE EARTH A BETTER PLACE TO LIVE

N O W in the morning, when Right-Handed Sun rode into the people's presence on the great horse Nightway, they recognized that he was indeed the son of the sun, and they gave a feast in his honor. There was food in abundance as the herds of animals that had vanished during the time he was gone were now returned: elk, deer, buffalo, and sheep in great numbers on all the fattened hills and in all the hollowed valleys. Right-Handed Sun accepted the honor bestowed upon him, the gifts of eagle feathers and elk teeth, fine turquoise that shone like the southern sun, well-woven blankets richly adorned with legends. All of these he accepted graciously, for he was glad that he had come home alive; his place in the eye of his father was assured.

And the people fed Nightway delicate flower blossoms and gave him mingled waters, holy waters—melted from spring snows, hail water and soft water from the four quarters of the world. The people honored Nightway by blessing his presence on earth; they placed sacred skins and silk scarves on the ground where he walked, and when he danced on the hills, they saw that he raised not clouds of common dust but the pollen mist of heaven. The holy men were then arranged in a line, and they sang Nightway songs, blessing all of him—his war-chant whinny, his jet-silk skin, the precious flowers that fell from the corner of his mouth when he fed, the dust of glittering grains that hovered over his muscled flanks and huge withers as the winds blew gales around him.

37

And thus was he praised; and honored among men was Right-Handed Sun, praised in song and chant. Yet he shrugged it off, saying that he had more important things to do than listen to ornamental words. The time had come, he said, to purge the land of monsters, to plough the soil, make it sacred. "How will you do this?" the people wanted to know. And Right-Handed Sun explained that the saddle-bags he had brought with him from the house of the sun contained implements of magic. He then put a war feather in his hair, which no woman or child should ever look upon, lest the warrior, in battle, be brought to an untimely end.

And upon his shoulders and chest, he put on the armored flint of the horned toad; in his quiver, he carried the zigzag lightnings that could strike the four directions at once, returning the way they came, having found their mark; and so it is, they say, that lightning always looks as if it flashes out and then goes back the way it came. Singing the songs of sorcery, the songs of war, Right-Handed Sun went out on the back of Nightway seeking to cleanse the land of stone giants, cactus monsters, flying devil birds, and the other grotesque creatures made by the women in their time of sexual transgression.

The people saw him ride off at dawn, clothed in sun prayer, a flint-hearted hero, heading into the desert with the dream charm of sorcery on his breath. So it was that he slew the big-winged shadow birds of the sky, the ancient evil ones that nested in the rocks. His zigzag lightnings returned and were quivered. And he aimed again and shot the dun-headed stone giants, who groaned like avalanches and crashed to the earth; and these became mesas and mountains that touch the sky to this day. The blood of the giants rivered across the dry land and froze into the plasmic lava flows of the purple desert.

In a black flint bonnet, flint leggings, and flint boots, Right-Handed Sun rode forth, slaying the cactus monsters, who, when he struck them, shrank down like mushrooms, shriveling piteously under the hot-bolted pinion of his zigzag lance. The blood boiled out of them, formed the pear-shaped pink fruit that the people eat today—cactus fruit. And all of these creatures died under the zigzag bolts that flashed and were quivered in the smoke sheath of the sun.

Afterward, when the land was ridded of all monsters, Right-Handed Sun took a sweat bath in a sweat lodge made of turquoise.

When the heat was great, he cooled off with bits of shell that he stored against the inside of his cheek.

Then came the time of real work: the plowing and fielding of the land. He called forth his brother, Moon Water Boy, and together they fashioned canyons with the four lightning bolts. Then they called upon Vulture to fan the lakes of fire that were left on the burning earth; and these the winds changed into lakes of mountain water. Out of their heads, they extracted lengths of hair, planted them, watched the grasses grow up, and cover the burned-out prairies.

Now, when the people asked them what they should do if there was a drought, Right-Handed Sun answered, "You must pull up the grass and the spruces by their roots, sing the rain songs; and the turned-up roots will draw down the rain and nourish the earth. After this, you must replace the root heads, put them back in the soil." And the people remembered this, for they knew that a time of plenty is always followed by a time of lack, and that the world is always changing, the hoop of life ever rolling. But now they had the songs of the sun brothers to sing, and when their voices were raised in song, the people knew that their prayers would be answered.

The Story of Bear Woman

IN WHICH BEAR WOMAN BECOMES BEAR GUARDIAN,
THE TRAVELING COMPANION OF MOTHER EARTH

WHEN Sun Father looked down from the house of the sun to see that his son had made it safely to earth, he was happy—as only a father who fears losing a son can be happy—and he surveyed then the warrior road of Right-Handed Sun, the killing of the monsters, the purging of the evil left on the earth, and was doubly proud. For all stood strong upon the enduring earth: the singing grass, the flickering leaves, the meandering rivers, the dark woodlands, the empty plains, and the sparkling deserts—all restored to loveliness, all put to order by his son. And so he rode out that day on Noonway, the blue horse of noon, to see for himself the harmony his son had brought to the land.

And as he sat astride the great turquoise horse whose muscles flexed like the clouds in the sky, he saw the land as it was meant to be seen: Where the stone giants had held out against his son, there were great bouldered hillocks with freshets of clean water coming out of them. And it was at such a place that he caught a glimpse of a pretty earth-surface girl who was from the Mountain Around Which Moving Was Done.

She was beautiful; the sight of her licked fire through his marrow-bones. She had no need of feather or quill for her hair, not this girl; her hair was the same gloss as the raven's wing. Nor did she require anything but daylight to enhance the color of her skin. What a sight she was for his famished eyes as she stood, waist-deep in maidenhair fern, picking berries for her shoulder-slung basket. He hid himself

40

behind a tree, watching until her basket was full. Then, when she put it down and, sighing, made a pillow of fern to lie down on, he wanted her as he had never wanted a woman before—but he waited. Disguising himself as another berry-picking girl from a neighboring village, he appeared cloaked, hidden, and entered the little clearing, asking her name. She started up from her sunny reverie, surprised to see anyone in so remote a place. Rising from the fern-pale pallet, she asked the newcomer where she was from. "I come from over the hill," Sun Father said in his trick voice, that of a youthful girl. Then he said, "We are the people who crossed the river twice, made our home on the other side of the hill. You've always called us They Who Crossed Twice, but we call ourselves the people."

"I come," the pretty girl said, "from this side of the river; you've always called us Those Who Would Not Cross Over. But, like you, we call ourselves the people."

"May I know your name?" Sun Father asked politely.

"I am called Bear Woman," she replied.

Listening, Sun Father rejoiced in his perfect deception.

"And may I know your name?"

"You may call me Sunlit Water," he lied. Then he said, "It's so terribly hot; wouldn't you like to swim in that spring over there by the alders?"

Bear Woman, who had been thinking the same thing, assented immediately. And they shed their deerskin dresses and started into the cold spring. The gentle murmur of the spring as Bear Woman waded into it and the startling beauty of her naked form made a fiery fever in Sun Father's skull.

He saw clearly the clean throat, the young breasts. He trembled, thinking, If Mother Earth saw me here with her, she would loathe me. But it was really himself he loathed; nonetheless, he could do nothing about it. Timidly, Bear Woman entered the spring, crouching against the leaf-grown bank, tenderly clutching a shock of grass as she lowered herself. Now the vast bower of alder boughs shielded them from the bright light of day; once inside the secret pool, it was nearly night. Sun Father watched with delight as his companion's nipples grew hard as the cold water crept up her thighs. Throwing off his disguise, he came into the spring quickly, making a loud, sudden splash. Bear Woman spun around in surprise and landed,

by accident, in his arms, her hair outspread like a huge black blossom.
She was steadying herself by holding on to his shoulders, but the
pool had a slippery bottom and she kept losing her balance. He had
his hands on her delicate shoulders, laughing at her awkwardness.
She felt foolish and so turned away. But he could stand it no longer,
and, lowering his face to her neck, began kissing her as no woman
kisses a newly met friend.

And, at the same time, he became what he was, an unbridled god,
with a god's inordinate love for mortal flesh. Catching the double
arcs of her shoulders with a powerful grip, he pulled her to him,
kissing her hard on the mouth. She fought with him briefly, but it
was no good—he was much too strong. And so they wrestled for a
short time on the muddy bank, and he parted her at the knees, made
her thighs come open.

Then her body quivered as he entered her—not roughly, as she
had feared, but surely, placing his maleness perfectly. Holding her
breasts in his hands, he raised her up, gently pressing her back
against the bank. She arched herself, bending under him, face
turned, eyes closed so she wouldn't have to see. He caught her at
the hips; she rose, then subsided. And he devoured her frightened
flesh, which smelled of wine-dark berries fermented in the sun, and
tasted her sweetness on his tongue, ravishing her, spreading her,
half in water, half on the grass, until finally she held back no longer,
accepted a god's lust, the whole of him inside her. He saw her then,
clawing and crying, fearful no longer, desiring their mutual naked-
ness under the alder-starred boughs, the bright-needled pines.

But when, afterward, she awoke with a start on the bank, she was
overcome with a shameful shivering. He was gone—if he had ever
been there at all, her wild mind said—and she, mud-pasted, wrapped
in waterweeds, glanced around, fearful now, at the forest itself: the
knowing leaves, the shady, watchful trees.

It was nine moons to the day before Bear Woman happened, by
chance, to see that treacherous spring again. She was out mushroom
hunting with some of her friends when, all of a sudden, they came
upon that haunted glade, that secret spring. There in the cool grove
of alder, the unblinking eye of the pool stared up at them. Praising
the place, the other girls dipped their toes in the spring. "No one
can see us here," one of them said. "Let's go in." And, as youths

will, they did—all but one, that is; and that one, of course, was Bear Woman. She did not remove her clothes as the others had, but stood reluctant on the grassy bank, hesitant, wide-eyed with fear. Giggling at their rude game, the others stripped her and then saw plainly the startling truth: what she had been hiding. She held herself pathetically, arms hugging her ripe belly, but then, panicking, she fled from that scene of naked truth. She ran off through the spruce scrub, crying. Now, Mother Earth, knowing all things—and one thing not less than another—saw this, took in what had happened at the spring. She was aware of what had gone on there before, as well, and so she went after Bear Woman the way a mother will run after a frightened child.

When she caught up to her, the poor girl came apart in their embrace, sobbing. And as she wept, she was mothered by the mother of all creation. Then, as Mother Earth stroked her head, the girl's face grew round as a stone; her arms blackened, growing rough with fur; her hands curled inward; her lips turned black, slick; her nose wrinkled up; and her voice grew into a growl.

"Listen, my child," Mother Earth said, "you will now be my traveling companion; wherever I go, you will be there with me, watching. In time to come, you will watch over all who visit the forest, for just as Wolf was named Wanderer, you will be named Bear Guardian."

And so it was; and so, they say, it always will be: The bear of the blue-green forest watches over all who go there, the likely to be lost, the hopelessly lost, those who embrace for the first time, those who have parted for the last time. Bear is there, watching, and since a bear person was once one of the people, it is important to say the name with gentleness and respect. For she and the others of her kind are the watchful guardians of the wood. When you step into their world, you must remember what once happened long ago: A woman was here who became a bear, but she later married a man from the mountain lake country and they had a child who yearned to walk among men. But that, they say, is a story for another fire.

BOOK 3

The Story of the Raven, and the Raven's Story

The Story of Old Woman Moon

The Story of Owl Boy

The Story of the Raven, and the Raven's Story

HOW RAVEN BECOMES A SHAPESHIFTER, A TRICKSTER,
AND A STORYTELLER ALL AT THE SAME TIME

N this way, Bear Woman became Bear Guardian of forests and mountains, traveling companion of Mother Earth. After this, when the people saw her, they called her many names: Honey Foot, Black Food, Bee Fur. But all of these names seem to say that she is much like them and they are much like her.

To all of the animal people who would listen, Bear Woman told the tale of how her beauty had been her ruin. Sun Father, she told them, took advantage of her. Everyone knows, of course, how powerful the sun is and how the carrier of the sun is a god of powerful dimension. And it is well known that, of all the deities, Sun Father wields the greatest power—for just think of what life would be like if he withheld the sun from us, or how damaging would be the rays of the sun if he let them shine day and night without cessation.

Now one day, as was her wont, Bear Guardian was retelling the story of her ravishment to some of her friends when one of them, that blackest, most contentious and raucous of all bird people, Raven, spoke up.

"You are not the only one who was blessed, or cursed, by beauty. Your luck, Bear Guardian, was to have Mother Earth rescue you. But look what happened to me. My beauty was truly my ruin, as surely as you say yours was your own. Once, long ago, before there was any light in the heavens and when I was still lovely, a god came after me. It was the one they called Shapeshifter, who is now Guardian of the Game.

"I ignored him as much as possible, but he didn't take no for an answer. He kept changing into various forms, so I never knew whom I was refusing. One day, he was a clam; another day, a hill of sand; yet another, an old discarded basket. Well, one time I was walking along the shore of the great sea, and he came after me in a rush. First, he wrapped himself around my ankle—a bit of seaweed that I kicked away. Second, he changed into a sand crab that danced around me, clicking his claws. I threw sand on him and ran off. Third, though, he became a monstrous green wave that dazzled and doused me, tugging me into the tidewater. I could feel his wet, bubbly hands all over me.

"I cried for help—but who was there to hear? No one came. Seeing my helplessness, he turned brutish; he took me into deeper water, folding his lengthy limbs over me. He was everywhere at once, a hovering shadow, a monster of manacles, tugging me to the bottom, where I couldn't breathe. His shifts of shape were much too rapid to keep up with; sudden fins quivered between my thighs, then a loud crash of brine, rolling me over, tumbling me onto my back. Finally, he dragged me to the foam-shaking shoreline, became a glowering, hulking saltwater wave beast, his enormous shoulders foaming with spray. He was through playing; now he took me, giving me a terrible grinding on the hard sand. I heard the sea roar in my ear; I felt the sea inside my loins, slipping up and up. He spread me out, had the salt and sweet of me, and he loved me—if you could call it that—and left off loving me, then loved me again, not ever tiring of having me, again and again.

"In the end, his sea changes altered me: My arms darkened with soft plumage. My shoulders shadowed; little feathers started poking out of my soft skin. I screamed; my voice croaked. Whatever I tried to do to stop the feathered fury from overtaking me proved in vain; as I beat my naked breasts, they hardened into quill, blanketed over with blackness. Soon I had neither soft breasts nor beating hands: I was touched with feathers from head to foot.

"I ran away from him, and he let me go, for his rough play was done. I ran—but not as I used to. I skimmed across the breakers,

water's light reflecting off my skin. Did I say skin? I mean feathers—
for I had changed completely: I flapped, grawked, grew into myself,
became at last what you see before you now: this poor bedraggled
raven person."

It was at this point that several other animal people wished to tell
their own stories, but Raven silenced them, as often she does, with
a flap of her wings and a loud croak of "Quiet!" She had more to
say, as she always does. She went on to explain that the tale was
only half-told. Having been shapeshifted herself by the creator of
that deed, she discovered that she might do it again, at will. And
once the first shift was made, it was quickly followed by others, which
explains why Raven is such a tricky bird person. As she put it, "The
world turns, and all things turn with it; the shape shifts, and all
things shift with it."

Then she finished her tale.

"One day, I noticed there was only a small amount of light in the
world. And that light was being hoarded by a miserly old medicine
man who lived in a lodge on top of a hill, surrounded by a great
forest. This medicine man lived with his daughter, and together they
had all the light in the world; and they kept it greedily to themselves.
"So I changed myself into a tiny speck of dirt and dropped down
their smoke hole into a pot of drinking water. Now, just a little after
that, the medicine man's daughter took a drink of that water, and
she unsuspectingly drank me down. In four days' time, she found
herself pregnant, and soon she gave birth to a noisy, nasty dark little
baby. The baby grew up in four more days. But she was spoiled by
the medicine man and his daughter, who gave her anything she
pointed to. They couldn't stand her crying, which sounded like pine
trees cracking in a storm.
"Now it didn't take her long to point to all of the sacred medicine
bundles hanging on the walls of the lodge. She'd cry, and they'd
give her a bundle to keep her quiet; she'd cry again, and so on and
so forth, until she had all the bundles in front of her. Now one of
the bundles had stars made of crushed shells in it. She took these
out and threw them up the smoke hole; and that is how the stars

came into the heavens. Then she opened another bundle, and in this one she picked up the moon, which was made of abalone, and she tossed this up the smoke hole; and that is how the moon came into the heavens. The last bundle had the sun, which was a piece of turquoise, inside it, and she threw that up the smoke hole; and that is how the sun came into the heavens."

Thus, Raven concluded her story. But the animal people wanted to know what happened to the medicine man's granddaughter. "Oh, that one," Raven said disinterestedly, "she went croaking up the smoke hole and was never seen again." But we know that is not true, for Raven, like Coyote, can spin a tale that makes the world turn with it; can shape a shift of thought so that all thoughts shape around it. Even the Maker must smile when Raven puts tongue to the telling of how the world began.

The Story of Old Woman Moon

OF THE STORYTELLING GIFTS OF OLD MAN GOPHER AND
OF HIS TALE ABOUT OLD WOMAN MOON, THE SPINSTER
SISTER WHO IS ALSO A SEER

N O W Old Man Gopher had heard some things and seen some things, for he was the one who, they say, brought toothache into the world. Well, he listened politely to Raven's story, but he wanted to know more. "What happened to that selfish medicine man?" he asked. "And what about the rest of his family?" Raven did not—or would not—say, because the story was already told, the part she liked, anyway.

"You tell it, Brother Gopher, if you know anything about it," she commented, and went off looking for pretty baubles to hang in her lodge. That was the way she was; and the way Old Man Gopher was . . . well, as his tunnels and caves always prove, he will stop at nothing to get to the bottom of things. Whatever it is, he will dig down until he finds it. So the following tale belongs—as much as any story can belong to anyone—to him. And that is why this one has so much aching in it. But you must remember, he did bring toothache into the world.

"Now the medicine man, who had kept the light of the world in his lodge, had a spinster sister who became known as a seer. She knew all about the mystic arts: the power of chants, dreams, potions. Her teachers, though, were the sacred objects that her brother had hoarded in his medicine bundles: the stars, the moon, the sun. She listened to the stars at night, studied the curvature of the moon, the sun's arc across the heavens—these were her mentors, from whom she learned the secrets of the universe. And in the course of time, she grew as wise as the ways of the heavenly bodies.

"So the mountain people and the people of the river valleys came from afar to see the old woman with moon-white hair whose predictions of the weather, the death of a relative, the coming of a child were so often true. Someone might journey days and nights, wearing moccasins thin, just to ask the old woman a simple question, such as, 'Why is the moon a friend?' And she would answer in that tired, soft voice of the river wind that the people had come to expect: 'The moon shows lovers where to lie, children how to dream, thieves where to meet; so the moon, you see, is friend to all.'

" 'Tell us of the sun,' someone would ask.

" 'The sun has given us the gift of shadow, without which we would never know if we were going forward or back.'

" 'What of the stars?'

" 'The stars show the path to the pathless.'

"And so for every question, the old woman, who became known as Old Woman Moon, had an answer. So it seemed there was nothing she didn't know; and the people thought the world was contained in the whorls of the palm of her hand. However, there was one thing she didn't know, one question she couldn't answer; and this troubled her, gave her no rest. One day someone asked her, 'When do you think the world will come to an end?' Old Woman Moon thought about this for a long time, and in the end, all she could say was, 'That is the one thing I don't know!' But such was her nature, her need to know everything that there was, that the matter of the end of the world became a nervous twitch, then a weeping sore, and finally an expression of dumbfoundedness. 'Why,' she cried, 'was I given all but this one small piece of knowledge?' And she would rant and rave at Sun Father, shaking her fist with the fury of self-righteous madness. 'Tell me when the world will end!' she demanded, looking up at the sky. But this always happened at night when Sun Father was asleep, and after she woke him up, he'd holler down, 'Can't you see that I'm trying to get some rest?' But she was so bitter—the question of when the world was going to end having turned into a stone in her stomach—that she paid him no mind. But one night as she was carrying on, he got up, resolved to do something about it. I'll find a place where that old woman can occupy herself with something other than the end of the world, he decided. And he built a lodge on the moon, rode to the earth on his roan horse, Sundownway, and carried the old woman into the high mesas of the clouds, then put her down on the moon's silver sand. Here was quiet dust, white silence. By day, the moon burned pale; by night, the moon burned bright. But always the moon burned its lunar lamp in silence, impenetrable layers of ocean deep, feather down, smokeless stillness.

"So after this, Old Woman Moon was . . . well, you might say, almost happy. Since no one came to ask her questions anymore, she forgot all about the great unanswerable end of the world. She had nothing to do but boil corn in a great copper pot and, once in a while, stir it with a wooden spoon. One day, though, she saw Sun Father riding across a moony dune on his spotted horse, Dawnway, and she called to him, saying, 'I'm growing weary of life here, Sun Father. It is just so lonely on the moon. Can't you think of something for me to do?'

"Sun Father saw that all the old resistance had gone out of her; the moon-quiet had completely beaten her down. Thinking for a moment, he replied, 'I think you should weave a great long head strap, one as long as the moon is still.'

" 'All right,' she agreed, 'but I ought to have a friend.'

" 'I'll get someone to keep you company,' he offered, and rode off in puffs of powdery moon dust.

"Shortly after, Sun Father brought Bobcat to her door, and Old Woman Moon thanked him, for now she had much to do—boil corn, weave a head strap—and here was a fine person to talk to, Bobcat. And that, I should think, ought to have ended the tale happily, but, sad to say, there is no happiness to be had on the moon, only sheets of nocturnal fire, slow-burning in the cold light of the hidden sun. She was very busy, however. All day long, she shucked corn, tossing it in her boiling pot. And when she wasn't doing this, she was weaving that endless head strap. Stir the pot, shuck the corn, put it in the pot—under, over, over, under, weaver weave the threads together—that, I'm told, was her whole life. However, let's not forget Bobcat. He got so bored that whenever Old Woman Moon turned her back to stir the corn, he pounced on her head strap and pulled it undone. And she was getting so old and forgetful, she thought she'd never gotten around to finishing the thing, so she'd start weaving it all over again. Then she'd stir the corn, and Bobcat would take the head strap all apart again. As you can see, this goes on forever, which is why the work of Old Woman Moon is never done, why she appears always to be changing from thin to full, to thin, and back again, once again, to full.

"And now you know why the moon is thought to be a lonely old woman, foolish, wise, and more than a little mad. But the people still remember when she once lived in their village and answered all their questions—all but that one about the end of the world. And that, they say, is better left alone."

The Story of Owl Boy

IN WHICH OWL BOY LEARNS THAT THE WORLD OF MAN
IS NOT WHAT IT SEEMS TO BE AND THAT THE WORLDS
OF DAY AND NIGHT MUST REMAIN APART

O W L is the right person to tell the next story, for who, other than Owl, can tell what happens at night when everyone else is asleep? They say Owl sees all, and that is probably true, if half is to be considered the whole. You see, Owl is known for having certain sympathies, night being one of them. Once, long ago, she cheated at the moccasin game when the bet was down for a whole day's night, which meant, if she won, no day at all for the rest of us. Good thing, they say, that Owl's gambit failed. Who would want darkness all day long? But this is getting far afield. The story Owl told marks another beginning in the world. Once, as we know, the people were one, be they man or animal, two-legged or four. The animals, so they say, had hands, and the people had fur. Yet in time, one turned away from the other, and now Owl always asks, "Who is listening, who?" She alone claims to know the thing that split the people apart, putting animals and two-leggeds in different camps.

"Now it was Bear Woman who, you'll recall, was changed into Bear Guardian, protector of the forest. She accompanied Mother Earth on some of her star travels; once they even visited Old Woman Moon and ate some of her famous moon-white hominy. But after their adventures together, which are another story, Bear Guardian met a man, a member of the mountain lake people, and they settled down and had a family—or tried to; it wasn't that easy for her, as you'll soon see.

"It happened that Bear Guardian and her husband lived somewhat apart from the village. In the winter months, she softened the autumn elk hides, chewing the tough skin, wetting it with her mouth, so that her husband could do the delicate beadwork with his fine five-fingered hands. In the summer, she brought him hives of succulent honey. The honeybees hid in her fur, and she had to sit in the lake to drown them. One autumn, she gave birth to a son. She couldn't wait for her husband to come home from hunting so that she could show him their newborn.

"That night, when her husband entered the lodge, bringing arm-loads of fresh meat, Bear Guardian proudly showed him their son. At first, his face showed no emotion; he looked at the little round face, set in the cradle board, as if it were a stone. Then his neutral face showed something like fear. Turning away from the cradle board in disgust, he placed his head in his hands, crying out, 'For what reason, my wife, have you shown me this monster?'

"Whereupon Bear Guardian recoiled from him in surprise. Hurt, she hid her feelings, clutching the cradle board close to her furry breast. And for the rest of the evening, they said nothing to one another. They roasted the meat he had brought home, hung the rest on lodgepoles, and went to bed without speaking. But Bear Guardian tucked the cradle board close to her side of their sleeping robe, away from her husband, who, tired from the long day's hunt, was soon asleep. Bear Guardian, however, stayed awake most of the night, thinking about what she must do before dawn.

"Now they say a mother is *usually* blind to the faults of her child—but I want to know what mother isn't? After all, the child was created in the depth of her being. Her soul nurtured it; her flesh fed it; her heartbeat was the only music, until the moment of birth, that it ever heard.

"And then Bear Guardian thought about her husband. Did he ever feel the secret expansion, the mystic weight, as it increases, day by night and night by day? Did he—except for selfish reasons—ever eat for two, or more, if such there be? Did he feel the quickening kick of feet from within, pushing at the warm walls of confinement; did he feel the twoness, threeness, fourness of persons, unknown to him, filling up and rounding out his swollen belly?

"Bear Guardian knew, upon first examining him, that her son was different from her husband and herself.

"Yes, he had claws—not long like hers, but short and hooked, sharp as needles. Yes, he had a beak, a face claw, set on his face where his nose would have been. And as for his body, well, that, too, she had to admit, was round and feathered, fully made for flying. The child, in point of fact, was not a bit man, not a bit bear. He was all, if truth be told, owl.

"But a monster? Never. She would not hear of it; she'd die first.

"And so that crisp dawn, before the sun rose, Bear Guardian gathered up her owl child and headed out for the deep forest, where she thought to hide him from his father, because she knew that he meant, that very morning, to end the child's life. She took him, therefore, far away to spare his life, to give him another chance. She reasoned thus: If an owl is what he resembles, an owl he must be. And she took him to a place where the sunlight never penetrates the dark tangle of interwoven branch and overgrown needle—a pine forest where no men go, where no animals are safe, where the feathered cat of the night pine, Mother Owl, lives with her brood in a nest full of moon-splashed shadows.

"So she left her son there and slipped away, then roamed the upland hills, blazed her claw mark on half the trees of the forest, tore others down, raked the earth in sorrow and rage, frightened the timid birds from the tops of the high-branched aspens, and alarmed the bickering jays, who flashed insults at her but kept their squalling distance just the same. And she raged and roved, crying for her lost one, until, home at last, she saw her husband and thought again of having a child, which she did, and this one was born white and brown, a mixture of her and her husband, which was what they wanted in the first place. So all was well with them, but that is yet another story.

"Now Owl Boy grew up with all the advantages of an owl person. He learned the art of hunting from Mother Owl, the death feather falling out of the moonlight, claws extended; the clutching of a helpless heart. He learned the art of seeing in darkness, and his gold eyes grew big and round. He learned to sleep days, to hate sunlight and everything connected with the day, especially the hunting pat-

terns of ravens and crows, who tried to peck his eyes out while he
dozed in the dark.

"Time passed, and as he grew too large for his adopted mother's
nest, she asked him what he was going to do. 'I've raised you like
one of my own,' she said, 'no better, no worse, but now you've
outgrown the nest, as they have not. They're still children, and you're
full-grown.' And it was true: Owl Boy was so tall, after only four
days, that he had to sleep outside the nest, holding on to a leafless
branch, while his adopted brothers and sisters were still safe and
snug under their mother's wing. But he didn't mind—why should
he? His mother took him on her hunting trips, and, after he took to
sleeping by himself in a nearby tree, they went hunting together,
like husband and wife. Sometimes his eyes were even keener than
hers; he'd spot a nibbling mouse, a rabbit still as a stone, or a bird
dreaming of the coming day. Any and all were fair game for either
of them; the coils of their claws were the only nightly law they knew.

"However, though they enjoyed these hunts together, Owl Boy
grew restless. On nights when the moon was full and the valley filled
with milky light, he could see the faraway camp fires of the mountain
lake people, and a sensation would come back to him, something he
did not understand.

"He told his mother of this thing. 'When I'm out on the night's
broad wing,' he told her, 'I sometimes see the dancers in the dark
who make circles around fires as they sing. I hear them singing far
off when I'm just going to sleep, when the sun makes the lash of
pain across our eyes and we close them, keep them tight.'

"Mother Owl warned him then: 'You mustn't ever get too close to
the people of whom you speak, for they are evil. If they see you,
they'll kill you. They are of the day; we are of the night. It's always
been that way; it always will. I warn you, son, to keep your distance.'
So saying, she closed her eyes, for the moon was now a pared-down
stripling, a skinny thing, all skin and bone; and the sun would soon
be riding the mountain ridge, throwing out lances of hurting light.

"They slept and dreamed, and it happened that one day Owl Boy
took leave of his mother's sanctuary in the blue-black forest of spruce.
He flew by night to a forgotten village where the people used to
gather; it was a summer hunting camp, long since abandoned. In
the half-light, half-dark, he found a broken pot made of clay, a comb

made of shell, and these things spoke to him, telling him where to go.

" 'If you go south,' said the comb, 'you will find the people of your mother, the bear people.'

" 'If you go north,' said the pot, 'you will find the people of your father, the two-legged people.'

" 'Which way should I go?' Owl Boy asked.

" 'Which way do you dream to go?' asked the comb.

" 'The way home,' said Owl Boy.

" 'That way,' spoke the pot, 'leads to madness.'

" 'Why?'

" 'Because,' replied the comb, 'you are made of both bear and man. . . .'

" 'And yet,' added the pot, 'you are neither of these; you are the child of the owl.'

"Owl Boy looked at his hands for the first time. He plainly saw that they were hooked, not good for anything but hunting and slaying.

" 'I'm not afraid of either of my parents' people. You see, I have claws that kill and maim; I have wings that carve the night.'

" 'And still you are no match for the two-legged people. They will hunt you down and kill you as surely as the sun will come over the mountain in the morning.'

" 'We shall see,' Owl Boy said bravely. 'We shall see.'

"Owl Boy slept all that day, hidden in a hemlock. When night came, he flew over the abandoned village and found an old man's useless robe. It was frayed and old, but he threw it over his shoulders, anyway. And he added to this unseemly disguise a rotted fur hat with a broken eagle feather hanging off one side. So dressed, he flew through the skeleton trees; winter was just coming on and the frosted air had knives in it.

"When he arrived at the village of the mountain lake people, he saw that they were having a huge feast, accompanied by much dancing and singing. He had had a dream of this in his blood for a long time now; more than anything, he wanted to see if he could pass for one of these mysterious beings who acted as if the world were theirs and theirs alone.

"Flying down to a clearing just outside the village, he hobbled out

of the forest and joined the celebrants, pretending that he was one
of them. When he tried to dance, however, the spurs of his feet
tripped him, and he stumbled and fell. When he couldn't get up
quickly, nobody helped him; many of the people laughed in his face.
This angered Owl Boy as he'd never been angered before. Afterward,
when the people were going off to their separate lodges, Owl Boy
threw off his robe, shook off his hat, and leapt to the lash of his
wings. Flushing a small child out of the crowd, he easily killed it
with his claws, then carried it into the forest with him, where he ate
it. He did not take his usual precautions about finding a suitable
place to sleep. Overcome with tiredness, he chose to rest on the same
bare limb where he'd eaten his meal.

"Day came suddenly, for the night had been almost completely
used. And with the first light came hunters looking for the assassin
in the trees. 'There,' shouted the father of the boy who had been
taken, 'look to that tree and you'll see our enemy.' And there was
Owl Boy, eyes shut to the light of day, face red from the night feast
of the stolen child.

"The furious father notched his bow and let fly an arrow, which
struck Owl Boy in the shoulder, waking him up. Outraged, full of
pain, he dived down and raked the man across the head, but as he
glided away into the gloom of the forest, another arrow struck him
in the back. He floundered through the moss-grown trunks; then
the bright light of day assaulted his night-trained eyes. He cried
bitterly for Mother Owl, yet she was too far away to hear.

"It was his real mother who heard his cry; she came bounding out
of the glen, raging at the hunters, who soon fled, leaving her to her
natural-born yet unnatural child. And so Bear Guardian was again,
if only briefly, reunited with her boy. Gently, she withdrew the
pointed tips of the arrows, biting them out with her teeth, casting
them away. Then, licking his wounds over and over, as bear mothers
do, she gradually restored him to a condition that would permit him
to fly.

"How he staggered and fell; how clumsy her son looked, he who
could cut the night wind.

"Owl Boy stumbled and fell, begged to be put to death. And in
the end, there was nothing Bear Guardian could do about it. Her

son could not fly and would not try to work his wings, and she had no way of knowing how to coax them into action.

"It was then she sought out his other mother; she found the tree she'd long ago located and begged her to help.

" 'Your son—and mine,' she said, weeping, 'is hurt by a hunter's arrow. Please come and get him to fly.'

"Mother Owl blinked; the day was still hard and bright.

" 'I will come when it gets dark,' she promised, then closed her heavy-lidded golden eyes.

"That night, Mother Owl taught her wounded son how to fly with a broken, swollen wing, one which, nevertheless, got him off the ground and into the fortress of a pine tree. The wing would mend, but going home was a matter of winging from tree to tree, throwing the hurt body, catching it with winged madness. It was a fury of flapping.

"And so to home. Owl Boy didn't have a chance to look back and see his real mother, Bear Guardian, one last time; and that was the only time she ever saw her son again. For he kept to the dark leafy and piney places after that, never seeking the company of two-leggeds again. He turned all owl, grew out his feathers, healed the gristle bone shattered by the arrow point, and lived the life of a nighttime hunter, pouncing and piercing, never dreaming of anything but dancing mice, winter snow, and full-moon nights.

"Now, the two-legged people say Owl Boy deserved his fate, that they chased him away, off into the night where he belonged. They say that when a man or woman sees a red-faced owl in a tree, it means someone is going to die. They say Owl Boy had his chance to be friendly and lost it. And they add to this the fact that long, long ago, Mother Owl herself once played the moccasin game when the stakes were night and day. That is, the winner, if a night animal, would order the world to be always night; and the winner, if a day animal, would order the world to be always day. Good thing, the two-legged people say, Mother Owl was caught cheating, hiding the little stone that is used in the game under her wing instead of in the moccasin where it belonged.

"However, two-legged people say lots of things to suit themselves; they seldom listen anymore to what the animal people have to say.

Poor Owl Boy, he never got over being driven away from that mean-footed dancing ground. And, to hear the owl side of it, he never stole any child; it was nothing more than an old rat person who was out stealing rotten meat. The way the owl people tell it, all Owl Boy wanted to do was dance one dance around the fire without being made fun of. But look, an owl is an owl; a man is a man—isn't that the way of the world? Or does it just depend on whether you have feathers, fur, or skin? Our differences, they say, once kept us together but now keep us apart."

And so saying, Owl finished her tale and shut her night-shaped eyes, for as all could see, the sun was beginning to rise.

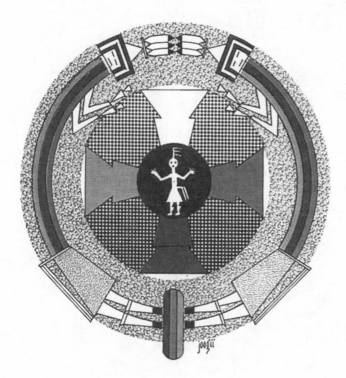

PART TWO

MYTHS OF LOVE, LOSS, AND LEAVING

BOOK 4

The Story of Sees-in-the-Night
The Story of First Light and Morning Glow
The Story of Rock Water Boy
The Story of Chicken Hawk Man

The Story of Sees-in-the-Night

OF SEES-IN-THE-NIGHT, WHO LOVES AND LOSES THE
BEAUTIFUL YOUNG WOMAN QUAIL'S CRY AND OF THEIR
LOVE FOR EACH OTHER, WHICH FUSES INTO A FLOWER

N the days of the long grass, there lived the people
of the plains, those whose lives made the rounds,
summer and winter, spring and fall, of the great
herds of big-shouldered buffalo. On nights when
the wind howled like a thousand wolves and the
wolves howled like a thousand winds, the plains
people stayed warm in their round houses made of stretched, dried
buffalo hide. They gathered round fires made of buffalo dung, drinking broth made from buffalo marrow. To the plains people, Buffalo
was elder, master, medicine; Buffalo was food, fire, prayer.

And the other great power of the plains was Eagle; a deed of honor
was rewarded by giving a sacred feather of Father Eagle, while a deed
of dishonor was punished by taking that same feather from the
shamed warrior. From the eagle bone, lighter than willow, prettier
than water, a medicine man carved many things: a bone whistle, a
sucking pipe for drawing out sickness, a sweet flute for making love.
And it was the love flute that Sees-in-the-Night played for the beautiful young Quail's Cry. These two, so the story goes, had grown
up, only tepees apart, in the roundness of their people's camp. Their
hearts were bound from the first moment they had ever laid eyes on
each other, yet their fate was that they seldom touched, hardly ever
showed their feelings openly to one another. At first dark, he looked
through the taut walls of his tepee, and saw the red coal glow of her
fire; they lived that close. In the conical skin house a stone's throw

67

away, he pressed his eye to the shadow movement of that perfect firelit form as she slipped, naked, under her buffalo robe. And she, through a place where the taut hide of her family's tepee had worn smooth as the silk of a summer stream, peered through the star-frosted night at that other naked form, strong-muscled, large, looming on the shadowy tent walls.

Their parents couldn't keep them apart—even if they had wanted to, which they didn't—but the fact was, they were cousins and thus not suitable for marriage. So they remained childhood friends who had bathed together, played together since birth, but whose love for one another had, by force of will, to be kept still. Nonetheless, they were a couple of playful ponies, touched by the sun, heads and tails flashing in the wind. They moved identically, as only lovers can, or do, unconsciously. And there grew in them a passion, a ferment, a deep desire to draw away from their families, to breathe the heady, heart-filled, forbidden air of their own idyllic camp, set in their minds somewhere off in the sage meadows where no one would see them making love through the long late-summer afternoon.

So it happened that whenever Quail's Cry gathered dry wood for the fire or rubbed a flint knife across the drawn, pegged hide of a buffalo skin, she daydreamed of her would-be lover, Sees-in-the-Night. And whenever he came back from the hunt, an arrow-pierced buck slung over his shoulder, he had thoughts of her.

She would think, If only I might touch him now, let him know how my heart thinks. And he, in turn, thought, If only my hand might feel her heart beat beneath her breast. And always when the sharp stars burned on the dark prairie night, the two pressed their faces to the hidden peepholes through which their eyes could lay claim to their dream: to press not faces but bodies in hot embrace, to roll under the autumn-furred buffalo robes, to feel the firelit reflections, the dancing shadows on their mingling skin, to love without fear of being caught. Instead, the cries of the nighthawk in their ear, they fell asleep in separate robes, tepees cut off by the great river of darkness. Then, as water turns over the stones of a riverbed, they drifted, dreamed. And at last, in spirit, lay in each other's arms.

The time came when Sees-in-the-Night set out upon his manhood calling: to trap an eagle. Hidden in a hole in the earth, he secreted himself. Above his head, a webbing of branches, overlaid with sod grass, was already in place; and, tied to a thong, a rabbit was strung out, alive, placed there as bait to draw the circling eagle down.

Time passed; he thought of the thing ahead of him, the thing he must do to prove his manhood. When the scream of the rabbit made its ghostly sound, he must leap up and out, straight and true, clutch the yellow-scaled feet of the taloned bird and pull it down, capture it, alive. Thus would prove his power. However, if he should fail, miss the feet, not grab them fully, then the stabbing beak would wreak havoc on his face, disfigure him, and the claws would rend him to shreds.

He sat cross-legged in the pit, waiting through the dove-quiet morning and into the locust-trilling afternoon. Thinking of his love, Quail's Cry, he began to doze, to dream, to see her soft skin under the deer dress she wore.

Suddenly, the loud flapping of dark wings tore him from his dream, where he was lying beside her on the riverbank, and through the webbing, he heard the shrill rabbit's cry, imagined he saw the well-sunk claws take the rabbit, jerk the thong. Now, he thought, before the proud bird discovers it is caught. Before the eagle could open its claws, unattach itself, Sees-in-the-Night leapt. Then, through the trickery of branches, he grabbed the thick-tendoned legs. He pulled them, crashing, wings flapping, down into the darkness of the hole. Quickly, he released the startled bird, flung a blanket over it, gave it the hood of night, roped it round with a gut-string tether.

He had caught the great sky eagle, and afterward a hero's welcome rang out in his village as he came home with his prize. His ears, however, were deaf to praise. His eyes waited on Quail's Cry, and when she whispered, "I'll meet you by the night river," he knew his dream had come true. After the feast in his honor, he left the village and went out across the level land, the hollow hills. White antelope heads lifted above the grass as he ran past; the first stars pricked the darkening sky; the late swallows swooped down through the lilac night. He crept toward the river—she was not there! His heart was frantic as his dream melted before his eyes. There in the river grass were her empty moccasins, side by side, as if she had kicked them off.

He knew the sign: All around them were many heavy footprints. Enemies, he thought, have taken my Quail's Cry. And it was written in the clay of the riverside, a tale bold as blood; there she had waited; there she had been taken. Running along the river, he sought further sign. There was none. His throat dry, his heart heavy, he stopped running, for he knew the law of the long grass, the law of the hunter, the hunted. Would he now return the eagle he had so recently taken from the sky? He, thief of eagles; his enemy, thief of hearts. Shedding bitter tears, he turned toward home.

But love, the first ember to light the heart, doesn't go gray and cold when dreams are ruined. As night came on, Sees-in-the-Night saw only a bleak line between sky and earth; the grass went dry; the burned hills died. He took out his knife and stabbed himself in the heart. He fell then by the river, the innocent blood running down the clay banks that looked like snow. And where his blood gushed out, guttered away into the water, a red-petaled flower grew, the one we call paintbrush, the lover's flower.

The Story of First Light and Morning Glow

IN WHICH THE TWO SISTERS FIRST LIGHT AND
MORNING GLOW HAVE A CONTEST FOR SUN FATHER'S
LOVE, WHEREIN THE LOSER IS SORROWFUL AND
MOTHER EARTH IS KIND; IN WHICH A CHANGE COMES
OVER MORNING GLOW AS SHE BECOMES
WOOD RAT GIRL

IN the desert under the Mountain Around Which Moving Was Done, there stood a great storied house made of mud, sand, and stone. The people who lived there were peaceful and as close to one another as the centuries of cedars that graced the windy sand hills of the desert. The peaceful people's days were spent growing and grinding corn, making thin leaves of fine blue bread, light as the dry mountain air, baked in the round sand-colored clay ovens that looked like beehives sitting in the sun.

One day, so they say, there were two sisters called First Light and Morning Glow who agreed to have a contest. First Light, the taller and elder sister, said, "Whoever Sun Father sees *first*, shall be the winner." Then she added, "Whoever Sun Father sees *last* will have worthless children."

What harsh rules to be laid down by such a lovely girl, but, such was her nature, firm and demanding, while her younger sister, Morning Glow, took things as they came, not thinking of the outcome, the presence of luck or loss or any other fateful thing. Well, these two sisters, having agreed on this unforgiving contest, waited through the night for Sun Father's morning visit. Finally, dawn came: the bright band of a sand-cast abalone bracelet. Then the sky reddened to crimson flush, and Sun Father rode out of the clouds on the great dawn roan with the flaming mane. Quickly then, the warmth of his greeting fell upon the fallen hair of First Light and she was bathed in the sun's glow. Next, his blessing fell on Morning

Glow, slipping down her face and shoulders, where, suddenly and unexpectedly, it stopped, leaving the rest of her body stranded in blue shadow. First Light stood proud, but there was a meanness in her demeanor, for she was the one who was all aglitter, all aglow, standing like a statue in the sun.

And there stood her poor sister, Morning Glow, a cold shadow blanket loosely thrown upon her, as if she was one not even worthy of Sun Father's kind attention. "Why am I," she cried sorrowfully, "cast off in shadow, while you are richly robed in light? What have I done to so displease our father?"

"You speak as if it was my fault," First Light chided. Then she added, "Remember the rules—whoever Sun Father sees *last* will have worthless children."

Hearing this, Morning Glow broke down, bursting into tears. And Mother Earth, who was watching the contest from afar, took pity on her daughter Morning Glow and changed her into a quick little wood rat that scampered off into the crack of a rock and disappeared from sight.

"I have won!" First Light decreed—and she had; the victory was clearly hers, but although she didn't know it at the time, without her sister to share it with her, her gain was really a loss. For, as you remember, the peaceful people, those who lived in the many-storied mud and stone house, were all one family, one blood. The taking of anything, without mutual benefit, was meaningless. First Light, as she soon learned, was miserable, for she missed her sister as much as she loved her father.

Little wood rat, though, was not forgotten. As the people tell us, she didn't go very far away; she lived in the big rocks outside her family's door. And though she lived in shadow most of the time, she enjoyed seeing her sister in the sun. For life, they say, is made of equal measure: sister of sun, sister of shadow. And that is why the people leave little crumbs on the rocks and why they find piñon nuts when they return.

The Story of Rock Water Boy

HOW THE YOUNGER BROTHER OF MORNING GLOW,
WHOSE NAME IS ROCK WATER BOY, SEDUCES HIS
SISTER WOOD RAT GIRL, AND HOW THEY ARE CAUGHT
AND PUNISHED BY SUN FATHER

O N E day, Rock Water Boy, who was the younger brother of Morning Glow, set a snare in the bare lichen-splashed rocks in the hope of catching his sister. He was more than curious; he wanted to see her close up in her wood rat's skin, touch her, and know that she was real. He was a rough person, with roughness in him, like a rock that has been pawed by the wind, suffered by the lashes of rain, the bite of snow. He knew that he was not supposed to capture Wood Rat Girl, but he was compelled to try. So he set a snare with string from the yucca plant, hid himself in the shade of the sun-spilled rocks, and waited out the glare of day. The snare, baited with sunflower seed, was irresistible; it worked, catching little Wood Rat Girl. "Ha!" Rock Water Boy shouted from his hiding place in the rocks. "I see you, my sister!" But Mother Earth saw her son's mischief. Pitying her poor daughter, as she had done once before, she turned Wood Rat Girl back into beautiful Morning Glow. And thus the clever brother saw his sister the way she once was, yet she was now more lovely than he remembered her.

Morning Glow, startled by the sudden change, discovered her body growing warm in the arms of her brother. She coaxed him then, helplessly and haplessly, to love. They moved among the rocks, seeking the shade. She, acknowledging a need she didn't know she had, exulting in a body she had forgotten was hers. Where no eyes would see them, they made raptured love, then rose from slumber and

73

began again. So it was that Rock Water Boy made love to his sister, not once but many times. And in the fire of the noonday air, her passion swelled, subsided, grew, faded, yet never seemed to stop until Sun Father, looking down from the midday sky, saw the rampant boy, his son, loving the spellbound girl, his daughter. And he passed between them the shock of recognition, so that they knew—suddenly and irrevocably—who they were and what they were doing.

"Oh" said Wood Rat Girl, "it is you!" And she turned back into a wood rat and scampered away.

Rock Water Boy turned from her, from what he had done, in shame. Then with his big toe, he drew a line in the sand and watched as it filled with water, made a river, a great roaring river. And the people came to see the fast river run. Rock Water Boy told them, "You must now cross over this river I have made, or something terrible will happen to us."

So the people entered the water, prepared to swim across, but halfway, the children began to bite their mothers. Some grew the round domelike shells of turtles, while others grew scaly-skinned, lost arms and legs, became snakes; and some sprouted feathers, beaks, talons. All were madly beating their mothers with wings and claws; silver-scaled, diamond-patterned, feather-crested, they fountained the water, made whirlpools, sprayed white froth in the four directions. The children were stronger than their parents and thus subdued them—hissing, singing, croaking, beating them with their webbed, clawed, hooked feet. As the frightened parents tried desperately to escape from them, the children swam underwater to the bottom of the river. They swam down to the root of the mountains, which extend all the way up to the sky.

"Our children," a mother wailed on the other side of the river, "turned on us." But Rock Water Boy told them, "Your children are now river spirits and mountain spirits. Those lights at the bottom of the river are their camp fires. One day, you'll see them come out of the tops of the mountains. They'll come to you and ask for a great dance. And just as you were their parents, they will now be yours—for all time."

Now, when they return today, just before darkness, the people honor them by sprinkling cornmeal beside the river. For it was on this sacred place that the middle ground was found, the place where balance among all life could be achieved. So now when darkness falls and fires burn, the people wait. And their children, the old ones, come again, through the roots of the rivers and the mountains, across the sky and into the village, the many-storied house of mud, sand, and stone.

The Story of Chicken Hawk Man

IN WHICH CHICKEN HAWK MAN TEACHES A LESSON TO
HIS UNFAITHFUL WIFE, BIRD WOMAN, WHO,
AFTER MAKING LOVE TO WATER MONSTER,
IS FOREVER CHANGED BY HER HUSBAND'S ARROW
INTO A THING OF GOODNESS CALLED GROUSE

A s the stories of heroes spread around the world, all were honored
in their own way and in their own time. But there was one who was
given no recognition because he claimed he wanted none. This was
Chicken Hawk Man, who lived in the north country. No less a shaper
of change than Rock Water Boy, Chicken Hawk Man, however, preferred to keep to himself. "Hunters who are seen too much become
the watched rather than the watchful," he would say, and that is
why he goes about his business on the sly. Yet he is known for one
great and famous deed, reported by Little Hawk—Kestrel, you may
call him—who, they say, tells all that he sees, which is quite a lot,
because he gets around. This is his story, told his way and in his
words.

"Chicken Hawk Man lived in a house made of bark, built in a clearing
of moss and pine. In the morning when he woke, the scent of balsam
and fir came to his nostrils and sweetened his breakfast of huckleberries, gathered fresh each day by his wife, Bird Woman. After
saying her morning prayers, she would go along the knotty path that
led to the lake of Water Monster, the one who has control of lakes
and rivers and, they say, all other bodies of water.

"Well, after filling her baskets full of ripe huckleberries, Bird
Woman went to the lake's edge to refresh herself. Usually, the sun-
warm shallow water was the color of wet bark, but when the sun

76

climbed higher in the sky, the sand was yellow and the deep water got so clear, you could see the stones on the bottom.

"Now, Bird Woman loved nothing more than to swim out into the center of the lake. But she feared to do so because of the stories people told of the Water Monster. He was known to be a greedy fellow, hot-tempered and unpredictable. So she stayed close to the shore, wading at first, then going in deeper, swimming farther out each day, until she was quite far from shore.

"One time, when she was standing halfway in and halfway out, she saw the one who lived there, the one whose water it was; and he came quickly to her. She tried to cover herself from him, but he had seen her, all of her, and it was too late. 'What do you want of me?' she asked him.

"He moved midway between water and shore, coming slowly toward her; she saw the color of his skin was like the bark brown lake and that his hair was long and unkempt, full of stringy water plants. His face, smeared with a claylike slime, was bumpy, pockmarked, and when he grinned broadly, she saw that he had no teeth.

" 'You swim in my lake each day, but you never give me anything,' he said sullenly, drawing closer to her.

" 'I pick berries for my husband,' she said, trembling.

"He was now close enough to touch her, and he did, leaving a stickiness where his hand met her skin. He smelled foully of the swamp, his slime-slickened features shining darkly in the sun.

" 'What you do, you do only for your husband, then,' he said, placing his oily hand on her breast.

"She shuddered under his touch as he put his other hand on her other breast. Again her body quaked, and an odd feeling went through her at the same time, a sense of powerlessness.

" 'Would you do for me what you do for him?' Water Monster asked.

" 'Gather berries?'

" 'No,' he sneered, pulling her toward him so that her face was pressed against his swamp-smelling chest.

"Bird Woman's fright was so great then that she slid out of his rubbery grasp, wriggled out of his mud-caked arms, and went running up the beach. He ran after, humping awkwardly along on his great, flat, toeless feet, and finally caught her at the edge of the huckleberry meadow.

" 'Are these the berries you've been gathering?' he asked, panting, as he held her tightly at the waist.

" 'Take them,' she stammered, dragging herself away into the meadow grass. But he had a hold of her foot now, and he let her struggle as he devoured the berries, throwing them, basket after basket, down his throat, leaving only one small basket untouched. Then, berry juices rippling in rivulets from his mouth, he climbed on top of her, forcing her legs apart. He groaned, as if he'd never had a woman; and she, for her part, screamed, for she'd never had a Water Monster. Afterward, they rolled away from each other. He lay on his back, rasping through his watery lips, and put his arm over his eyes, which were sensitive to the sun. Soon he was asleep, snoring louder than a bear and exhaling an odor of fishes and snails.

" 'He is like my husband,' Bird Woman said, 'only bigger.' Gathering her dress in her arms, picking up the baskets, and running away into the forest, she took the path that led to the bark house where she and her husband lived. And there he was at the door, waiting for her with a wondering look in his eyes.

" 'I've just taken a bath in the lake,' she said breathlessly.

" 'And how did you get mud all over your back?'

" 'That was when I tried to find the ripest berries for you, my husband.'

" 'Why is it, then, that you have only one basketful and all the others are empty?'

" 'That was when I got hungry from so much berry picking,' she answered, yawning.

"Then she curled up on the bear robe by the firestones that were still warm from the morning's fire. 'Don't worry, husband,' she murmured sleepily, 'tomorrow I'll get you plenty of huckleberries.'

"Now he sat disconsolately on a willow-backed brace, watching his wife sleep, and it seemed to him that her sleep was troubled, for her hands twitched like the paws of a dreaming dog. 'I will know more about this,' he said to himself. In the four days that followed, he said nothing, but always it was the same: His wife came home with empty berry baskets, clutching her clothes to her breast, her skin soiled with clay. Once, after she was asleep, he smelled her skin; it was rank with sodden waterweed, sour with the fish stench of the marsh. In her hair were bits of crushed water root, and he observed that her body was covered with claw marks and welts.

" 'We'll see,' Chicken Hawk Man said, 'who handles my wife so roughly.' So the next morning as Bird Woman set out, he followed her through the spruce, down the balsam-and-fern-lined path to the edge of the lake. There, the thing he already suspected was waiting, standing in the tule grass, grinning toothlessly, anticipating Bird Woman's arrival. He watched as his wife went singing, going freely to the thing's bidding. 'Bird Woman,' he whispered, 'is a traitor,' but he remained hidden behind the leaves of an alder. As Water Monster took her by the lakeside, grunting as he placed himself into her, she cried out, but not, her husband thought, in pain.

"Afterward, Water Monster fell asleep as usual, rattling horribly through his open mouth. Bird Woman, suddenly sensing her husband's presence, gathered her dress and ran for the path, but Chicken Hawk Man stepped quietly out of the shade and into the sun-dappled pathway, blocking her escape. 'Have you no feeling for us, Bird Woman?' he asked, looking away from her. She hung her head, not because she was sorry for what she had done but because she was so tired from her exertions with Water Monster; since he'd laid claim to her, she let him do what he would in his presence, but she did nothing but sleep in his absence. Now she was just too tired to talk; her head drooped and she thought she would fall asleep on her feet. Chicken Hawk Man, meanwhile, selected the finest sun arrow from his quiver, and as his wife weaved to and fro with her eyes half open, he shot her through the breast. Then her eyes came open, and, staring wide, startled, she sprang away in surprise, tugging at the arrow that was all the way through her. Then she fell softly into the fern brake, collapsing quietly, no sound from her lips except a breathy *cheep*, her head dropping back as she tried to breathe, her eyes staring deeply at her husband. Now, stepping clear of the hip-deep ferns, he walked away from his wounded wife and down to the lake, where Water Monster was stirring from sleep. 'Oh, friend,' Chicken Hawk Man called out playfully. Water Monster awoke, heaving himself foolishly to his feet, his drooling mouth gaping in surprise.

" 'How did you come upon me so quietly?' he asked. Chicken Hawk Man circled him, smiling.

" 'It was not hard. Now, are you prepared to die?'

"Water Monster laughed until gray foam curdled over his lower lip.

" 'Are *you*?' Water Monster hissed.

"Chicken Hawk Man laughed dryly, and he let fly the second of his sun arrows, those blessed with the first light of the sun, and the shaft went deep into the neck of Water Monster. He clung to the arrow with his pulpy hands, trying unsuccessfully to rip it out of his throat. Then he turned and fled toward the swamp, thrashing, plunging, sinking, and finally crawling under the sedgy leaves. Yet even after he was gone into the backwater, bubbles came to the surface, emitting the hiss of the dying creature.

"After this, Chicken Hawk Man climbed up the path where his wife lay bleeding in the ferns. Now her eyes were large and clear and beginning to glaze with death.

" 'My husband,' she cried, 'though you've killed me, I love you still.'

" 'Bird Woman,' he whispered, cradling her in his arms, 'why did you bring me to this?'

"She didn't answer, though, for her spirit left her then, soaring darkly out of the sweet-smelling fern brake. From the blood-soaked bracken, Chicken Hawk Man saw his wife's spirit turn into a beautiful golden brown bird, a bird with wings that drummed as they rose and fell, wings that shuddered and made a lovely-sounding noise.

" 'Ah,' he said in recognition. 'Bird Woman, you've become the one we will call Spruce Grouse.'

"And ever since that time, the people of the forest have eaten grouse and liked the earthy taste that comes with it—the flavor of ripe huckleberries and damp grass, wild ferns and wet spruce. And some say there is the taste of something else, as well—something, they say, that cannot be described any better than the tameness that has made Spruce Grouse such an easy target for hunters."

BOOK 5

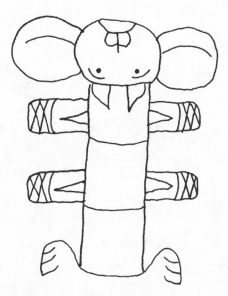

The Contest between Coyote and Spider Woman

HOW MAGPIE TELLS OF THE CONTEST BETWEEN COYOTE
AND SPIDER WOMAN AND THE GRIEF THAT COMES OF
COYOTE'S NAME-CALLING

N E time, Magpie was complaining that she was as good a storyteller as anyone else, maybe better, and since Raven and Coyote were not around to challenge her—their storytelling efforts being the loudest, if not the best—Magpie launched into a narrative that did no harm to her reputation and did more than a little damage to Coyote's. You may wonder how it is possible to damage something that is already ruined. For Coyote's reputation was off to a bad start from the very first—as this tale amply shows. Here, anyway, is Magpie's version of the contest between Coyote and Spider Woman.

"They say that First Man sent Coyote to discover the source of the dawn. The first thing he did was to steal two of Water Monster's children, keeping them tucked under his arm while the great flood ravaged the land, but that certainly isn't the worst thing he did.

"First Man gave him the name Coyote, which ruffled his fur the wrong way, so he renamed him First Angry, which, in the end, he accepted, and went on his way. It was after that, however, that he stole the polestar, which First Man and First Woman had laid out on a piece of blue velvet; then he tried to steal the sun, but it was too hot to hold on his tongue, and he had to spit it out.

83

"Now the people say Coyote's wife was just as troublesome as he was. She was the one who begged Mother Deer to tell how she put white spots on her children's coats. Mother Deer told her to fan some ashes on their fur, but when Mother Coyote tried it, she used red-hot coals instead of cold gray ashes; as a result, she burned all their fur off. And that's not all: One time, after she'd had another batch of children, she was bringing water to them, one mouthful at a time, and she walked under this aspen tree where Bluejay was waiting for her. 'My, aren't you dressed up tonight!' he said. Whereupon, Mother Coyote forgot all about her babies and swallowed the water she was bringing home to them. Bluejay's foolish remark went straight to her head every time; and after a few dozen passes under the aspen, with Bluejay always making that same remark and Mother Coyote always swallowing the water intended for her babies, her poor, parched children died of thirst! That is what they say, anyway; and so now you understand why the people shake their heads when they hear the name Coyote. But did you know that one time Coyote had a battle with Spider Woman? Of all Coyote stories—and there are a great many—this is the most outrageous, because Spider Woman never hurt anyone—almost. On the other hand, Coyote could make a stone roar with rage, always.

"The way it happened was that Coyote was out bragging, telling people there wasn't anything he couldn't do better than someone else. Buzzard asked if he could weave as well as Wood Rat, and he replied, 'Better.' So he asked if he could weave as well as Spider Woman, who is the world's best weaver, and Coyote answered, 'You set up the loom and I'll weave the webbing right out from under her!'

"Now Turkey was present while this was going on, and he suggested that the two of them play the weaving game, the one where you have to always tell the truth. 'It's well known that you like to lie,' Turkey said. 'Therefore, you may weave only when you say something truthful. One word of truth, one strand of wool. Of course, Spider Woman will do the same.' Having agreed upon these rules, Coyote and Spider Woman took their places before their looms. The first thing that Coyote said was, 'Bear is the one who brought coughs into the world.'

" 'This is true,' Turkey replied, and he gave Coyote a strand of wool, which he threaded into his loom.

"Then Spider Woman said, 'Old Man Gopher brought toothaches into the world.'

" 'True,' said Turkey, and so it went, back and forth, like a game of handball. And for a while, it sounded just like this:

COYOTE: Magpie's white feather is named Dawn.
SPIDER WOMAN: Owl's house is called Darkness.
COYOTE: Bobcat's coat is covered with stars.
SPIDER WOMAN: Wolf is called Big Roamer.
COYOTE: Elk is called Food.
SPIDER WOMAN: You are known as Coyote.
COYOTE: You are called Ugly Teeth.
SPIDER WOMAN: You are called Piss Pants.
COYOTE: You are called Fat Ass.

"And so it went, the weaving game turning into a battle of insults, which Coyote was probably going to win because he always knows the meanest things to say about someone. So Turkey stopped the weaving game by declaring that neither one of them had won, and the contest was over. However, it didn't stop there. Coyote kept calling Spider Woman names, while she just sat still and didn't say a word. Her hands were weaving the whole time Coyote was heaving insults at her, though, and she was making a very fine web, so fine, in fact, that you couldn't see it. This web was as thin as breath, as strong as sunlight, as sharp as the horns of the moon. And she wove the web for days, while Coyote went around calling her names, which, much to her credit, she just ignored. However, finally he decided to kill her. That way, he wouldn't have to call her names anymore. So Coyote ran at her, baring his teeth, but he ran right into that invisible web she'd made. And that web, thinner than a thought, cut Coyote into a thousand little pieces. So Spider Woman got the last laugh. But Little Wind, who always has a good heart, felt sorry for old First Angry; he picked him up and put him back together again. Then he called forth some of the other wind people—Left-Handed Wind, Summer Wind, Big Wind Coming, and Wind-in-the-Air—and they blew the life back into Coyote. After that, he vowed never to insult Spider Woman again, and he hasn't said a bad word to her to this day, at least not to her face. That is what they say, anyway."

The Story of Slim Girl and Mountain Wing

OF THE CHASE OF SLIM GIRL BY A SERPENT OF THE
EARTH, A WITCH WHO IS ALSO A HANDSOME YOUNG
MAN, AND OF SLIM GIRL'S RESCUE BY MOUNTAIN
WING, A GOD OF EARTH AND SKY

N O W there is the contest of foolishness, as in the previous Coyote story, and the contest of love, as in the following tale of Slim Girl and Mountain Wing. Here is the tale of a beautiful girl, much like Bear Woman when she was still a maiden, who drew the powerful god of the mountain to her. One who listens carefully to this one will understand something of the mystery of life. Mystery, to the mountain people, those who lived in the ring of mountains to the north and who later moved down to the southern plain, was a way of acknowledging the inexpressible and inexhaustible beauty of existence. For all of life was beauty, and all of beauty was mystery. Nothing to the mountain people was strange or impossible, since all things came from the same source. And that source, both beautiful and mysterious, was the great, unknowable, mysterious way.

Now if all of life was born at the same source, or fount, then it shouldn't seem strange—and it didn't to the mountain people—that a common stone should speak with the uncommon voice of a man. For what, after all, is a stone but a little chip off the mountain's shoulder? But let the tale be told by the one who lived it, the way the people tell it today, in the remembered words of Slim Girl, the woman who was embraced by the great mountain of mystery.

"One day, I was tired from nut gathering. I remember that the day was warm, the sun high, the sky without cloud. There was a stream that I knew, far off in the depth of the butternut woods, where I used to go as a child. The water of that stream was as transparent as the broth made of marrowbones. You could see the white pebbles clear to the bottom, and the water was cold and there were no ripples on the surface of the stream.

"I put my nut baskets down on the bank and dipped my toes into the coolness. It felt so good, and I was so hot that I waded a little way in, holding up my skin dress. Tiny minnows nibbled my toes. The leaves of the willows whitened as they fanned back in the gentle breeze. Then I took my dress off, pulling it over my head, threw it on the bank, and entered the water without a sound. The minnows scattered from my shadow, which rippled like a great dark fish across the pebbled bottom. I glided, turned, glided again, and thought I saw in the corner of my eye a handsome young man sunbathing on a bark-stripped log on the streamside.

"I blinked and then, suddenly, I saw the streamside roll and flow like a great serpent. The moss-muscled bank heaved again, growing enormous. Then the whole sloping green-scaled bank of summer fern heaved up and came after me. I ran from the stream, naked, no time to fetch my garment. And the thing, swollen up and rolling, plunged ahead, surrounding me. I climbed up over it, but it changed shape, swirling around the very ground I was standing on, rising up, falling down, turning and blocking my path. I skirted around it wherever I could, dodging its advances.

"Cutting my hands on thicket and thorn, I ran on through the shape-shifting forest. And it kept changing as I ran—here, a bank of purple primrose, swelling huge as I passed; there, an oak thicket, a sudden explosion of bark chips, leaves, catkins, and lichens. I heard roots ripping apart; grass—if grass could scream—screaming! Listening to the shredding of the earth, the molten mouths of ten thousand hissing serpents, I ran, on and on.

"As night came, I knew that I was tiring, losing heart. My burning skin was spotted from the earth's mad eruptions, and always the stalking thing rolled on, changing form as if the land were its own skin. Once it sought to ensnare me with a fold of belly—white scales, the underside of a grassy hillock, it looked to be—but I fought to get over it, grasping the heads of tussocks, scrabbling, scrambling

to get free. I felt then like the poor hunted rabbit in the center of
the stick-throwing circle, the hunters closing in, singing the rabbit song. I felt like the wounded deer leaving blood spoor as the
hunters close in, arrows notched in tightly strung bows. My body
was all one cold sweat now, for I knew it had me; there was no way
to escape it.

"Then I heard a kind voice say, 'Come now, child, no dark thing
with night scales will come after you where I go.'

" 'Who are you?' I said.

"It said, 'I am called Mountain Wing. Come, I will protect you.'

"So I let Mountain Wing, a presence like a great storm cloud, enfold
me with his wings, and as he carried me into the upper air, I saw
the serpent thing writhe and rage, charging at us with furious coils,
a spiked, hammering, pointed head. But though it was powerful on
earth, it had no power in the sky. Mountain Wing rose higher and
higher, taking me up where the rainbow people bend beneath the
sun; where the winds store their magic breaths; where Sun Father
sheaths his bolts of lightning; where Old Woman Moon stirs her pot
of boiled corn; and where the star people dream of the pretty girls
they left on earth.

"Then Mountain Wing carried me back down, but far, far away
from the serpent thing. His sheltering wings of darkness were all
around me, and I felt myself settling at the foot of a great mountain.
The moment my feet touched the earth, Mountain Wing changed
into hard seamless stone, glittering in the starlight. And you can see
him there today, rising over the moonlit plain, towering over the
rivers and streams that wander aimless at his feet. His wings have
grown still, but they enfold our people with power, just as they once
lifted me out of danger and put me back on the earth, where I
belonged.

"And now I tell all young girls who will listen not to swim in the
stream by the butternut woods, for an old evil serpent man lives
there to this day; he was once a two-legged child like any one of us,
but his grandmother, they say, was a witch who fed him sumac milk,
boiled corn, snake intestines; taught him to sing through his throat
like a snake person; made him bathe in that secret stream until the
day when he became a serpent witch himself. So if you should see

a handsome young man lying on a log by the streamside, beware, for he is not what he appears to be; he is the evil spirit twin of the serpent thing that haunts those woods. Keep an eye to the mountain, I say, and remember that Mountain Wing will come if you call his name."

The Story of Rain Boy and Butterfly Boy

IN WHICH THE SHAPESHIFTER, BUTTERFLY BOY, CASTS
AN EVIL SPELL OVER DAWN COMING, THE WIFE OF
RAIN BOY, AND IN WHICH THERE IS A GREAT RACE
BETWEEN RAIN BOY AND BUTTERFLY BOY AND THE
GOOD THAT COMES OF IT

THE stories of spells and spellmakers got around, and it was not long before it became known that there was a woman, Dawn Coming, who lived in the desert under the great arch of Rainbow Bridge. She was the wife of a watchful and often jealous husband named Rain Boy, who kept her weaving blankets for him, safe at home. She never spoke of her talent on the loom, the curious power that made the spindle sing, for to do so would be to insult Spider Woman; and only Coyote was capable of that. Better, by far, to let one's gift flower in silence.

When it came to designs, she breathed life into the thing she wove; a mesa on her loom was a brow of gold surrounded by the smoke of dusk; a cactus wore a halo of silver spines, thumbed with budding purple fruit. Whatever she chose to weave came alive under the nimble magic of her spidery fingers. And when she dyed the thirsty wool red, it stayed that color as long as the threads of the blanket stayed together. Children watched in wonder as Dawn Coming wove a portrait of First Man. Sun-blessed, agleam with golden grains of corn pollen, he stood in beauty, as if alive and ready to speak.

Word got around—the people say Hummingbird told all of the flowers—that Dawn Coming was not only a wonderful weaver but a wonderful-looking woman, as well. And one day, such talk brought a wicked person to her door. His name was Butterfly Boy, and though he was as handsome as the day, he was also as tricky as the night. However, Dawn Coming knew nothing of him. She didn't yet know

91

of his mysterious powers, his passion for playing tricks on those who were unaware of his spells; and so she was like Slim Girl, innocently gathering nuts in the woods. One morning when her husband, Rain Boy, was not around, Butterfly Boy paid her a surprise visit. Another idle admirer, she thought, not really thinking or paying attention. Now, as he saw the loom was set to frame a new creation—the weft bound to the juniper beam, the threads carded and spun, the shuttle ready to sing through the waiting warp—he was much impressed. Her workmanship had such personal grace, her hands so fully under her command, that he stopped and looked deeply at her face, and immediately he found himself—the enchanter—enchanted with her beauty. As he observed her hands fly to their threaded goal, he witnessed the miracle of Dawn Coming's vision—a rainbow burning through the haze, a blue deer dancing on a cloud. Amazed, he said, "The eye cannot see the difference between your art and the real thing!" She, saying nothing, plied her spindly fingers to the magic work of making art, turning that which is unreal into a shining vision of reality. Now, as he admired, spellbound, each furrow in the woolen earth sprang up into radiant, incandescent life. Butterfly Boy began to spill unwanted praise upon her ear, but his words of sweetest honey were wasted, for she worked not for praise or blame but only to honor the beauty of that which she saw around her.

Finally, failing to gain her attention by his gift of speech, Butterfly Boy said, "If you would but take your eyes from your work, I would show you what you've missed!" This being a new thought to her, she glanced in his direction, catching sight of his trickster's eye. And then the wind-burned breath of the desert died down; the dry cicada song sank back into the farthest cornstalks of the faraway afternoon.

He had her in his power: His evil butterfly's spell was complete. Straight away, her wondrous fingers got caught in her own dreaming wool, which turned into a wicked garden of pumpkin vines, shooting up and binding her hands so she could not move. It was then, at this treacherous moment, that Rain Boy returned from the hunt, standing confidently, legs apart, leaning and grinning. His enemy, Butterfly Boy, was about to take away his wife; and yet, he had only disdainful mirth for this despicable act.

"Let me challenge you to a race," he offered casually. "The first one to get to Thunder Mountain will take Dawn Coming for his own—"

"That's fair," Butterfly Boy said, smiling whimsically, for there was nothing that he enjoyed more than a race.

Well, as soon as Rain Boy ran off, the sky darkened and it began to rain. Butterfly Boy, fearful of getting wet, flew to a cliff and found a dry overhang to shelter his pollen-dusted wings. Rain Boy, though, ran on, and as he flashed darkly across the desert, the sky blackened and rivers of rain ran in the parched arroyo beds of mocha-colored sand.

And when he reached Thunder Mountain, a rainbow person greeted him, curving artfully out of the sky.

A little later, he met Butterfly Boy wandering dizzily along the wet road. His soft wings drooped; his head hung down. "You've beaten me," he said emptily.

And Rain Boy, who could not have explained why, felt sorry for him. You see, it wasn't Rain Boy's way to break a man down, especially one so obviously undone by his own wretched deeds. He showed, therefore, his usual mercy, telling Butterfly Boy they could have another race, for the same stakes. Yet, as plainly as Rain Boy showed kindness, Butterfly Boy concealed cunningness. "Let's not race just yet," he pleaded. "Let me catch my breath first."

Oh, the foolish things we must learn in order to live in the world. What traps we set for ourselves, what snares of sympathy, which cost us so dearly. Rain Boy, disposed toward doing right, set himself up to fall under the evil spell of the magician's fluttery wing. Better he had broken him than trusted him, for now Butterfly Boy made the sun shine bright and hot. This quickly weakened Rain Boy, drained him of his rainy magic, his personal power.

Butterfly Boy then raised up his sun-soaked wings; the day glowed, honed to the shine of a killer's blade. "I can't see!" Rain Boy cried, stumbling in the sun. He tripped and fell. "Too bright, too bright!" he wailed, his power gone.

"So, it's true, what I thought," Butterfly Boy whispered wickedly. "Rain Boy can't run in the bright sun!"

And thus Rain Boy would have lost his lovely wife, had not Dawn Coming seen the pitiful sight from afar. From where he had imprisoned her, she saw the butterfly's evil spell. Rising to save her husband, she carded and spun the very vines that held her captive. And now her art served her once again: She wove her captor into a design of her own, the picture of his undoing. Up from the earth leapt the pumpkin flowers, the plump green stalks that snared her hands. Now they ran rampant, snaked across the sands, seized Butterfly Boy, and threw him to the ground, binding him into a helpless ball.

Then Rain Boy rose, got to his feet, staggered, and shook off the bad spell. "Now it's my turn to deal," he said softly, raising his ax over his head. But Butterfly Boy, helpless as the day he was born, twisted and writhed, begging for one last gesture of sympathy. "Let me die by the blade of my own ax," he wheedled, "that's all I ask."

Well, as everyone knows, Butterfly Boy's ax always does his master's bidding; that is, anyone other than Butterfly Boy who holds that ax in his hands would, if Butterfly Boy gave the order, cleave his own skull. "Your ax looks rusted," Rain Boy said. "I think it's better we use mine." And so saying, he again raised his own weapon over his head and brought it down hard. The blow struck clean; Butterfly Boy's skull split like an overripe melon into two perfect oval halves.

And out of this cracked skull came a funnel of baby butterflies, an upflung scarf of beautiful bright-winged creatures, and they scattered across the sky, becoming the butterflies of this world. As the people say, they are better off being small and unaware of their fragile, spellbinding beauty.

BOOK 6

The Story of Great Snake, Blue Racer, and
Younger Sister
The Story of Deer Boy
The Story of the First Animal Council

The Story of Great Snake, Blue Racer, and Younger Sister

OF SUN FATHER'S GIFT OF THE POWER OF LIGHTNING
TO GREAT SNAKE AND OF YOUNGER SISTER'S
SEDUCTION BY BLUE RACER OF THE TWO-LEGGED
PEOPLE WHO LEARN THAT ALL SNAKE PEOPLE ARE
THEIR RELATIONS, WHO MUST BE ADDRESSED WITH
TRUE KINDNESS

 o w it happened that the animal people and the two-legged people began to feel estranged from one another. For the two-leggeds had flint and fire and bows to send arrows from where they stood. But the animals had only tooth and claw, and they had to rush to use them.

It was after Sun Father had given his quiver of crooked lightning arrows to his son to carry to earth that he realized that the animal people had no arrows for themselves. "Who among you shall carry my lightning arrows?" he asked those animals assembled in the sun grove on top of the Mountain Around Which Moving Was Done.

And there came a voice from a hole in the earth, which said, "I shall carry them."

"Who speaks?" Sun Father asked.

"It is I, Great Snake," the voice answered.

"Why should you be the carrier of sacred arrows?"

"I am a lowly creature without arms and without legs, but I would like to carry the arrows."

"And how would you hold them?" Sun Father asked.

"I would hold them in my mouth," Great Snake replied.

Sun Father considered this seriously, for it was a matter of great moment: The animal people needed his arrows as much as the two-legged people did, and there was no animal person, as yet, who was meant to carry them. Without fire from the heavens, there would be

97

no rain; without rain, the creatures of the earth would soon die. All opposite elements were needed—fire and frost, water and lightning, heat and cold, day and night—if the world was to stay in harmony. And, in addition, Sun Father was certain that if the two-leggeds kept the power of lightning arrows all to themselves, the animal people would be the worse for it.

"Very well," he said, "I have thought this thing over, and if you, Great Snake, believe that you are equal to the burden of the sacred arrows, then you may try to carry them now. But first show me how you walk upon the earth."

Great Snake stretched himself to his full length, and, rolling his seemingly boneless body along the sandy plain, he ebbed away like a ribbon of water.

"Ah," Sun Father said, amused, "so that's how you do it. Well, you're not much better off than a worm, just faster."

Great Snake stopped, hissing with evident displeasure and drawing his coils around him in a mass of protective loops. He lay there, a mixture of sun and scales and bone-lapsed coils, but there was a fidgeting at the end of his tail.

"What is that?" Sun Father asked.

"That is my temper sounding," Great Snake said, rising up in height and opening wide his large white mouth. He was so hot-headed, and always had been, that he was barely able to suppress his wrath. This always happened when anyone or anything challenged him.

Sun Father looked at Great Snake and thought to himself, I do not believe he is the right representative, somehow, for the arrows, yet who of the animal people gathered here is better? There is Badger, much too dirty; the caked mud of the first world still stuck to his rough, matted belly fur. There is Coyote, who already had the responsibility for rainmaking and childbirth, both risky prospects, at best; the fellow is too unreliable to be trusted with lightning arrows. There is Lizard, much too lazy and too preoccupied with himself. And there is Bear, already a guardian, but moody and unrelenting most of the time.

Sun Father looked at Great Snake, examining the tip of his tail, which was making a whirring sound like hard seeds in a dry gourd.

"Still angry?" Sun Father asked.

"Can't be helped," said Great Snake.

"Very well, then," Sun Father said, reaching into his quiver and notching a lightning arrow into his bow. "We'll see how well you hold one of these." And he let loose a shaft of lightning that zinged into the open mouth of Great Snake. The arrow struck, knocked back his head, unhinged his jaws, which is why, they say, that Rattlesnake's mouth opens so wide, why his jaws come apart the way they do, and why he still has lightning coming out of his mouth.

But yet when Sun Father's arrow went down Great Snake's throat, it didn't stop there but traveled all the way to the tip of his tail, and the bolt, being crooked in three places, made Great Snake jerk forward and back and side to side. And that is why Rattlesnake always moves the way he does, first one way, then another, crooked, like lightning.

"You're pretty strong to take such powerful medicine," Sun Father said, "and so, I suppose, it is settled. You may carry a quiver of sacred lightning arrows for the animal people." And so it was—at least for a time; but things have a way of unsettling themselves, falling out of balance. Great Snake's medicine power, they say, turned him into a being of imperious behavior. Many of the animal people feared him and stayed well away from his lodge.

It happened, one day, that Younger Sister, a good-looking two-legged girl, was out looking for some quail eggs to take home for supper when she saw a wisp of smoke rising into the clear blue sky. I know what that is, she thought. It's the smoke of Great Snake's pipe. The thought of Great Snake made her shiver, and she ran in the direction of Sage Canyon, trying to get away from the sight of his smoke. Yet his was curious smoke, and, under his instructions, it followed her there.

When she got to Sage Canyon, she saw a tiny hole in the ground. If I could only fit into that, she thought. Then a voice told her that she could. "Blow four times on the hole," the voice said, and she did. The hole expanded, swallowing her up, and soon she found herself in a cave way under the ground. A slender, bluish-faced young man stepped up to her, and though she could not see him very well, she knew he was handsome.

"Step into the light so I can see you," she suggested, but he said that he preferred the dark. After a while, though, her eyes began to adjust and she saw the young man more clearly. He had narrow shoulders and a blue glow came off his face, but otherwise he looked like a man.

"My name is Blue Racer," he said.

"I am Younger Sister," she told him.

"Why are you here?"

"Great Snake's pipe smoke was following me. Didn't you see it?"

"No great snake comes here," Blue Racer said confidently.

"I am very grateful, then, for your protection."

But as she said this, there was a rumbling at the opening of the cave and a booming voice roared down to them: "I can see you hiding. Come out of there at once!" A huge golden eye filled the entranceway of the cave, its center like a black crescent moon. Blue Racer moved sinuously toward the hole. "You'll not like it if I decide to come out," he explained softly to Great Snake, who was astonished at his rudeness but who, taken by surprise, slid back, away from the hole. "You see," Blue Racer whispered to Younger Sister, "I'd wrap him with coils and squeeze him to death. He might shoot me with his five arrows, but these do me no harm; my blue armor protects me."

"I'm leaving now," Great Snake hissed in rage, his tail thrashing up a dust storm, "but I'll be back." Then he went away in the manner to which he was accustomed, gliding across the smooth sand like a furrow of forked lightning.

"Now we've gotten rid of him." Blue Racer smiled. "I'd like to see what you really look like. I think it would be best if you took off your clothes." This sudden talk, ripe with familiarity, surprised Younger Sister, but she realized there was nothing she could do. Her host, now that he'd saved her life, was in control of her; besides, his magical ways were not something you could run from. So she shed her dress and he took off his coat of iridescence, hung it on a peg on the cave wall, and came to her, naked. He was a handsome person, very well formed, and he moved with deliberate calm, surrounding her with his dreamlike presence. All at once, she was smothered in smoothly crafted movements; his flickery tongue tickled her eyelids, her chin, danced at the edge of her lips, and entered her mouth. As he dreamed himself into her flesh, she heard the rustling of cast-off clothes— dry, discarded coats that crackled crisply as they lay on them. The pair locked in an embrace of slow-rolling love that made Younger

Sister dream she was on the shore of some great far-off lake, where, ever attended by the soft, eager lapping of the waves, she drifted, floated, let go of her mind, and seemed to dream deeply yet never drown. When it was over, if it ever was over, she slept.

And finally she awoke one morning, if morning it was, for the light inside the cave was all one unvarying shadow, neither light nor dark, but something of the two. Then she had a bad pain in her stomach, and her dream-husband, the bluish-faced man, Blue Racer, came and went, slipping in and out of the cave. She couldn't get through the hole because her hips were too wide, and then she grew too large in the stomach. She begged to go home, though she knew it was too late, but Blue Racer chuckled softly under his breath, saying, "It will be all right, you'll see." Then, dream of dreams, his whole sinewy family came to live with them. She kept stepping on them by mistake, but the way they curled up left her no choice. Then one day, she gave birth to two little snake people, who were her children as well as his. She knew then that this was no dream, that she had really married Blue Racer, who was her flesh-and-blood husband. Her children were blue and black and they had little copper-colored tongues like their father, and yet otherwise they were much like her. But being a mother, she raised them; and, being a wife, she honored her husband.

Now, in time, she went to visit her family on the other side of Sage Canyon. Hers were desert people, always on the move; just now they stayed by the canyon's rim, but soon they would go to another place, far away. When she arrived at her mother's earth house, her mother told her to leave. "You don't smell right anymore," her mother scolded, hiding behind the walls of their mud-plastered, juniper-roofed lodge.

"You'll be sorry, Mother, if you don't treat me well," Younger Sister said, much offended, but her mother stayed out of sight and didn't come out into the sun at all. That afternoon, as Younger Sister was going back to Sage Canyon, some children from her village threw rocks at her. And so it was that she returned to the secret hole of her cave dwelling, met her husband, and told him what had happened. Then his dark blue face, which in the sun went silvery, turned dark plum as he heard of his wife's treatment. "No member of our family has ever been treated so!" And his tongue danced angrily between his teeth. Then he lifted a deer-bone whistle to his lips, made a windy, reedy noise with it, and drew from the hills and rocks, and from all the cardinal directions, a great number of snake people. They were of all shapes and sizes—with bellies of white and yellow and backs of smooth plate and rough shield; with good and bad and unbearable breath; with heads square, flat, round, pointed, thin, and triangular. And they all came around Blue Racer, then writhed away when he told them to spread out and find a two-legged person's lodge and move into it. This was his decree, and this was what they did.

Well, what happened then anyone might wonder. Few, however, would guess. The two-legged people, just like Younger Sister in the cave of Blue Racer, tripped over the snake people, not out of inherent meanness but from outright clumsiness. Then the snake people went away as quickly as they had come. No one knew where they had gone; they just vanished into the ground. And the land changed after they left; it grew dry as tinder, dry as fallen leaves, a dead, dusty dry. The drought that followed was terrible, and whatever the people planted died. Whatever water they had dried up. Their lives were cursed with a dryness so absolutely unforgiving that it even entered the women's wombs, and then there were no more children. Finally, the people held a council, and the chief, whose name was Wind-in-the-Trees, asked his people what ought to be done. And the people said that all their bad luck had begun when the snake people went away in anger; it was after that, they said, that everything had dried up. So Wind-in-the-Trees called upon the mother of Younger Sister and told her to go to the home of Blue Racer to ask his forgiveness. She did this, receiving his word that the people must do the follow-ing. "First," he told her, "you must put pollen on all the snake trails so that the snake people know that they are welcome again. Then you must hold a great dance in their honor, and at this dance, you shall call all the snake children Grandchild."

The words of Blue Racer were thus returned to the ear of Wind-in-the-Trees. And he ordered that it be so, and it was done. The pollen paths were laden with the holy dust of sacred corn; the honors were given the snake people; and the dance was danced, the song sung. All the snake people showed up and joined in, exactly as they do today. And so lasting peace was finally made between the two-legged people and the snake people. And that is why today when a man sees a snake going along on the ground, he speaks to it gently, in a kindly way, remembering, so the people say, the ancient and honorable way of greeting a snake person. "Blessings upon you, Grandchild," he says, "and all your relations; may our days be made as long as our goodwill to one another."

The Story of Deer Boy

IN WHICH DEER BOY LEARNS THE LAW OF THE
HUNTER'S HEART BY TURNING INTO A DEER HIMSELF,
AND OF HIS LOVE AND SORROW

ONCE long ago, they say that the animal people ran off with the months, which were made out of leaves. First Man had a great pile of them. Some were red; others were gold, green, and brown. The leaves of months matched the seasons from which they came. And the animals were supposed to take the leaf month that suited them; they did this, but a big wind came up and blew the leaves all around. And that is why the animals had to make due with months they didn't always want or like.

That is what they say, anyway. However, as the animals took control of the seasons, the two-leggeds knew they could not hunt them without honoring them. This was what happened in the desert of the previous story—the song of honor for the snake people, whose season is summer, the time when Winter Thunder sleeps. Soon the people held dances for all of the animal people, each according to the proper season. The dances were, and still are, a blessing for the spirit of the animals, as well as for the spirit of the seasons, for without them—the harmony of the hunt, the bounty of meat—the people could not have survived.

Now it happened at one of the seasonal dances, a boy danced so hard and so long, doing the deer dance, that he turned into a deer himself, bounding away into the forest thickets on stiff, springy legs. And each year thereafter, in late winter, when the forest people danced the deer dance, the boy deer, Deer Boy, he was called, returned to gaze fondly on the village where he had grown up and been happy as a two-legged person. There was, in fact, a young woman of the village with whom, just before his enchantment, he had fallen deeply in love. He remembered well her incomparable beauty, her lovely two-leggedness; just thinking of her brought tears to his round, dark, deer-eyed face.

One year, shortly before the winter season gives way to spring, the time some of the people call false spring, Deer Boy returned, as he always did, to look down upon his former village. And when he reflected upon his sorrow, seeing the people prepare for the great midwinter deer dance, he felt a change pass through him; it was thus that he began to turn back into a two-legged person. From off his knobby head, heavy with velvet antler, went the young prongs of his tough deer's manhood; in their place came the black braided hair he had once had, and his feet, sharp-pointed and hoofed, melted back into the moccasins he'd always worn.

Thus the change was complete, and that evening in the light of late dusk when the deer dancers went down to the river to dig up their deer sticks, the forelegs of the deer they use in the dance, the changed youth saw his face in the clear water of the river. He could not believe what he saw: the young man, which was himself, bravely made, handsomely clad, sun-browned and strong. He felt his brow, where horns had so recently protruded, to prove that he was real, that he was actually flesh and blood. And, though he was, he could not accept it so quickly. He thought, If she whom I love would know and believe that I am really a man, then I would believe it with my own heart.

That night, he tried to bed down in a little glade under the flick of stars. And unsleeping, restless, he woke in the cold, his breath full of icy frost, asking himself if his wish—to see his love once more—might be granted. In the morning, he rose before the sun and peered through the gambel oak and wild holly by the spindrift fog of the river, and he saw the women come down, as they always do, to fill their baskets and pots with fresh water.

As luck would have it, his love came last, alone, lingering by the lazy, circling stream, herself lost in a dream of forgotten days. He broke from his concealment then, making an appearance before her. At first, shocked at the sight of him, she dropped her water jar, breaking it and spilling its contents on the sand. Then, turning from him, thinking that he was spirit and not real, she started to run, but he caught her; his clumsy feet, which were hands he had not gotten used to, battered her, forced her into the river.

He made fountains of foolish spray with his awkwardness; she dropped into the freezing water and swam away. He went after her, jumping as a deer jumps, in dizzy hops and feinting sprints; he caused such commotion that he accidentally summoned a hunter, who, as it happened, was none other than his lover's husband, to the panicked scene. Immediately notching an arrow, the husband took aim and let go; the bow twanged in the early-morning air. The arrow flew true and struck its mark—the upper shoulder of the poor youth—and Deer Boy, so lately changed by his heart's own magic, paid the price of two-legged love. Then, falling in the river, wounded, he let out a cry; she heard, turned to face him, and saw the shaft driven deep, the mortal wound in the side of the one she now tearfully remembered.

Deer Boy was more than half deer, more than half wild; the untimely arrow served to waken his hidden strength. Then his hooves seemed to strike up that ancient song, the deer song, the deer that runs for its half-spent life. Surging, heart burning, he felt his sinews light afire, his muscular flanks and stringy deer-flexed calves come to the fore, compelling him to run as he had never run before. Young and strong—and now under no illusion of who or what he was—he headed madly for the upper reaches of the unleafed woods. The tears that coursed his brown face were tears of love, mixed now with fear and shame, combining in his mind with the image of himself, that bold buck seeking to touch his own lost love. And so tears of love, burning with shame, coursed his face, wetting his fur; so now an alternate vision of himself came to him: the running deer, fleeing for its life, the shoulder-struck arrow forcing hot blood out, pelting the hard-tipped spring buds with a sorrow of red rain.

Through the forest mist he ran, spending his life, his stride gone but all four legs kicking and his deer's heart stronger than his man's mind. Now, limping, he fell, then struggled to get up. White foam mingled with red blood, smearing his black lips, until, unable to flee any longer, cornered and broken, he saw his foe, the pursuing hunter, his former best friend.

Seeing what was left of his life through a dim haze of reddish gold, his thick tongue hung down and he faced the hunter who had wounded him. "Dawn Boy," he tried to say, but the blood froth held back the words he could not manage to say. When the eye of the hunter fixed on the hunted, they stared at each other. The hunter approached; the hunted crouched. The lowered horns, daggered with arrow points, leveled at the waist of the bow-wielding man.

Then, once again, some mystic wind touched the wounded one, and though he was all deer, and dying, he spoke clearly and well. "I am Deer Boy," he said into the sun, "not a man, but a dying deer. I give myself now to you, as all deer in death must befriend their foe." Submissive, Deer Boy raised his head, shielding the hunter from his horn. "Friend," he said with a sigh, "I give you my breath."

And Deer Boy dropped then, the life gone out of him.

The hunter, Dawn Boy, cradled the deer's head in his arms and sang the deer's surrender song, the conquering hunter's plea for forgiveness. "The deer has given me his breath so that I may bring him back to the village and he may live again in all of our hearts. This deer gave me his life so that all may share, all may live: the deer, the mountain, the river, the sky. All of these are one in my song of thanks for the sacred deer that has given me his breath."

So singing, he finished. And the forest people say that his song is sung by all hunters who take a deer on the hunt. However, only those deer that give their breath are ever taken; the others bound away to live and grow and make more deer. After this, the animal people grew more wary; they say that no animal in his rightful mind would ever wish to be two-legged or to hold a bow in his hand. Nor would any man with a hunter's heart wish to bound away on stiff, springy legs and be a deer in the sun that is young but once in a lifetime.

The Story of the First Animal Council

OF PORCUPINE'S TALE OF THE FIRST ANIMAL COUNCIL,
WHEREIN IT IS SAID THAT THE ANCIENT FRIENDSHIP
BETWEEN THE TWO-LEGGED PEOPLE AND THE ANIMAL
PEOPLE HAS BEEN BROKEN

N O W Porcupine was not a greedy creature, except in his preference for salted wood: the sweat-stained handles of clubs, axes, knives, and bows. These he sought out wherever and whenever he could; but other than this single-minded passion, he was known as a slow-moving fellow whose meditative mood often led him on the path of wisdom. However, he was often disheartened, for the hunters were always stealing around his lodge, looking for quills to make decorations for their moccasins and shirts. It was not enough that he gave of these freely, leaving them around wherever he bumbled about, but the hunters always wanted more. Soon they began to hunt Porcupine and his kind down. And this he would not abide, reminding Grizzly Bear, who was also much prized by hunters for his claws, fur, and teeth, that the time had come for a great meeting of minds and hearts. So here, in Porcupine's words, is his account of the first animal council.

"It is now many years since the ancient friendship between the two-legged people and the animal people was broken, and since that time we have been hunted continually and go about in fear of our lives. All deer people remember the story of Deer Boy; all snake people remember the story of Blue Racer, his wife, and their children, who were turned away at the door of their two-legged grandmother. So

108

it goes that the mutual mistrust, occasionally healed but generally lingering in the minds of the animal people, is the cause for much sleeplessness among us.

"One day, on account of my prodding him, Grizzly Bear invited the animal people to a council high up in the mountains. All the mountain animals came when Grizzly Bear made his great speech, wherein he spoke of the constant dangers and perils faced daily by the unprotected members of his tribe and about the urgent need of finding a remedy.

" 'What would you have us do?' Timber Wolf asked.

"And Grizzly Bear answered, 'We must appeal, in our prayers, to Winter Maker, the god who makes the cold season, to lengthen this time of year so that the hunters are forced to stay by their fires and cannot hunt about so much.'

"All who were present—Timber Wolf, Gray Fox, Mountain Squirrel, and White-Tailed Deer, and, of course, myself—agreed. However, Mountain Squirrel suggested that before acting upon it, we ought to consult the smaller animal people, who should also have a say in the matter. 'If we do not include them now, worse things may happen later on,' he concluded, and we all agreed.

"So the next night, Beaver, Tree Squirrel, Mink, Weasel, Marten, Muskrat, and all the insect people met at the great night gathering, the most important animal council ever held. The larger animals sat on one side of the wide circle, under the trembling stars; the smaller animals spread their blankets opposite them. In the center of the circle, a big fire crackled and roared, and as before, Grizzly Bear led the proceedings, telling of the previous day's meeting and his suggestion about lengthening the winter days and nights so that the two-legged hunters would be confined to their fires and not hunt so much.

"His speech was followed by a long silence, during which we quietly meditated on his words. Even so, however, the insect people, led by Cricket, kept up a steady, popping beat with drums and rattles, keeping time. Cicada played his flute and Star-Nose Mole sang the mountain chant. Well, after a polite silence, I rose and asked, 'What of the little people here gathered, the ones with such thin coats? Won't they suffer terribly in a too-long winter?'

"Grizzly Bear never liked ideas that ran counter to his own; I watched the fur on the back of his neck come up, bristling darkly in the firelight. 'Who cares?' he said thoughtlessly. 'We big animals have decided to do this, anyhow. For us, it's already settled.'

"Now I looked at him narrowly, my own formidable bristles beginning to rise. 'I fear you're being shortsighted,' I told him dryly. 'Already there's not enough food around to feed you, and yet you'd have winter longer! The roots of the grass on which Deer lives would be frozen stiff; the berries you're so fond of wouldn't be out, nor would the nuts that Mountain Squirrel eats. As for me, porcupines pride themselves on living off bark—that we can do indefinitely. So can the insect people, if they have to, live longer underground. That is all I wish to say; I have spoken.' And, as it happened, the other animal people liked what I said. 'How wise!' the mice began to whisper, but Grizzly Bear, who has ears that hear even the smallest thing, felt slighted by these remarks, because he considered himself not only the largest but the wisest of all of us. Growling with displeasure, he grumbled, 'Let he who has the most votes stand and be counted.'

"And so the animal people decided to put their trust in me, Porcupine. The usual way a vote was cast was with grass straws or pine needles. However, Cricket said, 'Let's do away with the old way of counting. Porcupine's quills will stand for our unanimous decision.' And that, they say, is why I raise up my quills whenever I see someone coming; I like to show that the vote went my way, and that winter, long as it is, will not be any longer than it has to be."

That was where Porcupine concluded his story, but that was not really the end of it, for Grizzly Bear would not forget being voted down, and the mouse people saying that Porcupine was wise stuck ever so deeply in the back of his mind. So whenever Grizzly Bear caught sight of Porcupine, he tried to kick him with his foot—without getting stuck, of course—and one day, Grizzly Bear succeeded in kicking him into the air. And when Porcupine got rolling, he got scared and stuck his thumb in his mouth. He went soaring into the sky and banged into a birch tree, where, they say, he bit his thumb off, which is the reason that Porcupine has only four fingers to this day. But it is a good thing they went with Porcupine on that vote, because if Grizzly Bear had had his way, we would not be around to hear the next story, which tells what happened after the gods took up the tale.

BOOK 7

The Story of First Hunter and Abalone Girl

IN WHICH THE WISDOM OF MOUNTAIN OLD MAN AND
HIS TALE OF WOE SHOWS HOW FIRST HUNTER IS
CUCKOLDED BY ÀBALONE GIRL, WHOSE TRUE LOVE IS
KILLER WHALE, AND IN WHICH SUFFERING FALLS UPON
ALL THREE OF THEM

N E day, sometime after the first animal council, Sun Father was talking to Mother Earth on top of the Mountain Around Which Moving Was Done. "I believe I know what is wrong with the world," he avowed. "The problem is that men, at heart, are always unhappy." Mother Earth asked him if women were not the same, equally as unhappy as men, but he replied that he didn't think so. "From what I have seen," he concluded, "the man's position is worse."

"How can you say that, when you see how much the women suffer?" she asked.

"When the sexes separated at the river, if you remember, it was the women who did unnatural things."

"But it was the men, Coyote and his friend Shapeshifter, who had it both ways; separation from the women as a whole but sex whenever they wished it. The two of them, working together, got one of the women pregnant."

"And who brought monsters into the world?" Sun Father demanded.

"Look," Mother Earth said, "I know of someone who can settle the question of whose position is worse, the man's or the woman's, once and for all."

And so they appealed to the wisdom of Mountain Old Man, who had seen fire and rain before they were born. He had, they say, seen

115

Coyote come out of the sky in a canoe; he found Mother Earth wrapped in a swaddling blanket when she was a baby, the child of Horizontal Woman and Upper Darkness; he gave Sun Father his first turtle-shell rattle, his first lightning arrow. They went to him, then, with the ageless question of the unresolved burden of man and woman: Who was the greater sufferer of the two? And what effect did this have on the animal people and the two-legged people getting along in the world?

This is what they wanted to know, and they came to the lodge of Mountain Old Man and asked him these questions. He appeared at the east doorway of his lodge, a cave in the side of the oldest mountain on earth, First Mountain. Now, Mountain Old Man looked just like the ancient place where he lived: His shoulders sloped terribly, and it seemed he was melting away into the earth. His eyes, the color of glaciers, were blind. Yet in all the world, there was nothing going on anywhere that he didn't know about. When his visitors arrived, he came out of his cave and greeted them.

"Grandfather," Mother Earth said respectfully, "would you tell us who is worse off, man or woman? We have tried, but we can't resolve the matter."

Now, Mountain Old Man rubbed his head; a flock of dark birds flew out of his white hair and disappeared into the sky. He blinked; ice water ran out of his eyes and streaked across his face, forming frozen pools at his feet. Here, they say, was the oldest man alive, and when he spoke, even the light listened.

"Once, grandchildren, I had sight and saw many things. Once, I knew a woman, one of the gods, and her name was Abalone Girl. She was married to a man called First Hunter. Together, they lived at the edge of the world-holding sea, where the salt froth meets the headland shore.

"Each day, Abalone Girl went to the river mouth to gather shellfish for her husband's meal. There she stooped in the tawny sand, gathered what she could, broke the shells on a pointed rock, and took out the meat. But if that was all she did, all would've been well and I'd have no story to tell. The truth was, she broke the shells to attract her lover, Killer Whale. He'd come out of the surf with his smooth white-and-black spray face, and he'd carry Abalone Girl out into the sea troughs to sport with him. Afterward, when they were through playing, he'd bring her up on the sand and make love to her. Now, Abalone Girl could bear her lover well, but he was so large, as you will imagine, that she cried out in pleasure and in pain. First Hunter could hear her cries from the brow of the hill where he made his fishhooks, but he preferred to think they were the mewing cries of the fish-seeking gulls, whimpering after the running tide. Anyway, for a long time he didn't let on. In the end, though, he decided to see for himself what made these noises.

"One morning, quite early, before Abalone Girl rose from sleep, he took her blanket, wrapped it around him so that his head and body were hooded, went down to the dawn-colored sea, and broke shells on the upright rock where his wife would call for her lover. And as soon as Killer Whale heard the *chk-tsk, chk-tsk* of the shells, he leapt up, salt face freshened, full of eager gladness to see her. He came with the tide through the yellow-sand sun glow of the shallows, clear blue in the depths, rosy-hued in the distance. And he came out of the foam, the lacy spray glistening along his inky back. As he came up on the beach, heaving himself along, he was ready to have sex.

"From under the hooded shadow, First Hunter saw Killer Whale's rock-hard member thrusting up, red-curved, ready for fun. 'Is that all that you have for me today?' First Hunter spoke from his garment's concealment. Then, without warning, he rushed at Killer Whale, his shell knife flashing in his hand. And with a swift downstroke, he severed Killer Whale's member, chopped it off where it grew.

"Then Killer Whale rolled out to sea, flopping and wailing, red-dening the sea with his spilled blood, making noises that no earth person or sea person has ever heard or will hear again.

"So that day, for the first time, when Abalone Girl went to the shell-breaking rock and cracked shells, her lover, Killer Whale, never came. She went home sad, but her husband met her with a cruel smile; he was stirring a stew pot, wreathed in steam. 'Husband,' said Abalone Girl, 'what is that sweetness you're stirring there?' And he answered, 'Wife, it is something tender, something sweet—something I've made just for you.' And he served the thing that he'd cut off down at the beach. She ate all of it, begging for more, so that at the end of the meal, he had to show her the pot to prove there was nothing left. Then he said to her, 'Wife, was your lover's member sweet?'

"At this, she ran out of their lodge, and though a storm had started up, she went out into the waves, crying for her lover, who did not come. The great waves crashed, pulling her down, but still she swam, as best she could, until she could swim no more. Then, floundering in the sea drift, the breakers pounding all about her drowning face, she went down for the last time. And she turned into the reef the people call Woman."

And so the tale of Mountain Old Man ended, and, as with many such tales, the listeners were left with their own opinions about what it might or might not mean. Sun Father believed the story showed how perfidious women were, always tricking men with their deceitful ways; Mother Earth believed the story proved the lengths that men will go to wreak vengeance upon women. And they went off, arguing, as unsettled as ever. However, no god ever seeks to overthrow another's action or thought, and so the eternal debate continues. But to add one last thing to the eternal contention: The reef known as Woman is still there, ringing the world-holding sea, impartially protecting all that lives on both sides of her; and, as steadfast as ever, Woman keeps the water and the land at bay. As Mother Earth asked Sun Father: "What male god, forever rooted to his task, performs such work in the name of Man?"

The Story of
Mountain Old Man's Son

HOW THE VAIN SON OF MOUNTAIN OLD MAN, WHOSE
NAME IS BUTTERFLY DANCER, LEARNS THE ANCIENT
LESSON OF HUMILITY FROM A GHOST NAMED ECHO—
BUT TOO LATE

MOUNTAIN Old Man's son, Butterfly Dancer, is a good example of two-legged man's self-praise, his love of his own actions. This handsome young man had a bit of the Coyote spirit in him—he was completely taken with himself. The people of the canyon, where Butterfly Dancer lived, used to ask Mountain Old Man, "Do you think your son will live to a ripe old age?" To which he invariably answered, "Only if he does not seek knowledge of himself." Now this was not the advice you'd expect from a father, but this father knew his son's affection—or affliction—for himself, his strange, fragile, self-imposed vanity. He knew, as well, his son's longing to be left alone; that he enjoyed no company better than his own. Partly, at least, this was the outcome of the admiration Butterfly Dancer received from the girls of the village. Because he was so godly, all the young women adored him and followed him around everywhere—and yet he had no words for them except an occasional "Go away."

Often his father said to him, "Butterfly Dancer, it is time you enjoyed the company of people your own age. I am too old to be much comfort to you, and you ought to seek something other than your own selfish thoughts." Good advice, but not well taken. For Butterfly Dancer had no intention of breaking his favorite pastime, which was to ramble through Rainbow Canyon, attending to the amber-eyed flowers—not girls—that lay in such profusion on the path where he walked.

119

He liked nothing better than these solitary strolls through the swallow-filled afternoons within the deep russet walls of the great scarlet canyon. There among the locust trees and the dusky olives, against the glare of the salmon-pink cliffs, he passed his hours, daydreaming. Quiet on the buff sand, he watched the little lizards catch flies in the rock and sand hollows, musing to himself in the half-light until dusk drove him home. Then, walking by the clear green river, listening to the friendly song of the evening frogs, he counted his blessings, for though he felt alone in the world, he knew that he was unattached to anything, and was, therefore, quite happy.

One day, as he made his way through Rainbow Canyon, smelling the sweet honeysuckle vines that draped the box elders, he thought he heard something that he had not heard before, a voice of unusual clarity, sweet-sounding, mellow as a hive of bees. This was Echo, picking up his humming and imitating it. You see, Echo was the spirit of a girl who once lived in the village. When her family opposed her marriage to the young person she dearly loved, Echo leapt off the highest cliff; and now her spirit, cut off from all but the distant wanderers who follow the farthest recesses of the canyon, knows no peace. It was her habit, though, because her life had been so abruptly shortened, to say but half a thing she heard, an echo of it—thus the name given her spirit.

Echo, seeing the handsome Butterfly Dancer, who reminded her of her own lost love, followed him that day, making a song of his footsteps. She saw him and burned inwardly. Echo followed him secretly as he made his rounds from flower to flower. And she wished, poor thing, to say one natural word, one honest outpouring of her own heart, but all she was able to do was repeat the last part of something she had heard. There was no way to invent an utterance of her own. And Butterfly Dancer, unable to see her, only able to hear the vague drift of something occasioned by his own humming, ignored her. Yet as the afternoon wore on, he began to feel a hovering presence of some kind. Looking around, he saw the dry woods, droning in the arid wind, rippling in the heat of the flaming rocks. In the shadows, sitting under a tree in cool blue light, he almost dreamed he saw the flicker of a face, the gesture of a hand. Whatever it was, he never quite caught the source of it, the thing from which the gesture flowed, and thinking it might be an animal, he dismissed it.

One day, the presence was felt more strongly by him, and he even called out, "Anybody there?" Wild with desire to speak with him, Echo answered back: ". . . ere," which was the most she could say. But he heard this well and wheeled around in all directions, looking for the whereabouts of the volleying voice. "Someone there?" he said to the empty air. ". . . ere," she called back.

"There," he repeated, confused, still looking around, seeing nothing.

". . . ere," she replied. The word seemed stolen by the dead silence of the red stone canyon.

And so it was that he began to feel something *was* there, if ever he might *see* just a little of it. It happened that on full-moon nights, when the light lay like snow on the canyon floor, Echo could, in part, be seen, and was one night when he stayed late. The moon had worked her light into every crevice of the canyon; the shine of silken trees, moon-bent grasses, and gray-blue cliffs filled his eye with luster. The broom plants waved in the gullies of the closed hills, dancing in the wind. The sunflowers, nodding, dropped earthward, as if the dreaming wind had put them to sleep. The whole canyon, dreaming now, awake and dreaming at the same time, seemed to breathe with a special life.

And suddenly, Butterfly Dancer saw the faintest outline of the gossamer girl. The particles of her being, so long stored in cold canyon walls, came out, mad, in the moonlight. And she found on such a night, she could actually speak. "Let's make love," she begged, her desire for mortal ways overcoming her reticence.

"Let's not!" he said, backing away fearfully.

So she went to him, offering him her spirit's tempting body, moony, lovely, deliciously curved. But he kept backing away from her, saying in his thin voice, "Let's not touch each other." Repeating this, he went backward. She, going closer to him, arms open, anxious, coaxing, "Please." He said cruelly, "I'd sooner die than touch a ghost!"

Then she vanished; not a part of her remained.

"I don't love anyone but me," he shouted at the wind.

Echo, gone from sight, said, ". . . me."

Then, turning from the troublesome vision, Butterfly Dancer turned around and saw he had retreated all the way to the edge of the river. Another step and he would have fallen in. But now as he bent his face for a drink of the moon-filled water, his reflection looked back at him, wobbling eerily in the current. The face was so handsomely set, so perfectly formed, that it gave him a start to see it up so close; he bent to kiss the moon blue lips, returning, gaze for gaze, his fondest love of self, and, losing his balance, he fell into the river. Now Butterfly Dancer was half god and half mortal, but the mortal half couldn't swim a stroke. Helpless in the eddying swirl, he was swept downstream. Deathly pale, he began to drown; and the river, knowing nothing, carried him to where the white water makes a great roar on the beaten banks. There, in the backwash of spray and spume, Butterfly Dancer met his death, his beautiful face and body melting in the wild mix of pounding water, which tore him up. He was taken in the arms of Big Wind, up canyon to his father, Mountain Old Man, who wept when he saw his son so torn apart. "My son," he cried desolately, "if only I'd known you'd come to this." He said no more, for the word repeated itself—". . . this"—as though the very air had put tongue to lip and made the word.

The Story of the Girl Who Married a Fire Spirit

OF PINE SONG, THE DAUGHTER OF CHIEF MOON GONE
BY, WHO MARRIES FIRE SPIRIT, THE GOD OF FIRE

M O R T A L S have wanted to marry the mystery deities, the spirit gods and goddesses of rain and wind and fire, ever since the Maker took the seeds of life from his generous breast and planted them in the mist of the rolling void. The story of Butterfly Dancer and Echo notwithstanding, there are other, bolder tales of love, of passion not *lost* but *found*, here and on the opposite shore of life, the death path, the spirit world. And it seems there was once a chief, luckless, perhaps, though some might say merely marked by a sterner fate than that which had befallen others, whose daughter was incomparably lovely. His name was Moon Gone By; hers, Pine Song. They lived in the great northern country where the wind sings in the pines. One day, Pine Song was sitting by the fire in her father's lodge, thinking that none of her suitors had love enough to satisfy her taste, for she was one who really lived to love. Anyway, staring into the gleaming firelight made her think strangely. I wish I had a lover like that! she mused. No sooner had she said this, though, than Fire Spirit in his cloak of smoke leapt out of the fire pit, clasped Pine Song by the wrist, and jerked her into the writhing flames.

Thus she became the love prisoner of Fire Spirit, who decided, since she was as fiery as he was, to keep her for his wife. Now, Moon Gone By knew what had happened to his daughter, but he didn't wish to offend the fire deity, so he called for his most powerful shaman, who told him, "Let your fire go out; have everyone in your village do the same. Then you will hear something." Moon Gone By

123

then sent a crier to all of the lodges, saying that all the fires should be put out. After this had been done, Pine Song slipped out of the stones of her father's fire pit, followed by a wraith of smoke, which, afterward, returned to the fire. And there she was, the same as before, a beautiful mortal girl, seemingly untouched by Fire Spirit's red-faced passion.

Things went on the way they usually did in the lodge of Moon Gone By, but he observed a subtle change in his daughter that dismayed him. She would stare and dream before the fire, a song of disembodied love in her eyes. She had nothing to say to any of her friends. And she helped her mother with all the meals, but only so she could be closer to the fire pit. And late at night when the fire whistled, as it will when fed wet wood, Pine Song left her bed, adjourning to the twining flames. Then, since no one was looking, she would step barefoot into the red-gold tongues and let them lick her all over, caressing her feet, knees, and thighs. Not being burned but embracing the ghost of smoke, the spirit of the fire pit that rose from the flames, she would slip into the center of the firestones and be gone for the night. In the morning, though, she would be back in her bed, asleep, so it always seemed as if nothing had happened.

Now one day as she was stirring a bowl of boiling soapberries, a young man of the village, who had always been smitten with her sight, playfully took hold of her stirring spoon. When, surprised, she grabbed it back, the wooden spoon soaking with soapberries flew out of her hand and fell into the fire. Immediately, a fiery fist seized the spoon, crushed it to coals and devoured it, whistling angrily all the while. The young man, startled, stepped back, afraid.

"That's only my husband calling me," Pine Song said. Then she stepped into the flames that lapped at her legs. And as a vapor of smoke undulated all around her, she settled into the bed of burning coals. "He wants me," she murmured sleepily, her voice drowning in flame. Then she sank back down into the firestones, forever. Moon Gone By mourned the loss of his lovely daughter, Pine Song, but he told anyone who would listen the lesson of it: "Never offend a fire spirit with wet wood. Never, ever, let your daughter sit too close to the flames, for the temptation is too great, and the fire spirit will reach out of his cloak of smoke and take her for his wife."

After this, the people watched their fires more closely, for now they understood that fire is a great and jealous thing whose hunger is always unsatisfied. And yet they also knew that fire is life; and life itself is hunger that begins when we are born and continues even after we die, as the next story will show.

The Story of the Shadow Wife

IN WHICH MOON GONE BY GRIEVES FOR HIS ONLY SON,
HANDSOME LAKE, WHO FOLLOWS THE ROAD OF THE
SPIRITS IN SEARCH OF HIS DEAD WIFE, AND IN WHICH
THE SHADOW WORLD IS STRONGER THAN THE WORLD
OF THE LIVING

EVEN though he had lost his daughter, Moon Gone By still had a son, Handsome Lake, whose lovely wife had died when they had been married only a few days; this was about the same time that Pine Song was taken by Fire Spirit. But Handsome Lake wouldn't accept the loss of his wife as his father had accepted the loss of his daughter, and he hadn't anything like firelight to remind him of her. He had only their sleeping blanket, but he could not sleep under that, either. He spent the endless night in sorrow, tossing and listening to the low moan of the pines soughing outside the lodge.

One morning, Handsome Lake got up before the sun and walked away from his father's village; daylight found him still walking, head bowed, heavy with memory. A long way off, he heard voices. Following them, he came out of the pine wood and onto the shore of a quiet silver lake coldly washed in shafts of pale, particled blue. The moon had just risen; the lake looked flat, frozen white in the light. Handsome Lake didn't know it, but he had walked all day upon the death path, the road of the spirits. Now, on the other side of the still lake, he saw the phantom shapes of shadow people moving in and out of the moonlit pines; he called to these wraiths, but they didn't seem to hear his cries. After he had grown hoarse with calling, he whispered to himself: "Is it so far over there, that they can't hear me?" Then they heard him. One of the shadow people said, "I hear a person of the dream time; let's bring him over in our canoe." So

126

they parted the mist in their canoe and carried him across the moony lake. When he reached the other side, the first person he recognized was his own dear wife. She was wearing doeskin and the moonlight made her look pale as milk. She was overjoyed to see him and they embraced for a long time. Afterward, he asked if he might have something to eat, for he saw the other shadow people feasting, and she said, "My husband, don't eat this food. If you do, you'll never return to the dream time."

That night, after not eating anything, Handsome Lake lay with his wife under their robe, but she said that it was too hot to sleep that way; she liked it better with the blue chill of the night air on her naked skin. Then, shivering, he threw off their robe and began to plan their escape. We cannot stay here with these shadow people, he reasoned, we must get back where it's warm and the food is good. Early the next morning, he slipped out of that lodge, holding tightly to his wife's cold-boned hand. She showed him where the spirit canoes lay along the foggy shore, and he crept up and took one, but no one seemed to be following them. "Don't worry, my husband," his wife said as he paddled through the streamers of fog to the opposite side of the lake, "no one will come, for this way leads to the dream time." Again he found the death path, the spirit road through the pines that took them back to his father's village. Now when at last they got to Moon Gone By's lodge, he was most happy to see his son. Handsome Lake talked about his trip, showing his wife to all who gathered there, but they gave him darting smiles and said nothing to her. Trying to be polite, Moon Gone By said, "Why don't you bring her in?" and he set a place of ermine and marten pelts for her to sit on by the fireside. Handsome Lake stared at his father in surprise.

"Father, don't you see my wife?" he asked. The weary old chief looked but saw nothing, and neither did any other members of the family. "You've traveled long on a lonely path," he said. "Now you should rest and forget your troubles."

That night, Handsome Lake was worse off than at the night camp of the shadow people, for, once again, his wife made him throw off their sleeping robe. When she asked him to make love to her in the openness of the lodge, with everyone trying to sleep, he complained, shrinking back under the robe. But in the end, he gave in to his wife, making love to her, while his family, including Moon Gone By, left the lodge in dismay.

"The poor boy thinks the moonlight's his dead wife," he moaned, and he went outside and sat under a pine tree and wept over his son's madness. The next day, Handsome Lake, having found no solace in the dream time, took his wife and went back the way they had come, along the death path that led to the shadow camp on the shore of the fog-shrouded lake.

There, at last, he found peace. He learned to sleep on top of their sleeping robe and he never thought again of going across the lake, over the spirit road, and back to the village where the people dream they are alive.

PART THREE

MYTHS OF
POWER

BOOK 8

The Story of Sun Hawk

The Story of the Turtle People

The Story of He-Whose-Tail-Is-Gone and the

Storyteller of Scorn

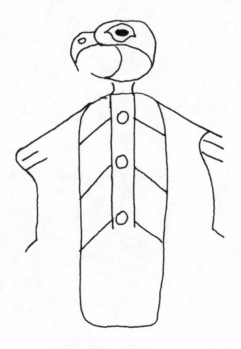

The Story of Sun Hawk

OF SUN HAWK'S SACRED VISIT TO THE CLOUD COUNTRY
AND HIS DREAM OF EAGLE POWER, WHICH SHOWS THE
COMING NEW WORLD GROWING OUT OF THE OLD AND
OF HIS GREAT AND POWERFUL NAME

H E people came to understand that the animals with whom they lived and shared the earth were messengers of the spirit world. The animals were guides whose lives were tied to the ancient song of the sun. And for each animal presence, just as there was a month in which that animal reigned, there was also an ancestor, a spirit that gave this animal power and cunning, as well as the will to live a long life.

It was seen by the people that when they hunted, the animals often knew they were coming, almost as if they had been warned. "What spirit gave us away?" an elder asked. "Who whispered our coming?" said the hunter. And the shaman, who prayed to know the secrets of the summer wood and the winter field, dreamed the answer, understanding that as Sun Father watched over his children, so did the animal spirits watch over theirs.

In finding out this secret, each man prayed, before and after the hunt, for the blessing of the spirit that guided his arrow. And this spirit guided his heart in love, giving wings to his feet and talons to his eye. A man, then, might call upon the power of the eagle ancestor to inform him and to give him eagle strength and eagle vision. There were those who quickly gained the quickness of the squirrel, the gravity of the cat, the fierceness of the wolf. Such men were named for the spirits that gave them their greatness.

It is two boys we turn to now—one called Weasel and the other

133

called Hawk. They had their names, and the spirits who knew them blessed them. However, they were as yet untried. With reckless hearts, they went about, wondering, wishing for a test of power. And thus it came, their wish. But only one of them emerged as a man of power. So, this is what happened when two untempered youths decided to climb the Mountain Around Which Moving Was Done.

At first, they went forth for the pleasure of the climb, but when they came to the top of the cliff where an ancient shrine leaned toward the midday sun, the boy named Weasel said to his friend Hawk, "We could, if we wanted, go even higher." Hawk, who was adventurous enough, scanned the clifftop and said, "I don't think so; I believe we've come far enough."

"Look at that old shrine," Weasel said, pointing it out, "I'd like to see what's over it."

Had the cloud cover lifted, he might have seen or known what awaited him, but as it was, the kind clouds had laid down a protective blanket, shrouding the shrine and what went up from it—a bare porphyry of slippery rock. "No one's allowed past this place," Hawk said, "it's forbidden." And he said again, "We've come far enough." Below, the corn lay clean in the sun's path, gold on green; the straight rows, when the wind moved them, looked like parted hair. Weasel cared little what others thought; he was brave beyond his means, or, some might say, foolish beyond his capacity to be cautious. Anyway, having made his decision, he climbed above the shrine, up, up, into the clouds, along the rock face, all the way to an eagle's aerie. Once there, boastful, he called down to Hawk. "I've reached the home of the eagle people. There's nestlings; I'm going to capture one and bring it down." Hawk called back, "Weasel, I see Mother Eagle coming." And as he spoke, a brown body cleaved the cloud mass, making a thin, high, wheedling warning cry.

Quickly, Weasel reached into the nest of sticks and grabbed a brown eaglet, who, beating him with untried wings, shrieked a warning, backing up into the rock ledge. Weasel caught it by the feet, closing his hand over the pincered claws. He took the young bird and started to crawl down the cliff. However, no sooner had he snatched the eaglet and started his descent then Mother Eagle dropped like a thunderbolt, striking the thief with uncoiled claws. Raked from his perch, Weasel tumbled into the clouds. And as he felt the loud rush of wind under his astonished feet, he tossed the helpless eaglet and fell.

Hawk saw all: his companion clawing the snowy clouds; Weasel's amazed face, his bare arms beating the air; and then the blue-green field far below opening and closing over his friend's fallen form. And into the arms of Hawk dropped the eaglet. Lucky catch, for a few feet more or less and the flightless bird would've joined Weasel in the parted sea of grass. Thinking then of returning the stolen eaglet to the nest, Hawk started up the cloud cliff, braving the rugged ascent with one hand. Slowly, he made his way up, at last reaching the stick-strewn nest that his dead friend had so recently pillaged. But just as he got there, the clouds surrounded him. Under his fingers, he felt the nest, heard the chittering of the nestlings. Then as he pushed the baby bird back onto the ledge, he heard the voice of Father Eagle: "We have waited," he said, "for one such as you." Then the voice of Mother Eagle added, "You are the first of the people to show such kindness." Suddenly, there came the gentle thunder of wings behind his head. In back of his shoulders, the two eagles caught hold and lifted him up. He rose above the clouds, and they carried him nearer the sun, to the sky country, where the corner-stones of the clouds support the upper world, which, though it is over and above this one, looks exactly like it.

"Remember," Father Eagle said as Hawk was put down on the sky ground, "listen to the bird people, for you are in their country now."

And Mother Eagle added, "Do as they do and not as you wish to do." Then they dropped back through the hole in the clouds that led to the lower world. The first thing Hawk noticed was how close the land was to the sun, how the sun struck the cloud hills and valleys, filling them with a burning glare. I must have water, he told himself, and he went searching over the gravel bars, bottomlands, sand sage, and saltbush hills; the land was dry and the sun lay low on it, making it gleam like a mica flake.

By and by, Old Man Sparrowhawk, who was the watchful spirit of that land, came around. "If you're thirsty, you should drink water," he said, but Hawk shook his head dismally. "There's no rain in this country," he complained, "only sun and more sun." Soon, however, he saw some black water jars, four of them, sitting beside a little gully. "Those are full of rain," Old Man Sparrowhawk remarked, "but you mustn't drink from them." Then he flew off, zigzagging across the sunburned plain. Each of the jars was filled to the brimming lip with rain; Hawk could smell the sweetness of the water. After Old Man Sparrowhawk left, he doused his face in one of the huge jars, sucking the rainwater down his throat. However, he was so thirsty, he tipped the jar, upsetting the water, which ran off into a gully, disappearing in the sand. Ashamed of himself for being so clumsy, Hawk sought another jar, yet in his eagerness he overturned this one, too. Then he accidentally turned over two more jars before he got his fill.

Now when the fourth jar had drained off into the desert scrub, the sun went behind a cloud. Suddenly, the bare ground was crawling with frogs and turtles; the frogs fired tongues of lightning at the turtles, and they ducked into their shells, tucked their feet in, and hid their heads. The sky grew black and hailstones rang on the rocks, rocketing about in all directions. The frogs and the turtles continued to fight, except that now when a turtle got hit in the head with a lightning bolt, there were buzzards who came down out of the glowering sky and tore the meat from their shells, eating it greedily.

Old Man Sparrowhawk, the wise elder, returned, battered by hailstones, and said to Hawk, "This is all your doing! You drank from the sacred water jars, didn't you?"

"I couldn't help myself," Hawk cried over the licking flames coming from the fierce frogs.

"Those are the jars that make rain!" Old Man Sparrowhawk told him.

"Isn't there anything we can do?" Hawk asked, shielding his head from the hard spell of hail.

"You must drink some sun," Old Man Sparrowhawk said, and he offered him a medicine pouch of cornmeal mush. "Eat the mush with your whole hand, just as we do." And the moment he did this, the sun came out from behind the cloud, the menacing frogs hopped back into their holes, and the turtles began bathing in the pools of melted hail.

"You may keep my medicine pouch," Old Man Sparrowhawk said, "but don't eat any more mush." Hawk promised not to, and Old Man Sparrowhawk said good-bye and flew away again.

For some time, Hawk walked along, enjoying the cooling air that moved across the land. However, after a while it grew hot again. The sun beat down as he walked and walked and walked. Finally, he came to a small rise; all around there were lakes of pale dust. Too tired to walk any farther, Hawk lay down, and before the sun had set, he was fast asleep. That night, he dreamed a wonderful dream; in the morning, he woke refreshed. Old Man Sparrowhawk was waiting for him. "Are you hungry?" he asked. When Hawk said he was, Old Man Sparrowhawk asked if he had had any of the mush in the sacred medicine pouch; Hawk said he had not.

"Well then, I believe it's time for you to go home." Then Old Man Sparrowhawk showed him how to uproot a certain tumbleweed bush, underneath which was the hole that went back to the earth world. "Take the bush with you," he recommended. "It is a medicine plant that will heal the people when they're sick."

"How do I get down?" Hawk asked.

"Take Spider Woman's climbing rope and lower yourself down with it." Old Man Sparrowhawk gave him the rope, tied it to a great stone, and lowered him down through the canopy of cloud, all the way down through the blue, to the top of the eagle's aerie, and down the Mountain Around Which Moving Was Done. Mother Eagle and Father Eagle greeted him on his descent, saying that he must remember his dream from the world above, that he must tell the people. Then they bid him good-bye, giving him sacred eagle plumes, breath feathers, to take with him. And so it was that Hawk returned to the people and became in time a great medicine man whose vision reflected the name he was given: Person-Above-the-Clouds.

The Story of the Turtle People

HOW THE LONG NIGHTS OF WINTER ARE SPOKEN OF
AND THE TELLING OF TALES BEGINS, AND HOW A
STORYTELLER FROM THE EAST, WHERE THE SUN IS
BORN, SOON SPEAKS OF STARS, STAR PEOPLE, AND
TURTLES WITH FIRES ON THEIR SHELLS

N O W , Person-Above-the-Clouds told his tale often and well. In time, others came forth and spoke of their journeys to the world of the animal spirits. And as they put words to mouth and tongues to tale, it happened that a new power came into being: the power of the storyteller. There came to be good ones and great ones and those whose stories lived lives of their own and grew larger with each telling. In the season of summer nights, the people smoked and talked and left off telling tales. But in winter weather, when the winds crept around their lodges, the storytellers gathered by their fires and spoke from the heart.

One winter's night, a visitor from the eastern sun listened as Person-Above-the-Clouds told the story of his visit to the country of the bird people. The visitor from the east considered what he heard. Then he said that he no longer believed in the wisdom of animal spirits or animal elders. "Eagles are eagles," he said sadly, "and they have no more power than the gift of flight. In our village, such a tale would be heard only by children, for no one wiser than a child would listen to it."

No one spoke for a long while, during which time the winter winds, outside the lodge, did all the talking. But, you see, the man from the east was a guest, and good manners forbade that his remark, short-visioned though it was, be challenged or even commented upon. Silent faces stored silent thoughts. The wind and the fire did all the talking, yet, after an appropriate interval, another guest rose from the friendly circle, the hospitable fire. This was a man from the southern sun. And it appeared from his winter-worn face that he was, perhaps, older than anyone present. His face swarmed with wrinkles, and when he smiled, it looked like brown clay cracked in the sun.

There was silence when, at last, he spoke. "The power of the gods has no limit," he said quietly. "Whatever they wish will happen. May my days be shorter if I do not tell the truth." So saying, he drew himself nearer the fire, and again the man from the east spoke up. "The gods have grown old and weary," he said dispiritedly. "They're busy with their own affairs and forget what we look like." After he had said this, all that was heard was the crackling of the fire; all that was seen was the shadows of flames leaping on the earthen walls of the lodge. The old one from the south broke the silence, saying, "Friends, I offer you this story," and he began to tell of the country from which he came.

"We live in lodges that are set off the ground on poles, so if a flood comes, we remain safe and dry. All around us in the marsh, there are many animals—water birds, deer, bear, alligator, and turtle. So, as you see, there's no great hunger in our village; we always have plenty to eat.

"Now one night, there were strange fires moving around in the heavens. They traveled across the night sky. Our chief told his scouts to follow them and see where they were going. The scouts left that night in log boats, but they returned in the morning. The fires, they said, had come from two old turtle people. When the wind blew on their backs, their fur ruffled and little sparks came out of it. When the wind blew hard, the sparks leapt up and the furry turtles were all aglow.

"Now the chief of our village was a wise man. He hadn't any reason to question his scouts or their story, but, just the same, he believed they had dreamed it. He dismissed them, and soon the people forgot it had ever happened.

"However, not long after this, the two old turtle people came to our village. They went from lodge to lodge, looking for a place of rest, and when our people saw them—the sparks on the turtles' backs leaping up when the wind blew—they were afraid. They thought the turtles would set their houses ablaze, so they gave them no place to rest. The turtles traveled on, finally coming to the edge of the village, where there lived a poor couple. Theirs was a broken-down lodge in need of repair; the thatch on the roof leaked and the poles that supported it were rotten. Yet the poor people seemed happy to see the turtle people. They offered them alligator tail to eat, water to drink, and a soft bed of dry sedge to sleep on.

"Just before dawn, the turtle people arose and told their hosts they were going home. They thanked them for their kindness but said they missed their home in the sky and wanted very much to return to it. 'You've been kind,' the old turtle said, 'and we would like to give you something to remember us by.'

"The kindly couple said that what they already had was quite enough for them but that if they were granted a thing not wished for, it would simply be to live long and well. This, the turtle people granted them, and so they returned to their home in the sky, where they have lived ever since that time."

The old storyteller wrapped his blanket around his shoulders and seemed to draw himself within himself. His story finished, he returned to the silence from which he had come. No one said anything, not even the traveler from the east. But all who were seated before the fire saw that the old round-shouldered man was sitting beside an old round-shouldered woman, both of whom seemed, in the dance of the playful firelight, to be older and wiser than anyone in the lodge.

The Story of He-Whose-Tail-Is-Gone and the Storyteller of Scorn

OF THE STORYTELLER WHO REMEMBERS THE TIME OF
MONSTERS AND OF A GUEST WHO SPEAKS OUT OF TURN
AND BECOMES KNOWN AS THE STORYTELLER OF SCORN

N O W there was also present on that ice-cracking winter's night, a man from the western sun, who said, "I have seen a little of the east and a little of the south, but I should like you to hear of the people who live in the west." The man was tall, lean as a pine, with braided hair bound with otter fur and woven red cloth. He was from the people of the shell, those who live among the rivers that run to the sea. This is his story.

"A long time ago, before my people came out of the earth, the land was still unformed: a lump of clay in the hands of the potter. Now, at this time, so my people say, monsters walked the earth. These beings were so large that, at night, their heads were star-crowned. They say that when they slept, their heads reached the great water of the west, while their feet touched the great water of the east.

"Now, all things desire to live under the sun. In the fullness of life, all things must, one day, come to an end, and thus begin again. So goes the unbroken circle, the medicine wheel of our months. The days of which I speak were the end of the monsters' time; this, they somehow knew. No one told them, but they knew. And the monsters, so great in size, so heavily made with towering heads and lowering tails, which, when they swung them, could carve the earth, cut a river, mold a mountain.

"One day, the largest of the monster people said, 'Brothers, the

141

world grows old as we grow old. The time will come when we'll be
around no longer.'

"Hearing this, the other monsters looked up, raised their shaggy
brows, and cocked their enormous ears. 'Now, brothers,' he continued, 'I believe we ought to do good rather than evil. That way, when
we leave, we'll be remembered for something other than destruction.'

"The other monsters turned this over in their minds, but it made
no sense to them. They were made, they knew, for only one thing:
destruction. So, one by one, they roused themselves, got to their
clawed feet, snorted through their horned noses, and bellowed
through their big mouths. They bashed their clubs about in protest,
and there came upon them, all at once, a very dark and dangerous
mood. They struck each other with their stone clubs until the sky
quivered under their blows and the earth trembled.

"Some blew sheets of flame from their mouths; some snorted snow
out of their noses. And the earth went black, then white, and they
fought on, until at last the largest of them was struck down by the
rest. He found he could move only his tail, which he swung vigor-
ously from east to west; and that is, they say, what flattened the
mountains and made the great plains.

"The monsters sought to subdue that wayward tail, but before they
could do this, he lashed out in fury, and his tail carved the great
riverbed that runs all the way to the great sea. The monsters struggled, finally overcoming their brother, and they tore his tail into little
pieces and cast them into the salt water; and so, as the people of the
shell tell it, these tiny pieces of monster tail wiggled away, turning
into fish, which the people now call Swimmer, the Salmon. And
every year now, Swimmer remembers that he was once part of a
great moving thing, and the once-great tail of the monster brother
comes back together again, and, yearning for the place where it
originated, struggles upstream, trying to reach the mountains. But,
of course, that monster, whose heart turned good too late, became
the mountain that watches over our village, the mountain the people
named He-Whose-Tail-Is-Gone."

Thus, having finished his story, the man from the west sat quietly.
And those gathered nodded their heads in approval and there followed a long, polite moment of silence, which was temporarily bro-

ken, however, by a skinny person who sat away from the firelight, in the back of the lodge. Although he was dimly lit, the shadow of his face was long and narrow. "I come from the north, the south, the east, and the west," he rudely boasted, "and the words of your storyteller make me want to laugh; for none of it is anything but lies."

At this, a grumble of disapproval spread around the lodge, scouring even the darkest shadow-shaken corner. Now, as the rude speaker spoke, all eyes turned to the back of the lodge. Who was this man with the pointed ears that stuck out from his head? No one seemed to know; and he took advantage of the situation by boldly holding forth in the following manner: "I have lived a long time," he said in his wizened voice, "long enough to know the difference between a cedar shake and a shack of dung."

The sudden grumbling grew into outcries of disgust; now the people knew who the speaker was, for there was only one person who would dare to talk in such a way.

"Old scolder!" someone called.

"First Angry," said another.

"Piss breath," cried a third.

"Groin fur," sneered a fourth.

The man with the pointed ears seemed to revel in the name-calling. He rose on his heels, bantering back, "Children of vermin! Were you present when the water rose and covered the land? Did you save the day and help the people pass into the next world?"

An old woman said, "You who stole Talking God's voice, what right have you to speak?"

"Let it be known," crackled the pointed-eared one, "I was present when First Man mixed the stars—"

"Not this again," scoffed the old woman.

"And I was the one who made the mountain named He-Whose-Tail-Is-Gone. Beaver was there, piling mud, making hills; I struck up a fight with him and made that mountain—just Beaver and myself. He said, 'I'll be the builder of forts.' I told him 'No, I'll do that myself.' And after he made war on me, I swore to take apart every fort he ever built, and I'm still doing it—he builds them and I take them down—and that's why there are so many islands, hills, valleys, fields, rivers, mountains, forests, and—"

But by this time, the people had heard enough. They filed out of the storytelling lodge and went back to their own fires for the night; as they left, the pointed-eared one went on talking, as if no one were there except himself, which is the reason no one likes to listen to any of Coyote's stories. Yes, he was there in the beginning—no one will deny him that—but his trotting tongue is full of scorn; his manners are an expression of the misfortune of everyone. Whatever he tries to do turns to trickery, which is why the people always leave when he starts talking. Of course, there are those who say that when we turn away from that which displeases us, we sacrifice our ability to hear. They say, let the old crime contriver speak, for life is not all honor and kinship; life is tragic and brief, a handful of quick-caught water that runs between the fingers. Yes, it is well, they say, to listen to the laughter of Coyote; it is nervous laughter—our own.

BOOK 9

The Story of Mountain Singing

The Story of Red Shell and Tall Man

The Story of Blue Elk

The Story of Mountain Singing

IN WHICH THE CHIEF MOUNTAIN SINGING AND THE
GODDESS OF WETNESS, MORNING MIST, SHARE
PASSIONATE LOVE, AND IN WHICH THEIR SELF-SEEKING
DEVOTION CAUSES NEGLECT AND THEY ARE PUNISHED
BY SUN FATHER

o Coyote told his story and had his way, though whether the people listened or not was their business—he didn't much care. Mostly, they chose not to, because his stink was on everything world-made, proving that where there was sweet, there was also bitter. But aren't there places so remote, so impervious to defilement, that nothing bad happens there—only good? There was such a haven, one storyteller said. It was a hidden valley, on the other side of which lay a trackless country, a rough and endless woods so deep that no one had ever gone to the end of it.

The chief of this sacred valley was wise beyond his years; they say Sun Father favored him, but whether this is true or not, his name was Mountain Singing, and his village, which was south along the coast and inland from Mountain-Whose-Tail-Is-Gone, was certainly safe from Coyote's chaotic doings.

Mountain Singing would wake each morning and breathe the blessing of sunlight through his left nostril, then through his right nostril; then, facing the risen sun, he would ask that he might be brave enough to meet the coming day. Sprinkling pollen in a circle that began in the east and closed in the north, Mountain Singing blessed his village, sunwise, putting a pinch of pollen on his tongue and offering the rest to the sun. Such daily devotions aside, Mountain Singing could not have said why his people, who were known as the people of the mist—enclosed as they were each morning in a gray

147

fog—did not know ill health, drought, the dangers of war. He thought, in the roundness that was theirs, the middle ground, that all people the world over lived so. His power, born of the twelve unmoving mountains that barred all visitors, was as solid as if it were hewn of the same stone. His will was thus made of substance stronger than human will; mountain-watched, sun-kept, he had no adversary to wrest power from him, no fear to make a single restless night. And so the people of the mist lived quietly, secretly, and in sacred trust of all the elements.

Now the other guardian of the valley was named Morning Mist. In the morning, when the killdeer cried, Mountain Singing said his prayers, and Morning Mist always appeared. She was guardian of grass, moss, and fir. And when she shed her robe of spangled dew, she freshened the fragrant fields and the slanted mountain meadows. For though Sun Father watched over all, his mere glance scrubbed the sky, heated it. Knowing this, Mother Earth long ago had appointed Morning Mist to tend the green shoots and the tender plants so the woods would not be burned or harmed.

So each morning when Mountain Singing watched Morning Mist throw off her garment aglow with the shine of female rain, he shivered in the sun—not from cold but from the longing of lust. What he saw was not only of the spirit but of the flesh. Morning Mist had the body of a virgin daughter, the eyes of a wise mother, the simple goodness of a trustworthy sister.

Quickly now, as she shed her robe, Mountain Singing feasted his eyes on her naked form; then, his heart aflame, she fed herself into the thin air. The quick curves, the slim-hipped loveliness, the small-breasted beauty became a wisp of smoke floating up. Then, the sky clear, the last glimmer of the morning star faded out.

In her going, the green burned more green; the field grass, home of the meadow mouse, prickled with crystal fire; the aspen leaves glistened in the rain-wet. Everything—from moss to mouse—was fresh, newborn.

Now at night, as Mountain Singing prepared his lonely bed—he had not yet taken a wife—he wondered at the incalculable sorrow of life. Just how was it possible that he had fallen in love with a sprite, a spirit of the dawn? Any woman would have him, so why did he have to choose the ineluctable something of sweet rain and hot spark, of wind glitter? Drawing the skin of a mountain sheep about him, he stared into the red light of his fire. His lodge was a place of emptiness: No heart beat next to his; no hand reached out in the night; no caress took him into the deep of sleep.

The moons grew thin to full and back again to thin. The big grass moon of young summer went by, the last cicada-shell moon of old summer, too. Then the first frost moon came, and the in-between moon—the time when the people of the mist marked the first frost against the breath of winter. Now the people worked hard to make themselves ready for the long cold; skins were stretched, rubbed smooth with skinning stones; game was hunted, brought into camp, and smoked, as was fish. Bones were boiled, sinew softened, and children worked alongside their mothers and fathers. So it was that the people prepared for Mother Earth's change of dress; soon would come the little downy feathers of snow. Soon would she wear her long robe of softest, whitest doeskin. Soon would come the white owl of winter, the hungry moon, when bear sleep and deer stamp in the hollows and the idle flakes fall from the sky.

However, these things had not yet come. And one crisp dawn, at the end of autumn, Mountain Singing found that he could keep his passion no longer. At the moment when Morning Mist was about to shed her foggy cloak and rise to meet the sun, he ran toward her, crying out his longing. "Let old men have their ways," he cried. "Let them speak of right and wrong; let them gather round the council fire for days on end, talking of these things. But hear me now: Long have I watched your morning dance, the falling of your robe, the filling of the valley with light as you go up to him of whom I am envious."

Now the morning breeze clung to that fleece of fog, parting it at the front. Poised between the gray and the gold, coming and going, she listened.

"Pity me for saying these things," he cried, "but do not go to him yet. Stay on earth a little longer. Let me feel the softness of your skin, for I know now that I can't live without you." He wanted to say how much he needed to feel her face in the crook of his neck, the throb of her throat on his lip, her smooth skin and cool breasts, naked in the dawn. And she paused, poised, withholding herself from the anticipated sky. Now, for the first time ever in that valley ringed with mountains, Morning Mist did not rise to meet the sun, nor did she drop her sacred robe of misted fleece. She kept it on, inviting Mountain Singing to enter it with her so that he could share her vapor.

The days passed, long days, and longer nights. The people of the mist wondered what had happened to their chief; wondering, they waited for his return, but months passed, moons and moons, and still he did not return. The cycle was thus interrupted; winter never came to the mountain-ringed valley. Nor did the breath feathers of Mother Earth tickle the sky and fall to the dry, barren ground. The cold came, but the air held no moisture; the dry duff and the this-tledown hills hung suspended in a cold summery glow.

In the spring of the year, when fawns grow spots and eaglets grow down, the valley did not turn green; it remained golden brown. The trees raised bony fingers to the parched sky. A terrible drought came to the valley, staying through the spring and into the summer.

But Mountain Singing knew nothing of this, for his heart was blind with love. He knew of that, nothing more. Hidden from all, he alone was moist and warm, happy beyond measure in the mystic embrace of Morning Mist, who fed him love—all season, every season.

One day, when he had been away for twelve moons, he came out of Morning Mist's arms for a brief moment—and what he saw made his heart stop. The valley had dried up; all that was in it had died. All around lay the bare bones of the valley; time lay frozen in an undying corona of deathly summer sun. There was the village he had so lovingly tended for so many years; everywhere the dust of summer caught in the ice of no season. The tepees were ragged, flapping in a dead wind; the people were stripped of flesh, boneyards of them, caught in the net of sunlit death.

"Oh, what have I done?" he cried out. "Where once a beautiful village was, there's now the blank face of death."

It was then he heard the gentle voice of Mother Earth, heard the forgiving whisper in the fold of his ear. She told him, "Greatness is a lonely lodge mate; but love is the friend of ruin, when eyes are blind to all but beauty. You've tasted loneliness; you've wallowed in love. Which do you choose? The choice is yours." And, eyes roving, he pitied the poor marmot, dead in his lair, the fire-struck summer hawk, bone-bright on his winter branch.

"Oh, my poor people," he said, sobbing. "I've killed you with neglect."

"So has your lover, Morning Mist," Mother Earth said. "Look, Sun Father's burned everything to bones."

"What should I do?"

"You must face Sun Father, see what he says. He alone can undo what has already been done."

And so it was that Mountain Singing left the milkweed womb of the stillborn valley, climbed to the top of the highest peak, and there prayed for four days and four nights, asking Sun Father to see him. Long he fasted, suffering privations, praying for a chance to make right what was wrong; to offer himself, if necessary, his own poor flesh in payment for his selfishness.

After the fourth day, Sun Father came, riding his red bay horse, his sundown horse named Sunway.

Mountain Singing saw him, reined on a turf of burning cloud, laying a path of pollen on the wind. Then, seeing the path was good and gold, he got off his red horse and walked onto the mountain.

There are many things he might have done, given his power, his anger at the craven earth chief.

Yet only one thing he said and did. "You are mortal," he said.

"I am."

"And yet your name comes from this mountain."

Again Mountain Singing nodded. "That is true."

"You've loved a goddess, paid dearly for it," Sun Father said.

Mountain Singing lowered his head. The charges, as spoken, were true.

"Now the time has come for you to be watchful."

And Sun Father struck Mountain Singing in the heart with an arrow of lightning. And Mountain Singing turned to scree, rose up, big and bouldered, and became the thing he had been named for, Mountain Singing. And all around him, the other mountains, large though they were, looked small.

The following morning, as usual, Sun Father rode out upon his fire-white horse, Dawnway, surveying the earth. Again he came to the little mountain-ringed valley beneath the clouds. And Sun Father saw that Mist Woman was shedding her robe of fog, as was her custom, ritually rising into the sky.

When he saw her, he said, "You, too, have loved selfishly; now your lover is that mountain that stands out, vigilant, above all the others. So now, if you love stone, you may cling to him all seasons of the year. Have your lover, Morning Mist. Never leave his side."

Then he rode across the heavens, changing horses from blue noon to red dusk, leaving her there, stunned, stopped between rising and falling, drifting between heaven and earth.

Now in time, Morning Mist did embrace her stone lover, the man chief changed into a mountain. They say that when the sky fills with snowflakes, the two are making love. And every spring, the people know by the swelling of the rivers and streams that they are being watched over by Mountain Singing and his wife, Morning Mist, who still clings to him.

Yet there is a time, the people say, when Mountain Singing feels such remorse for his neglected village that Sun Father allows his spirit to walk once again among the grassy, flowery meadows of his forest valley. Then he remembers all that happened, and he sheds tears of kindness for his people, for the shame he brought upon himself. The tears he sheds, so they say, are the white violets that grow in the alpine grass where he walks, remembering those short days on earth when he loved an immortal woman with a mortal man's heart.

The Story of Red Shell and Tall Man

HOW RED SHELL, THE WIFE OF MOUNTAIN SINGING'S
BROTHER, TALL MAN, DISAPPEARS INTO THE SPIRIT
WORLD AND HOW TALL MAN GOES TO THAT WORLD TO
LEARN THAT LOVE IS STRONGER THAN DEATH

s o the people of the mist turned their thoughts once again to life in the mountain-ringed valley. And their story—that of a misguided chief whose loss of wisdom, in favor of self-indulgence, brought ruin upon his people—might be, and probably is, the story of any people under the sun. However, even after a whole forest is set aflame, the rain comes and the carrion of crows is swept away. Thus the cycle of rebirth starts afresh; through the burned bones of broken conifers, toothlike and stubbed, come the spears of grass, the shoots of shrubs. From charred logs come curled ferns; under the warm earth, the hot seeds crack; and life, which loves life, begins anew.

Now one evening, a woman named Red Shell, whose husband was brother of the unfortunate chief Mountain Singing, was coming home from a luckless day of fishing, when she discovered a curious thing.

Beneath a cedar tree, she saw a young female deer freshly killed, with no sign of death upon it. I will skin this deer, she thought, and, as there is no food at our lodge, I will tell my husband it was hunted meat, given to us by a friend. And she did this just as she planned, ignoring her people's vow not to eat the flesh of an animal unkilled by an arrow, spear, bow, or trap.

Now the meat tasted fine, but sometime after eating it, Tall Man fell ill. The next morning, his throat was dry. He begged for water, and she went to the creek to get some. While there, absorbed in her thoughts, she stepped on a rattlesnake, which bit her on the ankle.

153

She limped home, feverish and pale. That night, in spite of her husband's attempt to save her, she died.

Tall Man went into mourning—scarred his body, slashed his hair, blackened his face. Carrying a crow's bill and Red Shell's moccasins, he walked about in a daze, somehow believing that he would see her again. The song he sang morning, noon, and night, a prayer for Red Shell's journey to the spirit world, was sad beyond belief—so sad that even the dead, who walk backward, strained their ears to hear it.

One night while mournfully singing his dirge, Tall Man looked up from his fire and saw something stirring in the darkness. He got up from the fire and searched for it, but all he found was a dead rabbit with a line of cornmeal drawn around its mouth. The arrow that killed the rabbit was still in its flesh, yet it was like no arrow he had ever seen: The wood was of a strange tree; the notched feather was unknown to him. The arrow point seemed to have been cut from a dark cloud—when Tall Man removed the arrow from the rabbit, it disappeared.

For three nights, the same thing happened: the gift of the cornmeal-mouth rabbit, the mystery arrow that disappeared. On the fourth night, a man of dark color came out of the shadows. But for the white cowrie shells that jingled around his neck, he was darker than the outer darkness, and his hair hung long, completely masking his hidden face. His moccasins were on backward; so were his leggings. He stood before the fire without speaking, waiting for something to happen. The little cowries tinkled in the wind; otherwise, there was absolute silence. When the man of dark color spoke, his voice seemed to come from afar. "Your wife is happy in the spirit world," he said, "and when your life is complete, you may join her. For now, be content that she is well, that she loves you. Know that your grief is a great burden to her, who has gone on ahead along the spirit road. I have come to say this, and now I must go."

He started to walk backward, but Tall Man fell upon his knees, weeping bitterly, holding on to the fringe of his leggings.

"You cannot know," he cried, "how much I long to see her face. If only I might see her just once, then I would go back to living a normal life. As it is, you can see that I do nothing but mourn for her."

The man of dark color raised his left hand and waved at the darkness. "If I should take you on the spirit road, the trail of shadows,
would you promise to do what I told you?"

Tall Man, tears streaming down his face, nodded blankly.

"Then come as you are."

Deep into the night's mouth they went, passing through a great
gorge into the inner whorls of the earth. No more did Tall Man feel
the sun on his back or see the glint of fire on the blackened stones
of his fire pit. Nor did he roll in the warm robe that he liked to sleep
in; no more did his eye delight in the radiance of stones, the gleam
of willow branches bending in the breeze. For the underworld was
a strange and soundless place; the only noise was the dull tread of
their footsteps and the jingling of the cowries on the neck of his
night-faced guide. Darkness was upon them always; the veils of
which neither parted nor barred their mute passage. They walked
on, and it seemed to Tall Man that all but his heart had been given
to the darkness of the endless gorge.

At last, they came to a kiva ladder that led down into a great hole,
at the bottom of which they could see a small, flickering light. The
man of dark color took hold of the ladder and descended, his shells
ringing. Tall Man followed him ever deeper into the earth's belly,
farther into the warmth of the womb that enclosed them. Then Tall
Man heard birds singing. At the bottom of the kiva ladder, he saw
a river whose grayish light was the color of the sky when the moon
goes behind a cloud. There were people bathing, their hair hanging
down and covering their faces, just like the man of dark color. These,
thought Tall Man, must be the spirits of the dead. Then, sitting on
a little shelf of rock, he saw Red Shell holding her head. She appeared
to be crying. The man of dark color spoke then. "There, you see that
your wife is well. Now you must leave." But Tall Man did not move.
"She doesn't see me," he said bitterly. "We must return now to the
upper world," the man of dark color repeated tonelessly.

Yet though he was bound by sacred promise, Tall Man was not
content with the bargain he had made. He had to touch Red Shell
to make sure that she was real.

"Do not touch her," the man of dark color said, anticipating his
thought.

But Tall Man would not be stopped; he ran to the river, reached out, and took Red Shell by the shoulders. And as she looked up into his eyes through the parted curtain of her hair, he felt her presence dissolve. For an instant, he saw her eyes, tears running out of them, and then she disappeared.

"Her eyes!" he cried. "Her eyes were weeping for me!"

"I warned you," the man of dark color said as he took Tall Man to the ladder, bidding him go up, one rung at a time, to the upper world, where he belonged. Through blinding tears, Tall Man climbed, but he saw only the lost eyes of his wife as she had dissolved before him. On and on, up and up, he went, yet he kept asking himself, "Why did I come on this journey if not to look forever into my dear wife's eyes?" So saying, his foot slipped on a rung of the ladder and he let go of his handhold, falling from whence he had come, back into the spirit world.

And nothing, they say, was heard from him again. But that is not exactly true, for there is a place where the river's roar turns into tireless lapping, where, slackening out of the sunlight, it dips into the ground, whispering quietly until there are only doves calling and herons lifting off, big-winged, between the old gray walls of the canyon. Here, in this sequestered place, their call is heard, those two who fear to leave the safety of their isolated stone retreat. Here their tinkling song, like silver bells or cowrie shells, comes up the unseen ladder of the ages. And there, drifting off the rimrock, it fills the stony silence, then withdraws: canyon wrens, sweetest of all singers in the canyon country, trilling songbirds whose paired voices rise into the light, ringing down the evening breeze, tangling in the salt cedar, falling back mysteriously into the deeper walls from which they came.

The Story of Blue Elk

OF A GREAT ELK WHO IS BROTHER TO A BOY WHO
CANNOT SPEAK, AND OF HOW WHEN THE ELK TAKES
LEAVE OF HIM THE BOY BECOMES A MAN AND FINDS
HIS VOICE IN THE MAGIC OF HIS BROTHER'S HORNS

A boy was born in a village of sun-baked bricks not far from the country of the canyon wren. He was a perfect child, well formed in all ways but one: He could not utter a sound. He came out of silence into the noise of the world, born without crying. Nor did he try to cry, for he had no way to do it. The medicine man who looked at him smiled, as if recalling some forgotten myth: "Some," he said, "do not need to speak."

The day the boy was born, a great elk wandered into the village. The horns of that elk, like the branches of a black oak, cast a long blue shadow. It came into the village from the south, walking slow and proud, unconcerned.

"It is a magic elk," the medicine man said to the people of the pueblo who gathered to spread pollen on its path. The sun caught those fine outspread antlers, and around the elk's great muscled neck, the fur was thick and dark. The hooves made no sound as it walked through the village, stopping only once, pausing at the mud-brick house of the newborn boy, where it snorted loudly at the door-way, asking to be let in. The surprised parents came to the door, but when they opened it, the elk's antlered head was too large to pass through. A gold mist of flies had gathered around the elk's eyes, and it stood there, flicking its tail. Somehow, though, the mother knew what the elk had come for. "I think," she said to her husband, "he wants to see our boy." So the father picked up the child and carried him to the elk, who stamped his hoof eleven times, then once

157

more, deliberate, slow, leaving two hoof clefts in the dirt by the door. Then it turned around and walked through the noonday light as easily as it had come, more like a dream animal than a real one. And it was never seen at the pueblo again.

Now when the boy, who was named Blue Elk, was twelve years old—twelve stamps of the cloven hoof—he fell in love with a girl his own age. The boy had never been able to utter a sound, but those who knew him understood that he had been blessed by the great elk on the day of his birth. The power of speech, though sadly missing, was, they believed, reserved in him for some unknowable reason.

Anyway, Blue Elk was unable to tell the girl, Sunflower, how much he cared for her. In truth, he could not sleep for thinking of her; her smile made him weak, light-headed. Her movements so delighted him that he remembered them for days. He yearned to speak to her, but this was not meant to be, so he contented himself with watching her fetch water and bake bread with her mother. Whatever she did, wherever she did it, intrigued him. One day when he was walking in the upland meadows above the pueblo, Blue Elk caught sight of his name-giver, the great elk that had come to the door on the day that he was born. It came out of the spruces, walking into the heather, shoulder-deep, afloat in flowers. Slowly, the elk made its way to the boy, its horned head like a thicket of buckeye branches. Blue Elk watched as the great elk eclipsed the sun, coming closer and closer, until he felt its flowery breath on his face and smelled the sweetness of jumbled cliffs, sun paths, cloud-washed ponds. The breath of the mighty elk, warm with bark, bud, and scrub, was good, and it passed between them as a bond of love, an unbreakable link in the necklace of their lives.

For a long time, then, the pueblo people saw the silent-tongued boy walking the slanted hillsides beside his elk brother. Together, they roamed the highlands. Blue Elk made a headdress of wildflowers, placing them on the elk's antlered head, or he would be seen riding him bareback through the mountain passes, where hunters saw them emerge from the forest as one great inseparable shadow. Then one autumn day when the geese were singing their southerly song, the elk spoke to the boy for the first and only time.

"I must go now," he said, "but you must stay."

Blue Elk tried to say the words that tumbled, bubbled, to his lips, but his tongue refused them and they stuck in his throat like sticks in a spring torrent. "When I am gone," the elk said, "my horns will stay. Plant them in the earth and something good will happen."

Sometime after this happened, a hunter from the far west came into the land of the pueblo people. He sat around a camp fire one night, telling some hunters of the fine elk he had shot with the sinew-backed bow whose string was so well strung that none of the pueblo people could pull it back more than a few fingers. "The meat of that elk," he said, "would feed my village for a whole winter. Pity, I am so far from home."

"But how could you kill such an animal?" the people asked, in wonder, as well as fear.

The hunter said, "He gave me his breath, so I knew that he was ready to leave this world."

Now when Blue Elk heard the story, he ran for the mountains, not resting until he came to the place where he and his brother had always met. There he found droplets of blood on the matted grass; he followed them into the spruce trees where his brother had been brought down and had given his breath. And he saw where the hunter had planted the heavy horns in the black earth.

"What my brother wanted is done," Blue Elk said, and he left the mountain, returning to the pueblo to mourn the passing of his brother. That winter, the snows were deep, but when they melted at last, the rivers rose, overran their banks, and engorged the lowland streams with roaring runoff and swirling fog. Finally, when the snow-melt ended, summer came, the time when elks graze on clover in the mountain meadows; the time when Blue Elk, lonely for his brother, would climb up the steep slopes to see if his brother's horns had grown. The day he arrived beneath the blue boughs of the spruce, he saw that the horns, bone-bright and beautiful, made a white glow in the pine shadow. He drew closer. The horns had twined, limb to horn, horn to limb, into the trunk of a young red cedar.

Now this will be my place, Blue Elk thought, for as long as I shall live.

And he built himself a cabin where he could see the snowy horns grow with the feathered wings of the young cedar. In time, the horns grew into the tree and the tree grew into the horns, so that the two were one. One night, Blue Elk had a dream in which he saw his elk brother again, and his brother said to him, "You cannot mourn my passing forever."

"I can never forget you," Blue Elk told him.

"You shall have a voice," the elk replied, "one that comes from the horn and the cedar. When you speak with this voice, she, the one you loved, will come; then you will begin your family." Then the great elk faded into the hills of the dream, and Blue Elk woke, knowing, now what he had to do. Asking for the red cedar's blessing, he cut a portion of the sacred wood and carved it into a flute. From the end, he tied bands of elk string, with blue and red beads at the tip. Then he rubbed the smooth wood with the fat of the mountain sheep. And the red wood was a river in the sun, shining with the flowing grain.

Blue Elk did not so much play the flute as speak into it—as he would have as a child, had he been able to. And his breath gave voice to the flute, and a song came out of it that caused the animal people to stop what they were doing and listen to the pure notes. The people from the pueblo heard them, too, and it was not long before they said a new name when they came upon him in the woods. Red Cedar Man, they called him, and the name stuck.

One day as he was playing the song of the geese going home, a young woman came to his cabin. She sat at his feet, listening. He remembered her well; but now she was a woman, supple as a poplar, rain-glistened, lovely.

"Sunflower," he spoke with the flute, fashioning notes that climbed the air. The song touched the woman's heart and made her smile.

"I remember you, Blue Elk," she said softly.

Looking into her eyes, framed by her long blue-black hair, he heard. Then he spoke with the flute again, and she listened. The stellar jays and the blue warblers came, circling through the ingenuity of Blue Elk's song. Bear cubs, looking under stones, listened; and their mothers, chewing honeycomb, listened. And it seemed that the whole world was still; for a moment, life listened to Blue Elk's antlered song as it reached out and touched the elk on the slope, the deer in the glade, the bear in the bramble, the bird on the branch. And all across the mountain pastures, the dreaming land listened to the song of the red cedar flute, a gift of power from the great elk.

PART FOUR

MYTHS OF WAR

BOOK 10

The Story of the War on Earth

The Story of the Second Animal Council

The Story of the Making of the Warrior Young-
Man-Afraid-of-His-Horses

The Story of the War on Earth

IN WHICH THE SORROW OF WAR BEGUN BY THE ANT
PEOPLE IS CARRIED FOREVER IN THE HEARTS OF MEN

o w there came a day when Sun Father and Mother Earth met to talk about the ways of men and women in the world, and how the animal people were faring, and whether peace would outlast war. For it seemed to them that the world was ever on the edge of some unforeseen calamity. Unknown was that blissful time, before the emergence of the people, when there was no sound or any stirring thing; neither was there evil afoot then, nor any walker on foot, only the calm heaven and the empty sea. Nothing was but stillness, darkness, endless nothingness. . . .

"And wasn't it better then?" Sun Father began, but Mother Earth cut him short, saying, "Was the child better before birth?" Whereupon Sun Father challenged her, as he had once before when they had gone to seek the counsel of Mountain Old Man. "Tell me," he said, "of the accomplishments thus far achieved by the beings of the earth—the animals, men, and insects. What great good have they done?"

Mother Earth said, "They have grown into many people with many camps. They do not always get along, but they do not always fight."

"Your ant people," he concluded, "were the first to fight and the last to put down their weapons."

"And they were the first to build," Mother Earth reminded. But as he had no memory for this, she told him once again what he

165

should have remembered. And thus follows her story of how the thing called war came to be.

"They worked; their lives were consumed with labor and they thought of little else. When they slept, they were merely still, their eyes open, their feelers extending into the endless dream of work. But things set in motion are bound, sooner or later, to make contact, or, worse, to come into collision.

"It was only a matter of time before a scout for the first ant people discovered a scout for the second ant people. These scouts exchanged stories. Each looked the other in the eye, and afterward, the ant scouts told their chiefs what they'd learned. 'Look,' each one said, 'I have seen long columns of the . . .' Here they had to make up a new word, a word for something that tasted bad: The word came, and it was *enemy*. The chiefs then did something no chief had done before. To match the word *enemy*, each chief looked for another word. And this word was *kill*. Together, the words *enemy* and *kill* changed the world, which, up to then, had been calm and still. Now as the first ant people fought with the second ant people, the world was filled with suffering. The bodies of dead ant people covered the earth. As a result of this, another word came into being. And this word was *death*. So the chiefs were now named chiefs of war, so yet another word was added to the three, making four.

"First Man moved the people away from the ants, but wherever he took them, the bitter odor of the ant war hung in the air and poisoned it. I, Mother Earth, saw the disharmony, the danger to the earth, and I felt much sadness, for the ants were my children as much as the animals and men. So I created a great fire that would consume all of the ant people who wanted to make war, and I struck a sacred flint, the first the world had known, and set the earth ablaze, telling First Man and First Woman to take sanctuary within the core of the mountains. And they did the thing I asked. When they were safe within the mountains, I fanned the flames high into the sky, and the ants stopped fighting and looked at the black earth. As their jaws came open and their hands set free their foes, they saw an orange cloud of fire loom over them; it swept them up, turned them to ash, and for a time after that the earth lay quiet, undisturbed. The people came out of the mountains, remembering how they had been saved, and they moved about carefully, setting things right, and, for a while, the words and deeds of the ant people were all but forgotten."

Now when Mother Earth was through with her story, Sun Father said, "You've got it all wrong. You didn't strike the first flint; I did. You set the tinder; I lit the fire—that was how it was." And neither would give quarter to the other, and they continued to argue about the nature of war. The argument is unsettled to this day. Nor has any age, nor any mortal or immortal being, nor any creature above or below the sun, an answer that explains why, after so much devastation, we, the people, still indulge in war.

The Story of the Second Animal Council

HOW THE ANIMAL PEOPLE VOW TO WAGE WAR ON THE
TWO-LEGGED PEOPLE, AND HOW THREE ANIMAL
PEOPLE, GILA MONSTER, HUMMINGBIRD, AND
CHIPMUNK, REMAIN ON PEACEFUL TERMS WITH
EVERYONE

WHEN they held their second council, the animal people did not invite the ant people, for their concern was not who had started it but how to finish it. And their opinion was that the two-legged people were growing in number faster than they were, and the art of hunting was growing more dangerous with each passing day. At the second council, Old Man White Bear, who was a chief, asked the bear people what should be done, and right away, Grizzly Bear got up and started to speak.

"Long have we known the secret of life," he said. "The two-leggeds still do not know our secret. Before a hunter kills me, I hide my heart, my liver, my spleen. I put them in my tail. That way, if they kill me, I can come back to life again. I just draw all of my parts back together again, and I live."

"Where do you hide your parts?" Ground Squirrel asked.

Grizzly Bear said, "I put them in the tip of my tail."

Then Old Man White Bear said, "That will not work anymore. The two-leggeds know of that trick. They're cutting our tails into little pieces and giving them to their children to play with."

"They use our skins for blankets," Buffalo Old Man said in disgust.

"And moccasins," added Deer Woman.

So after much talk, the animal people decided that they needed weapons to defend themselves against the two-leggeds. One of the bear people offered his own sinew to furnish a bowstring, but when

Old Man White Bear tried to use the bow, his long claws caught on the string and got stuck.

"I know what to do," Grizzly Bear said. "We'll cut our claws and make them short."

"That won't work," said Porcupine. "How can we climb trees with short claws? We'll starve to death."

"True, true," agreed Buffalo Old Man, whose hooves were as valuable to him as his horns.

"I've got an idea," Old Man Gopher commented. "I'll give every two-legged person who comes along a toothache."

"Can you do this?" Old Man White Bear asked, surprised.

"It is within my power."

"Very well," Old Man White Bear said, smiling, "let us consider it done."

"I," offered Deer Woman, "will give sore joints to any two-legged hunter that I see."

And the animal people agreed to the desirablity of this as well, and it, too, was considered done. So each animal gave a charm of sorcery to protect his kind, and their sorceries were many and varied. Snake offered bad dreams; Eagle offered the evil eye; Bear offered coughing sickness; and so on. Now Little White Grub listened to all of these curses as they were piled high upon the two-legged miscreants, and he thought this was so funny that he fell on his back and laughed. And he has never gotten on his feet since that time, which is why he crawls about the way he does today.

The only animal who, for reasons of his own, would not cast a curse was Chipmunk.

"What have you to offer?" Old Man White Bear asked him, but Chipmunk shook his head. "The two-leggeds have done nothing to me," he said with indifference. But Grizzly Bear was not happy with this. He reached out, raked his claws across Chipmunk's back, and carved those telltale stripes all Chipmunk people have to this day. He wasn't the only one, though, who wouldn't make war on the two-leggeds, and that is a lucky thing, for if everyone had, there wouldn't be any more two-legged people left on earth. However, Gila Monster, Hummingbird, Chipmunk, Buffalo, Crane, and many others decided to stay on peaceful terms with the two-leggeds. In fact, these animals felt sorry for the sickness that was soon heaped upon the hunters and their families. And it spread so that all men and women felt the sting of blindness from the wing dust of the eagle; the bitter cough from the husky-voiced bear; the unruly mind, set upon with bad dreams, from the cackling coyote. So, were it not for the kindness of the medicine animals, who taught the two-legged medicine men everything they knew of plants and cures, potions and healings, the world would know only illness. Yet in time, the medicine men learned the cures of all the animal people, even the ones who had vowed to make them sick. Some of these cures were used in the wars the people waged against one another. And there was no cure for war.

The Story of the Making of the Warrior Young-Man-Afraid-of-His-Horses

HOW TALKS ASLEEP RECOUNTS THE PROWESS OF
YOUNG-MAN-AFRAID-OF-HIS-HORSES, ONE OF THE
GREAT HORSEMEN AND HORSE STEALERS OF THE
PEOPLE WHO CALL THEMSELVES CROW

THE horse was proud, but the man seated on the horse was prouder still. Together, the two were one. Therefore, the man who had a horse was counted a good man, not a poor one. And a man who had many horses was a rich man, most probably a warrior to be reckoned with, for how could he acquire so many horses without being brave?

To enter the enemies' camp for no reason was foolish. Yet to sneak up to it with the purpose of taking horses was a worthy thing, a thing that would embolden a man, make him prove himself. To fly as the wind flies while mounted on the horse of an enemy was a fine accomplishment, one that children dreamed of, one that men would risk their lives to attain.

And so the gift of the gods, the sacred horse, put man against man, woman against woman, and people against people.

"How many horses do your people have?" a warrior asked his enemy.

"How many horses does your young man have?" asked the father of the bride.

The horses learned to dance as men dance, and men learned to dance as horses dance. And there were medicine men for horses, and they followed them into battle. And horses were buried in battle with their riders; and old chiefs, soon to die, did not go to the next world alone, but they rode the spirit trail on the back of their favorite horse. Now there rose among the people a great warrior whose name

171

was Young-Man-Afraid-of-His-Horses. His brother, who rode with him, made a great reputation as a storyteller by telling of his great deeds on the war road. So here is the story of Young-Man-Afraid-of-His-Horses, as told by Talks Asleep.

"Young-Man-Afraid-of-His-Horses was called this name not because he feared his horse but because, as a child, he had never seen anything as beautiful as a horse. He grew afraid that one day such magnificence might pass from his hand, might pass from the land. He was, therefore, called this name; and he lived to prove that horses, his own especially, were there to increase and to make him rich. By the time he was an old man, he had a herd of them, and they followed him about like dogs.

"Once, when he was just a boy, Young-Man-Afraid-of-His-Horses went on a raid. He and others of his people, who called themselves Crow, journeyed out of the mountains, took to the plain, and rode to the edge of the River That Has No Rival. There they saw the camp of the Crooked Nose people.

"It was a large camp, with skin tents planted on the plain for as far as the eye could reach. Here were fierce warriors, fine horsemen; and they had many horses tethered in many different places around the camp. The finest of these, the racing horses, were kept inside the outer circle of the tents. There the great horse chief, Kills-with-His-Eye, had his best mounts, stallions and mares of much worth, but these were watched day and night, night and day by boys who were in training to be horsemen.

"Young-Man-Afraid-of-His-Horses reasoned thus: 'Am I not one of them, a young man earning rank? Am I not seeking the power of privilege? We are equal, then. If we are equal, we should respect one another, and I do.' So saying, he devised a cunning plan.

"He and his companions ate no meat that was not dried and mixed with berries, nor did they light a fire to warm themselves. They tethered their own horses beyond the tangle of cottonwood trees by the river and hid in the deep grass that grew by the bank. At dawn, they watched the Crooked Nose young men lead the fine horses into the morning sun, taking them to the river to be watered. Every day started the same—the freshening of the horses. After which, the young men drank heartily themselves, sometimes playfully splashing the clear water about their heads and shoulders. Once, one of them fell off the slippery bank, and the others went in after him.

"The morning came, as planned, and Young-Man-Afraid-of-His-Horses put on a great disguise. From an old buffalo skin hard-warped from the sun, he had made a giant fish fin, which he tied to his back with thongs of sinew. Over his arms and legs, he tied leggings and armlets of bark. Then he darkened his face with mud.

" 'I am going to be the biggest fish cat that ever lived in this water,' he told his friends with a smile.

" 'There is a story I have heard,' one of the boys said, 'of just such a monster. They say it is three times the length of a man.'

" 'Just so,' Young-Man-Afraid-of-His-Horses said with a laugh.

"And when the sun came up, they said their prayers and watched the Crooked Noses come, leading their dancing beauties along the ridge to the watering place. After the string of horses was watered, the young men tethered them to a tree and went a little upstream to refresh themselves. Momentarily, being boys at heart, they were playing in the water, having a good time. Suddenly, a huge fish went past them, a great cat as large as any one of them. One ran to get his bow and arrows; another fetched his lance; a third plunged into the river with a knife between his teeth. Soon all of them had forgotten their responsibilities: The chief's horses stood unwatched, untended.

"And yet they floundered about in the water, looking for the fish cat of their dreams. Poking and stabbing the river, they emerged from it, gasping for breath. Occasionally, the jagged fin would appear, always farther downstream; they would see it flash in the sun, then disappear into the depths. Then the chase was on with even more passion; they thrashed crazily, beating the water to get at it. Arrows zinged, bowstrings twanged, but the monster fish was always out of reach.

"Finally, they came to a place where the river widened. A forest of cattails grew there; they were tall, shiny, brown-topped, and big. And the swimmers got easily lost in them, shouting wildly when they saw the great fin, thinking they had it trapped in the cattail shallows.

"Young-Man-Afraid-of-His-Horses led the Crooked Nose young men into a terrible trap, for hidden in the cattails were his Crow companions, who struck them down, one at a time, without ever revealing their hiding places.

"When the last Crooked Nose was knocked unconscious, the Crow youths disappeared into the cottonwoods, where others of their band had already taken the fine band of stallions and mares.

"And so it was, my friends, that Young-Man-Afraid-of-His-Horses was known after this as Young-Man-Who-Knows-What-Is-His."

That was how the great storyteller Talks Asleep ended his narrative about his worthy brother, who became, once he laid down his lance, a storyteller in his own right. For as he said of himself, "Once a warrior, twice a teller of tales."

BOOK 11

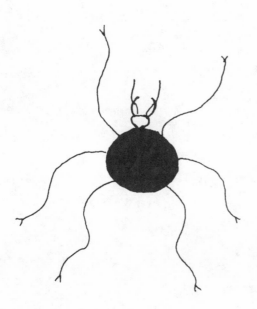

The Story of Hawk Storm

OF THE BOY DOVE RUNNING, WHO BECOMES THE GREAT
WARRIOR HAWK STORM, AS REMEMBERED BY THE OLD
STORYTELLER KNOWN AS MANY NAMES

FTER he was too old to go into battle any longer, a warrior often taught the young men the secrets of the hunt—how to steal horses; the art of touching an enemy on the breastbone, surprising but not killing him: what is called counting coups. When he grew older still, a warrior did not instruct young men; he told stories around the winter fire to children, and they listened, for they could see that his face was as the face of a rock that has been worn by wind, lashed by rain, and bitten by frost. Such was the old storyteller known as Many Names.

"When I was young, there lived a boy in the skin tent next to mine whose mother was killed soon after he was born. When I knew him, he lived with his grandmother. Now this boy had surprising powers for one so young. He liked to sit in the grass and watch the rock swallows. Once he told me, 'You see how they fly, bunched close; that is how we should run.' And this boy showed me how to run, elbow-to-elbow, drawing strength from one another.

"He became known as Dove Running because, even more than the rock swallows, he watched the doves, imitated their movements. Now one time when he was a little older, but not yet a young man, his grandmother was stolen by the ones they call the Wolf Eyes. The Wolf Eyes took her to the desert, where the people live who take silver out of the earth. The Wolf Eyes have a deserved reputation for cruelty; and they beat her when she brought them water from the river; they beat her when she brought them firewood. Sometimes they beat her for no reason, just because she was one of us, their enemy.

"Now Dove Running had followed his grandmother into the south country, where he called upon the power of the dove people to come to his aid. There he found that his prayer was answered, and one day he walked into the camp of the Wolf Eyes, unseen. The Wolf Eye women saw something and looked up from their work. They felt something come into their camp, yet they could not see it. What they saw was a small gray dove that ducked into one of the brush shelters. Ignoring the little bird, they went back to their pounding. Then Dove Running landed on the shoulder of his grandmother, and he saw, looking down on her scarred arms, that she had been freshly burned with fire sticks. Then he turned back into a boy, and his grandmother caressed and fondled him, but she said, 'You must fly home, little one. The Wolf Eye chief lives in this shelter, and soon he will return. Surely, when he sees you, he will kill you!'

" 'I am not afraid of the Wolf Eye, Grandmother,' the boy said. But, just then, as they were talking, the Wolf Eye chief suddenly entered the shelter.

" 'What do you mean by whispering to that dove?' he demanded of the old woman. Knocking her down, he grabbed up the gray dove and squeezed it until blood squirted out of its eyes and tiny white bones stuck out of the bloody feathers.

" 'Is that all there is to your sorcery?' The chief laughed fiercely and threw the bones and feathers out of the doorway of the brush shelter. Now when this happened, the grandmother let out such a wail that it could be heard from far away. She began to attack the Wolf Eye with her fists, but he pushed her away, saying, 'Pitiful old dog, your teeth have no bite.' Then he went outside, but he had not taken two steps when those little dove's bones lying in the dirt flew up into the air and came together in a dark cloud of dust, out of which flashed the wings of a great hawk that flew into the chief's face and tore out his eyes.

"But before the cruel chief fell to his knees and covered his face, the hawk whirled about and soared into the brush shelter, picked up the grandmother by the back of her buckskin dress, and flew away with her. That same day, he took her home. The people said it was a great thing that had happened down there in the desert. And after that, they knew Dove Running by the name of Hawk Storm."

The Story of Fire Storm

IN WHICH HAWK STORM FACES TRIALS AND RECEIVES
HIS SECOND WARRIOR'S NAME, FIRE STORM, AND IN
WHICH THE SPIRIT ALLIES SERVE HIM ON THE FIELD OF
BATTLE

WHEN next they met around the storyteller's fire, the children asked Many Names to tell of the worst danger that Hawk Storm ever faced; and so he told them of the time he got his second name, which is what this story is about.

"This was long ago, when the people called the Burnt Moccasins attacked Hawk Storm's hunting party. But today, as I tell it, it seems like yesterday. You see, my friend had been known by the name of Hawk Storm for some time, but it was a boy's name. He had done more impressive things after receiving the name, earning him even greater favor as a young warrior, but it was not until he met the Burnt Moccasins on the field of battle that he was given his man's name. You see, the Burnt Moccasins had been hunting Hawk Storm, and they finally caught him and tied him to a huge lightning-struck sycamore. Now, this is not a good-luck tree; and they tied him there in the middle of a thunderstorm, hoping the tree would be struck again by lightning—and presently it was, and it started to burn. Now Hawk Storm called for his ally, the hawk, but no hawk came."

"Why, Grandfather," one of the children asked, "did he not turn into a hawk himself?"

At this, the old chief scowled. "You mean to say you do not know the answer to that?"

Confused, the child shook his head.

180

"When you are a man of power," he said wisely, "you do not waste your power needlessly."

"But, Grandfather, he was going to die," the child protested.

"He was not given magic power to save his own life," the old chief admonished, "but to save the lives of others."

This seemed to satisfy the children, who, once again, fell silent, and Many Names then went on with his story.

"Now when Hawk Storm prayed for an ally to come, Raven heard his cry and came to him. Yet the flames from the burning sycamore blazed so close to his feathers, that he himself was caught on fire and burned black, just the way you see him today.

"When Hawk Storm prayed again for an ally to come, Screech Owl heard his cry and came. Yet the flames burned his eyes so badly, they turned red-orange, and they have been that way ever since that time.

"Again, Hawk Storm prayed for an ally to come, and Brown Snake appeared, wriggling into a hole in the burning sycamore tree. But he, too, was burned all over, and to this day, when we see him, we call him Black Snake.

"Now the fourth time Hawk Storm prayed for an ally to come, Spider Woman spun a fine silk thread and dropped it from a cloud. Then she came down from the sky, and with her sharp teeth she nibbled the bonds that bound Hawk Storm to the burning sycamore tree. And that, grandchildren, was how Hawk Storm escaped his death and bested the warriors of the Burnt Moccasin people."

"What happened to them, Grandfather?" one of the children asked.

"Well, they burned their moccasin feet black, walking all over looking for Hawk Storm," Many Names said. "And that is how they got the name Blackfeet, which is what we call them today."

"Grandfather, what of Hawk Storm's new name?" asked another child.

"That, grandchildren," the old chief said with a chuckle, "is for another time."

The Story of Water Spider

HOW MANY NAMES TELLS THE TALE OF HAWK STORM'S
THIRD WARRIOR NAME, WATER SPIDER, AND HOW OUR
HERO ACQUIRES IT

T H E next time the children gathered around Many Names, he told them that the new name of Hawk Storm was Water Spider.

"Why did they call him that?" a girl asked.

"Well," the old chief explained, "you remember how he was saved by Spider Woman? That meant that he was favored by the spider people. So his new name came from one of them."

"But why Water Spider?"

"They say that only Water Spider can come out of a fire without getting burned."

"What happened to him after that?"

And Many Names told them.

"Water Spider continued to be a great warrior. One time, he fought a long and hard battle, and was coming home with two of his friends. He had injured his leg, so his friends had to carry him between them. Their village was still a long way off. They were being followed, and night was coming on fast. At last, they came to a little canyon where a stream ran between the rocks, and one of the men said, 'I will go down there and bring up a water skin full of water.' But while he was climbing down into the canyon, he got the idea that they should leave Water Spider there; that way, they might still have a chance of eluding their enemies.

"And so these two cowardly companions pushed Water Spider over the edge of a cliff. Then they ran back to their village, arriving

182

safely, and told everyone that Water Spider had fought bravely but in the end had been overcome and had died with an arrow in his heart.

"Now, in the meantime, Water Spider found himself lying in a forsaken canyon with two broken legs. The only thing he could do was crawl along on his belly, seeking some kind of shelter for the night.

"After dragging himself for many hours, he found a small cave, pulled himself into it, and let out a long sigh of relief. At the back of the cave, he saw firelight flickering and an old naked man with no hair on his head sitting on a rock. The old man's legs, such as they were, were withered and useless, and his arms did not seem much better, being small as a child's.

" 'Welcome, grandson,' the old man said in the traditional way. He offered Water Spider a fresh-killed rabbit. Water Spider noticed that there were two fang marks at the rabbit's throat but no other mark on the body.

"The old man just smiled, saying, 'That is how I always kill them, right there on the neck. But I am getting too old to hunt; if only someone would drive the game to me, I might yet make a good hunter. But as you can see, I am just too old to move about the way I used to.'

"Water Spider let out a pained laugh. 'You are doing better than I, Old One,' he said, then added, 'In the morning, I will see what I can do to help you.' So they shared that rabbit, and soon after, they went to sleep. Water Spider noticed that the old man snored; and when he snored, he made a rattling noise that sounded as if it was coming from his backside.

"The next morning, the old man showed him how to slide out of the cave, how to move along the ground on his belly. 'We are not much good,' the old man said, snickering, 'but there are two of us.' That morning, they caught a quail by the river; Water Spider drove it in the direction of the old man, who killed it in the manner of the rabbit of the night before. Proudly, he showed off the puncture marks. 'I always get them like that,' he bragged.

"Now, in the days that followed, the two hunted together every morning, and always it was the same: Water Spider drove the game in the direction of the old man, who, somehow, managed to make the kill with just one shot. 'I would like to see the bow you use to do that,' Water Spider said, but the old man just replied, 'Sometime you will.'

"One night as they were preparing to go to sleep, Water Spider watched the old man place his head straight out in front of him, resting it on a rock. Soon he was snoring, with his eyes wide open and his tongue poking out and quivering as he slept. The next morning, Water Spider thanked the old man for sharing his lodge with him, but he said the time had come for him to go. The old man was sorry to hear this. 'We have hunted well together, grandson,' he said. 'But if you must leave, I want you to take this little bag; put it around your neck for safe-keeping.'

" 'What is it, grandfather?'

" 'It is the medicine I use to put my enemies to sleep.'

"So Water Spider thanked him very much, crawled out of the cave, and slowly climbed up out of the canyon. It took him a long time, but when he got to the top, he knew there was no sense in trying to walk; his legs still would not support him. But after all this time with the old man, Water Spider had gotten used to traveling in this way; in fact, he had gotten good at it. First, he moved his shoulders, then his belly, then his hips, gradually sliding himself along with his knees and toes. It was a slow way to go, but it worked, and he had no choice in the matter.

"So he traveled all day and all night, stopping only to drink water from a small spring. And the next day, he continued to travel steadily toward his village, stopping but once to eat service berries, then moving on. By nightfall of the fourth day, Water Spider saw the camp fires of his village, and tears came to his eyes because he never thought he would see them again. However, as he started down the hill through the grass, he was seen by some scouts—as it happened, the same ones who had tried to kill him.

" 'Look who comes crawling back after all this time,' the first said.

" 'Yes,' replied the second, 'it is Water Spider, who was once our friend but is now our enemy—for, given the chance, he will tell how we betrayed him.'

" 'I shall tell no one,' Water Spider said grimly, 'just help me get home the way you were supposed to.'

"But the two men could not take the chance that Water Spider would keep his tongue still on their behalf. Nodding evilly, they notched arrows and drew their bows on the unarmed man at their feet, who, seeing that they were about to kill him then, asked them to grant him one last request. The bows remained bent, but the traitors listened.

" 'In this bag I carry around my neck is the sacred medicine that has kept me alive all this time. If you will let me live now, I will let you have some of it.'

"The two sneered at Water Spider's childlike innocence. One said, 'First we take it from you, then we will kill you.' And they both laughed. Following this, one of them leaned down and cut the drawstring from Water Spider's neck, and as his partner drew near, he opened the small bag. Immediately, four porcupine quills flew out and stuck both in the throat. Reeling, they staggered, fell to their knees, turned purple-faced with poison, and died.

"Then Water Spider took back the bag and dragged himself through the grass on his belly until he reached his village. There, amidst much surprise, he was given a hero's welcome. In time, he told all that had happened to him. And this brought him a new name, one that I will share with you when the next big wind blows at the flap of our skin tent."

So saying, the old chief bade good night to the grandchildren gathered around the fire and left them wondering.

The Story of Snake's Medicine

OF WATER SPIDER, THE GREAT NAME-WINNING
WARRIOR WHO RECEIVES ONE LAST NAME OF HONOR
ON THE FIELD OF BATTLE, AND OF HIS NEW NAME,
SNAKE'S MEDICINE

"IN time, the warrior hero known as Snake's Medicine grew tired of having adventures. He was all but lame, and he wanted to settle down, have a family, and give up the warrior's way."

"Did he put his lance in the earth?" one of the children around the storyteller's camp fire asked.

"He did indeed," replied Many Names, "and became a chief known far and wide for his great wisdom and power."

"Did he ever have children, Grandfather?"

And Many Names told them.

"He married a young woman named Buffalo Calf, but it is hard to say why they did not have any children. They tried, but for them it was not possible. For many years, the two lived in a childless world, a world without stars, a world of winters without spring. And then one day while Snake's Medicine was gathering mushrooms in the woods, he saw something that caught his eye: a pine knot growing out of the trunk of a great pine tree. Now the more he studied it, the more he became convinced that this might be an answer to his, and his wife's, childless lodge. Here was a burl of twisted wood, a pine knot that looked just like the face of a child. He took out his knife and freed the knot, then sat down and carved the bark off it. Such a wonderful thing, he thought, this little pine knot looks just like a happy boy. When he was through whittling, he brought the

186

pine knot home to his wife, saying nothing of it except that he had found it on the trail.

"Buffalo Calf took the pine knot in her arms, hugged it to her breast, and placed it in a fine cradle board of bead and fur. 'Husband,' she said, 'speak to no one of this, for it is our secret and no one else's.' He agreed, and the two of them fed and clothed the pine knot, calling it Carving Boy. They talked to it and treated it tenderly, just as if it had been their own newborn son. Buffalo Calf fed it stew of boiled corn, and while this gruel, of course, ran out of the whittled mouth of Carving Boy, the two delighted parents did not really care, for at last their wish was granted—they had a child.

"Now, eleven moons grew from thin to full, and Snake's Medicine and Buffalo Calf pretended they had a son named Carving Boy. But one morning as Buffalo Calf was feeding him some crushed berries, he suddenly broke out of his cradle board, and roared, 'Mother, get me some meat!' Well, Buffalo Calf nearly fell over, she was so surprised, but her sense of devotion took over immediately, and she fed Carving Boy a piece of broiled buffalo hump, which he devoured in one bite, without even swallowing. For the rest of the day, he ate whatever she offered him. And he grew quite stout, so that by the time Snake's Medicine came home from hunting, deer slung over his shoulder, the starved boy wanted to eat all of it.

"Snake's Medicine was amazed. Here was the boy he had carved out of a pine knot, eating raw deer meat! Nor was that all: Carving Boy could not seem to fill his belly; he ate all of that deer—blood, bones, horns, hooves, even the fur—and there was nothing left for his mother and father, but still they did not complain, for this child was what they had always wanted.

"Now, Carving Boy grew very large; in four days he was as big as a skin tent. And by then, as you can imagine, he was eating horses, popping them into his mouth like strawberries. When his father's horses were gone, he ate the horses of other people. And when they were gone, he went out on a hunt and ate a whole buffalo herd. Nor was that all—for that Carving Boy now began to eat the hills and the mountains, the plains and the valleys."

At this, the children listening to the old chief Many Names became a little uneasy. They began to look over their shoulders, and as the wind moaned around the tepee walls, little shivers went up their spines and their eyes got big.

"Is he still out there somewhere?" one of the children wanted to know.

The old chief shook his head.

"He is no longer around," he said somewhat sadly.

"What happened to him?"

"Well, his father had to kill him with a stone ax. First, he chopped off one of his feet, so Carving Boy toppled over; then he chopped off one of his knees; and then he split open his belly. And what do you think happened then?"

The children looked at one another with great wondering eyes. No one could guess.

"Then," the old chief went on, "all the animals Carving Boy had ever eaten came out of his belly and ran away. There were deer, buffalo, elk, antelope, rabbits, mice, rats, and squirrels, not to mention the flocks of birds and the hills and mountains and valleys."

"Was that when he died?" a boy asked.

"Oh," said the old chief, "don't you know that a lie *never* dies, *never* goes away? That Carving Boy is still out there somewhere, and just like all the lies of this world, he is waiting, once again, to be born."

"Grandfather, what happened to the great warrior Snake's Medicine?" a girl questioned.

Many Names grinned and, stirring the fire, said, "He is still around."

The children looked all around them.

"You mean he is *still* alive?"

The old chief shrugged. "I suppose so."

"What keeps him alive?" asked the girl.

"Stories," the old chief said, chuckling, "stories and little children, just like yourselves."

BOOK 12

The Story of Turtle Dancer and His Sons

The Story of Fire-Is-Given

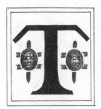

The Story of Turtle Dancer and His Sons

IN WHICH THE PLAINS WAR CHIEF TURTLE DANCER
REFLECTS ON LIFE AND WAR AND THE WARRIOR'S LIFE,
AND IN WHICH HE TELLS OF THE MAKING OF HIS OWN
GREAT NAME WHILE SWIMMING ACROSS A RIVER OF
TURTLE ISLAND

H E Cheyenne war chief Turtle Dancer made a great name for himself, but toward the end of his life, like many men who had ridden the battle road, he grew tired of fighting. Then he remembered how he had gotten his name, and the spirits of the earth who had always come to his aid when he needed them. Looking back on his long life, he asked himself, Who can know what life is unless he has truly lived? Who can know the power of war unless he is always prepared to die?

These were the thoughts of Turtle Dancer, the war chief who lived through many perilous battles and survived well into old age—into toothache, bent back, broken bone, but never broken will. He led his people well; he saw the sun rise and set on good times and bad, and times that were neither good nor bad.

Once, they say, he was chased by his enemies, and though he had wounds all over his body, he would not submit. He traveled like a turtle, burdened with its great round, cumbersome shell. But while he dragged himself along, listening to the hoofed thunder of his would-be captors, he thought of the time of the beginning, when Turtle went to the bottom of the world-holding sea and brought up a bit of clay to make the earth we live on. And in his mind, he saw the ridges on Turtle's back: They were the mountains. He saw the lines on Turtle's back: They were the rivers and streams. He saw

191

himself, a lump of clay in the middle of all the water, and, thinking this, he sang:

> Wading, I pass through yellow water;
> Wading, I pass through turtle water;
> Wading, I pass through enemy-arrow water;
> Wading, I pass through my life.

His song sung, he felt himself moving, not upon dry ground, but swimming easily, in spite of his wounds, across the great water of Turtle Island. Across the waking world, he saw his friends and family waiting for him, urging him to swim harder; yet right behind him, he heard the cries of his enemies, taunting him, trying to capture him. Then, as the voices of friend and foe turned into the same dull song, he heard the music of the crows, saw them gather overhead— a flock of protection, the good black crows, the messengers of the Father.

So he said to himself as he swam, "Ah, then, I am safe," for his enemies were no longer clamoring for him; his loved ones were no longer urging him on. And he heard only the sweet singing of the crows, and, swimming steadily forward, he saw that his bleeding hands were now brown paddles with long fingernails, and his back was a weighted dome, carrying the care-worn world, yet he swam effortlessly across the great water, the spirit water, moving ever forward, eyes shut to the light; so that when his eyes opened again, he found himself stretched out upon the sand of the safe shore.

His enemies had made camp on the other side of the river, and he could see the smoke of their camp fires as they watched him, but, for some reason, they would not come across. And all round him was the whirl of webbed tracks, turtle tracks, messengers of the Mother; and overhead was the song of crows, chanting, messengers of the Father.

In his later years, Turtle Dancer would not speak of his own days of battle, but he would sit for hours around the storytelling fire, telling of his two sons.

*   *   *

"When they were still young and playing at hunting, the younger said to the elder, 'If you could be any animal, which would it be?'

"And the elder answered, 'Why, Wolf Brother, of course.'

" 'Why Wolf Brother?'

" 'Because he is lean and strong, well formed for the hunt. He can travel miles without meat or water. A fierce fighter, he never runs from battle. But tell me, Brother, what animal would you choose to be?'

" 'I would choose Fox Brother. He is fast and tricky, knows every hiding place there is. His tracks are hard to follow; he does not fight unless he has to.'

"Now, when they were a little older, the younger one was captured by an enemy war party, and while his brother became known as Wolf Brother, a war chief who was feared throughout the land, his younger brother vanished before he could make a name for himself.

"One day, when Wolf Brother was on the warpath, he encountered an enemy leader whose warriors were in every way equal to his own. A vicious battle took place. Neither side was the winner; both sides suffered great losses. 'Who is the war chief who shows such cleverness on the field?' Wolf Brother asked one of his men.

" 'That is the one that cannot be tracked; they call him Fox Young Man.'

" 'I see,' Wolf Brother said.

"For twelve days, the fighting dragged on, neither side overcoming the other. The dead and dying were uncountable. Finally, Wolf Brother sent a messenger across to the other war chief. 'It is between the two of us,' he proclaimed. 'Tell your men to go home, and I will tell mine to do the same. Then, if I cannot find you in four days' time, we will declare a truce and put down our bows.'

"Fox Young Man sent word back that he agreed to these terms. And on a day when the sun shone on the first frost of winter, Wolf Brother, alone, went after Fox Young Man.

"The trail should be easy to follow, Wolf Brother thought, for the hand of Cold Maker has whitened the grass. But by noon, the trail of Fox Young Man had melted away into the thin, dry air, and there was nothing left to follow. The next day, there was a light prickling of rain. Wolf Brother again picked up the trail, yet by dusk, the tracks, moving in a tightly wound circle, had doubled back to the place where they had begun that morning. On the following day, Wolf Brother tracked Fox Young Man into a frozen swamp where rising steam made the trail impossible to follow; it meandered from one tussock of grass to another, finally slipping into the cold, trackless water where no trail is ever left behind. That night, under the winter stars, Wolf Brother prayed for his wolf spirit, his ally, to come and help him.

"In the morning, before dawn, he shed his warm robe, leggings, and shirt. Then he rolled on the frozen ground, stinging his skin with nettles of ice. 'Grant me sight of him; that is all I ask,' he said, breathing the risen sun into his being and praying to the Father. But that day was harder than any other. Fox Young Man, it seemed, was playing with Wolf Brother, leading him in and out of the leafless trees, making him ford the ice-bound streams, taking him up hill and down, tiring him out. So that, by the end of the day, his eyes were weak and he missed many signs. That night, a fever came upon him, and he shivered the night away. Just before the dawn, he glimpsed the smoky form of a gray fox standing over him, laughing, but he was certain it was a fever dream, teasing his mind, taunting him like the fox chief he was chasing.

" 'This day grant his death to me,' Wolf Brother prayed to the wolf spirit, his ally. Then he cut a piece of his little finger off and left it on a sun stone in a pool of blood. Yet by noon, he had made no progress. The fox tracks appeared to increase; wherever he glanced, there were more and more of them. 'I must have the heart of him,' Wolf Brother swore, slashing his chest with his knife and leaving a piece of flayed skin on yet another sun stone. By nightfall, he was no better off; all day the tricky fox had led him around by the nose, promising him plenty, giving him nothing but tracks and more tracks. That night, he was in too much pain to make a fire. He shook all over with a raging fever. I believe I am going to die, he thought, and he sang the death song of the wolf through his clenched teeth. But even as he sang, a shadow stole across the camp, and he saw it out of the corner of his eye. The shadow thickened in the starlight. Wolf Brother, trembling, readied his bow underneath his robe. The shadow came close, sniffing at the stars. Then, with the bow drawn under his robe, Wolf Brother waited and the shadow of the fox washed over him. Suddenly, he released the bowstring. The arrow struck and the fox dropped in his tracks, dead. 'I have killed you!' Wolf Brother cried, throwing off his robe, though when he went to inspect the body of the slain fox, he found only a little patch of gray fur stuck to some rabbitbrush.

" 'Enemy, I call you out!' he cried, his voice ringing hollow in the empty hills.

" 'I am here,' came a soft-voiced reply, and as Wolf Brother turned around, he saw that Fox Young Man greeted him with smiling teeth.

" 'Did you think I would give myself up so easily?'

"Wolf Brother, still holding the small patch of fox skin, flapped it in the face of his adversary; then he fell to his knees, for the fever still had him in its claws.

" 'My brother,' said Fox Young Man, 'you have been fooled by a spirit fox, my double, whom you have been chasing all this time while I was safe and warm in my lodge.'

"He laughed as Wolf Brother grew furious. He growled, 'I would have your blood.' But Fox Young Man only shook his head in a gentle, mocking manner.

" 'Do you not understand, Brother?' Fox Young Man asked.

" 'I understand that you have won, and I have lost.'

"Fox Young Man looked at his brother and pity filled his heart. 'We once traveled together, you and I,' he said. 'Yet it seems we have grown far apart. I do not live to fight; I fight only so that I may live.'

"Wolf Brother, teeth rattling with the fever that was burning his bones, rasped, 'I shall honor the peace between us, but I will not acknowledge you as my brother.'

" 'The peace is enough,' Fox Young Man whispered softly, sadly, and he disappeared into the falling night of prairie stars."

Turtle Dancer ended his story with this afterthought: "And though the truce was kept for the rest of their lives, after that night, my sons, who were once so close, did not see each other, face-to-face, ever again."

The Story of Fire-Is-Given

OF THE WOMAN WARRIOR FIRE-IS-GIVEN, WHO
RECEIVES HER WARRIOR'S NAME, GIVES-UP-HER-
HORSES, AS TOLD BY HER GRANDFATHER TURTLE
DANCER

S O M E say, of the people of the plains, that the man ruled and the woman served. But it was not always so: There were men-women, no less valuable than men, who behaved in their own natural way. Some distinguished themselves in battle, but most did what pleased them, women's work. And there were, they say, women-men, though few of these were ever storied, as such, because they knew that men and women were equal partners in the struggle to live, and it made little difference to them how they were talked about around the fire. After all, they dared to live as men. Their lives were ever on the line, which was how they liked to live, and thus they managed to stay alive. This story of the woman warrior Fire-Is-Given comes, once again, from Turtle Dancer, the elder who sired more than the story, as you will see:

"Now Wolf Brother and Fox Young Man both lived to old age, but Wolf Brother's sons were killed in battle, while Fox Young Man had four daughters, three of whom bore him grandchildren. The fourth daughter was different from her sisters. Her name was Fire-Is-Given, and from the start, she liked doing things that boys do. She enjoyed hunting, wrestling, even pretending to steal horses. There was no dare she would not try to fulfill; as for fear, she had none.

"When Fire-Is-Given was a youth, she was as strong, brave, and restless as any of her companions. She could handle herself on a horse better than her friends, however, and they respected her for it. One day, without telling her father or mother, she and a few others took some horses and rode from hilltop to hilltop to the hunting camp of their enemy, the Pierced Noses. They had awakened before sunup to sing the sun songs of warriors on a mission of holiness. Then each one of them prayed for success in a personal way, relying on the ally who watched over them. When they came to the Pierced Nose camp, it was nearly evening, with the red light of afterglow painting the hills. The riders hid in a thick grove of cottonwoods and chokecherry bushes. All the Pierced Nose horses had been turned out to graze. The other youths gathered around Fire-Is-Given, for she was the only one they looked up to, since luck and the wind of war were always one with her.

"A boy named Mountain Talking, who wore a wolf skin over his head and shoulders, asked her to sing a medicine song for them, which she did, singing softly in her throat, so as not to give away their hiding place.

> We come bearing flint;
> with hearts of flint, we come, bearing flint;
> with songs of flint and lightning in our feet,
> we come with trickery to hurl upon our foes.

"After singing the song, she asked them to follow her out of the grove. The Pierced Nose horses were grazing a little apart from the camp. They did not seem to be watched. Crawling on hands and knees, Fire-Is-Given and her friends got close to the horses, who did not bolt because the youths moved slowly, lying down in the grass every so often while the horses got used to their smell.

"The horses were handsome, well muscled, many hands high; there were buckskins, sorrels, pintos, bays, and chestnuts. The braided horsehair nooses slipped over their heads without startling them, and the hobbles on their feet were easily severed. Then, still crawling, the youths led them into the upland meadow, then off to the north where the thick grove of trees would hide them.

"As she crawled, careful not to get stepped on, Fire-Is-Given looked over her shoulder. She could see the flames of the enemy camp fires and heard the talking and carrying-on; she could smell the savory smoke of elk meat being roasted. All of this she put behind her, thinking of one thing: the ride home. They rode all night, leading the stolen horses behind them. At dawn, while they were singing the sun songs of praise, the blessing for reaching home safely, they saw the Pierced Noses, many horsemen mounted with bow and arrow, coming on them across the ridge. Quickly, they leapt to their own mounts. All eyes were on Fire-Is-Given.

" 'The straight road home is blocked off now; they come too fast for us. We must ride to Blind Woman Canyon,' she said. Mountain Talking shook his head. 'I go the other way,' and he kicked his horse into a gallop. Immediately, an arrow caught him off-guard. He dropped off his horse, falling limply to the grass, dead.

"The other three riders followed Fire-Is-Given down a grassy slope, across a small stream, and up an incline of balding grass, shale, and smaller loose-fallen stones. The horses slipped, lost footing, snorted, balked, but they whipped them on, drew them off the open hill and down into the mouth of the canyon, where they broke into a gallop. The way was narrow, a tunnel that moved like a snake, sliding first into the light, then slipping back into the dark.

"Finally, they came to the place where the canyon was blocked off, where a wall of stone came straight up from the graveled earth, towering over their heads, throwing out a great shadow like a blanket of death. It was in this place, they say, that the blind woman of legend had been unable to get out, where a stone monster had once trapped her. Now Fire-Is-Given and her friends were caught in the same snare, just like their ancient ancestor.

" 'We are dead,' they said.

"But Fire-Is-Given revealed a quick, secretive half smile, showing them that life and death are two different things. They were, her smile said, alive, not dead. 'My father taught me that when a fox has nothing to lose, it still wishes to lose everything but its life. So now, when I give the signal, cut loose the stolen horses.' In the time it had taken them to reach the canyon's end, the moon was up, burning coldly along the upper edge of the rocks.

"She waited on the sound of the moon-stalking hunters coming up the canyon, and as the Pierced Noses came out of the dark and into the light, and back again into the dark, the shift of shadow light made them see things that were not really there. Then, suddenly, the canyon walls were wracked with drumming echoes; horses streamed from all sides. There was no room to run. Their own horses came on them like the headwaters of a great flood, and the Pierced Noses, blinded by the moon, saw them coming too late. They ran, unseeing, into the oncoming hooves, which broke their bodies against the sharp rocks. And thus there was no fight, no flight, no burial. After this, so they say, Fire-Is-Given was known by the name Gives-Up-Her-Horses; and no man looked upon her who did not also look up to her, for she was fully accepted as a warrior.

"Now, only as an old man, a veteran of many battles, can I say that the same blood is always spilled; the same bloodstains are left on the same earth. So it is that in war, the sun rises and sets on the same faces of death. And who has lived who can tell us of the Maker's praise for having killed and then for having been killed? Of what use is dying when one's loved ones are left behind? Do not fear death, I say, but do not run to it, either. Fear only the bad spirit; love only the good spirit, that which keeps us out of harm's way. Life is but the brief glow of the firefly on a summer's night; but death we cannot say, for what do we know until we have walked that way in our own moccasins?"

BOOK 13

The Story of Rolling Thunder

The Story of White Buffalo Calf

The Story of Rolling Thunder

IN WHICH THE GREATEST WARRIOR OF THEM ALL,
ROLLING THUNDER, HAS A MEDICINE DREAM THAT
SAVES HIS PEOPLE, FOR WHICH HE IS REMEMBERED TO
THIS DAY

A thousand snows ago, they say there was a warrior more brave than any who lived. His name was Rolling Thunder, a great warrior, a great dreamer, and a storyteller of power. Here, then, is his account—not of the bravery of men but of courageous women and children, and the favor of the gods.

"In the country where the buffalo grass never withers, the Crow people lived and thrived. The land gave them all they needed, in spite of the long snow winters. Mother Earth's bounty provided rich harvest year in, year out: geese, duck, sage hen, deer, antelope. In the plum thickets and bullberry bushes, there was plenty of sweetness; and in spring, when strawberries were ripe, everyone's mouth was red.

"Now, in the time of the plains wars, when we were doing battle with the people called Pawnee, I was sent to scout their camp and take their picketed horses, and make coup, if I could. But when I crept up to their camp in the pines, I saw a Pawnee girl whose face made my heart beat loud. I heard her voice: night wind in the pines. Her loveliness was the sun rising over the mountains in the morning; the sun dipping down the mountains at the end of day.

"And she made me forget my mission. I gave myself up; the Pawnee took me prisoner. But in this I was fortunate, for she was always in sight, and, seeing her, I confess that the land of my father's fathers,

203

Crow country, was all but forgotten. In time, I rose from a prisoner to a free man, and proved my prowess as hunter and provider. One day, I was given the hand of that girl I had already given my heart to, South Wind, so we made our lodge together and were as happy as our lives were whole.

"Then one day, the Pawnee made me a member of their warrior band, their soldier lodge. I sat in council with them, as I would have with my own people. They had taken me fully into their confidence by then; I was one with them, though I knew, if it should ever happen, I could not fight with them against my people. It happened, then, at one of the council meetings that I heard of the Pawnee plan to surround and kill all of the Crow. What I had always dreaded would now, I feared, come to pass: to raise my hand against my own blood.

"The following day, I told my Pawnee wife, South Wind, that I was going to the warm spring to bathe, and she went with me. There, in the steamy water, I told her of her people's plan to scatter my people like leaves in the wind. 'Yes,' she said, 'I know. That is why I wish to go with you.' Shaking my head, I told her no. But she said, 'I ride not like a woman, but like a man.' And so we were young; we loved each other; we knew happiness together—and now, I supposed, we would know war together. Still, I told her, 'You are Pawnee; I am Crow.' Her eyes flashed then. 'Your heart is not speaking, only your lips. I am your woman and you are my man.' Trying to make her understand, I said, 'I go back to *my* father to fight against *your* father.'

"And she replied, 'Where you go, I go.'

"So it was that night that we rode out of the camp where we had first been happy, on two swift buffalo ponies. We rode far up into the canyons where my people's camp lay at the foot of the mountains. The longer we traveled on the dark trail toward my home, the more I wanted to sing the home song of the Crow, to let the old words flow from my lips, but when I would look over at South Wind, my heart would sink. 'Won't you grieve for your people?' I asked. And she answered, 'You left your people for me; now I leave my people for you.'

"And we rode into the narrow valley with mountains on one side and buttes on the other, and my blood was warming at the sight of so much familiar ground, every rock, tree, and stream singing my name, and me singing back praises. Finally, we came to the high-walled canyon that runs west with the sun. We were at last in Crow country. The level land, spotted with pine, sparkling with rivers, greeted my eye, as if I had never gone from it. And it welcomed me, the lost son, into the presence of my father's fathers.

"How much feasting and dancing do you think we did then? The lost son returned—and with a beautiful wife—and the criers rode through the village chanting our presence to all who would listen. Then came all of the Mountain Crows and River Crows, wearing their finest feast clothes, and there was night-long dancing, feasting, singing, and speech making. The firelight sprang at the stars as medicine men, runners, and wolf scouts came to see our faces, looking first at me, then at my beautiful wife whose hair shone in the firelight.

"We puffed the red stone pipe until the dawn sun; we pointed that pipe east, west, north, and south, speaking of many things, among them the coming of our enemies. I told them then, 'They are as many as the blades of grass. We are strong of heart, but few beside their great numbers. They desire our land, our buffalo and sheep, our grass and water; and before the next moon has gone, they will come from the north, pass into our valley. They will come with murder in their hearts. As everyone knows, our mountains do not move; they shelter us; they wall us in. And our enemies will trap us here and slaughter us in the shadow of our mountains.'

"Many good men spoke that night, and their words were much the same: To fight an enemy of such number out in the open would mean but one thing—death. Then each night when Old Woman Moon was high in the star-scattered sky, the wise men met and talked war talk, but nothing was won from this; it was the rattle of dry leaves when the wind is at play.

"The night came, however, when I had a dream, a vision that would save my people. The dream went much like this: I saw the windy river where we lived, the shadow mountains, the blue cedars and pines, the black-necked buffalo. All were alive in the dream, tumbling in confusion, whirling in the dust. The cedars were warriors; they moved as one, holding their heads high. And the buffalo were warriors, too, using their horns as lances. I told my dream to the old chief Sits-Down-Spotted, and he proclaimed it a great dream, saying,

'Your heart is young, but your head is old. This dream was sent by our father's fathers to save their children's children.'

"Soon everyone in the camp of the Two Crows knew of this dream, and all prepared for the war that would come—but now we had a great weapon, one that our enemies would not suspect. The night before the attack, our wolf scouts said the enemy was less than one sleep away. However, in the morning we heard a dull rumbling, the beat of thousands of hooves upon the earth. Soon a great herd of buffalo poured through the mountain pass, darkening the valley with their rough, shaggy coats.

" 'You see,' the women said, 'the Great Maker is fond of his children the Two Crows. Look, he is sending all the buffalo in the world to help us.'

"This was true, for now the buffalo would confuse the fight, as well as offering us cover in battle. Now the time drew near when we knew the Pawnees, thousands of them, were coming. And we were but five hundred strong, including women and children. Still, South Wind, because she knew of my dream, believed that the power of victory lay in our favor.

" 'You are going to fight my people,' she said. 'It is well, for I am your woman, but you must try to do one thing for me. My father, the chief Red Tomahawk, is old; his heart beats slow. He desired peace with your people, but when the young men demanded war, he could do nothing to stop them. I ask that if you win the battle, you spare the life of my father.'

"I looked long—and longingly—into the eyes of my woman, for I knew that I might not see her again. Then I told her, 'If I live, I will return your father safely to you.'

"She answered, 'If an arrow should find your heart, my husband, then I will end my own life, for I won't let you go to the Spirit World alone.'

"Now when the enemy came, they flooded into the valley like the waters of a great river. What the warriors saw as they came in on thunder horses—their pointed lances raised, their bows notched with feathered death—was a small band of Two Crows scattering toward the blind canyon's north end. Seeing the false panic in our faces as we—offering no resistance—fled in fear, they quirted their horses and filled the air with the noise of loosed arrows. And we ran, drawing them ever deeper into the canyon of death. The arrows showered down, hailing upon us, but we dived under them, using the buffalo, which were everywhere—the bulls charging at the horsemen with lowered heads of horned fury; the cows wheeling in circles, throwing up plumes of dust—getting in the way. We rolled, danced, and dodged around their huge brown bellies and jutting shoulders, yet because we were on foot and few in number, we outmaneuvered both the hot-tempered buffalo and the death-dealing horsemen.

"So when the enemy's arrows were spent and their horses lathered and winded, we had, at last, reached the mouth of the canyon—the place where there can be no retreat, for anyone. It was to be, then, a fight to the death. However, what the Pawnees had come to conquer, what they had witnessed from their mounts, was a fleeing band of men—perhaps two hundred in number—and they rode on them at once, sending their arrows into the clouds of hoof-beaten dust.

"But then it happened: My dream vision come to life. As the Pawnees pounded into the canyon, the cedar trees sprang to life. It was a forest of cedar-robed Crows, and though they were still outnumbered, five to one, every man, woman, and child was present, fighting. The many-branched trees gave the enemy pause, for they were cut at the root and fully limbed, and they made an armored cover that lifted from the earth and moved as one. Now as a woman moved forward, shielding her man, he, carefully taking aim with his bow, fired upon the larger target, the mounted warrior coming at him. The whine of flying arrows was drowned in the whinny of wounded horses; and into the foray were clotted the dark brown shapes of the desperate buffalo, charging and goring with abandon. Sunken neck-deep arrows were torn from the throats of fallen horses and used again, until the battle bore down into the long afternoon and turned to a hand-to-hand fight with war clubs and knives.

"Then as the sun sank in the notch of the western peaks, the Pawnees withdrew, beaten, they believed, by a foe too powerful to resist. On our side were moving cedars, angry buffalo, and fighting men, women, and children. And it was as if, in their sweat and tear-stung eyes, what they saw was the truth: The very earth had turned against them. And with the red dust of evening clouding their retreat, they headed home, leaving their dead and dying where they lay.

"In the dust of the battle, the cries settling all around him, I found the old man, Red Tomahawk, lying facedown in the dirt. A woman of my clan was already hacking at his white hair with her knife. Shoving her away, I faced the others—women, all of them—who would cut up the old warrior, as custom would demand.

" 'He is the father of my wife,' I told them, 'and, enemy or not, he is my father also. For when I was alone in enemy country, he took me in and made me his son. I can do no less for him now.'

"I rolled him over then and saw that though his wounds were many, Red Tomahawk was yet alive and would live. Then I carried him back on a stolen horse. When he saw South Wind, he came out of the trance he had been in. His mouth moved but no words came. I spoke for us all when I told them both, 'We are one family now.' South Wind and her father both wept openly, and the three of us held each other as the red dust of war settled all around the dead and the dying."

So ended Rolling Thunder's story, and you may think it is embroidered, a work of words, a thing of spoken art rather than a piece of proven history. However, if you travel one day to the Wind River country and chance to find the valley of the Two Crows, you may hear a ghostly singing as the sun sets over the Pryor Mountains. For it is certainly possible to hear the spirit chant on a full-moon night when the mountains themselves seem to sing. And if you look, you will see the earth swollen in places from the heaped-up stones below the headland of Lookout Butte, where the bones of the dead lie under their mounds to this day. Many snows have fallen in the four hundred years since Rolling Thunder dreamed his dream of the warrior cedars that rose up and walked, of the buffalo that fought, of the women and children who would not give up their land.

The Story of White Buffalo Calf

HOW THE GRANDSON OF ROLLING THUNDER, EAGLE
COUP, MEETS HIS SPIRIT-ALLIES IN A POWERFUL
MEDICINE DREAM—AND HOW HE LOSES HIS BEST
FRIEND WHILE COUNTING COUP AND THEREBY GAINS
GREAT WISDOM ON THE NATURE OF LIFE IN DEATH
AND DEATH IN LIFE

THE grandson of Rolling Thunder was named Eagle Coup, a boy whose heart and sinew were made strong like those of his grandfather. He had a friend, Big Neck, and the two of them were born with the same dream, the same desire: to possess a sure eye and hand, to be alert to all things, to fast in solitude, to revel in games with others, to love the body and praise the mind, to worship the father and be grateful for the mother. Sun and earth, this was how they lived, breathed, and made the most of their brief days on earth.

One day, during a fast, Eagle Coup saw his spirit ally, the eagle, in a vision. He lay upon a rock, facing the sun; sweat issued from every pore. He had been three days without food or water, his eyes troubled by fragmentary dreams. Now as he lay in the sun, shivering from the cold fire of the fast, the weakness that comes with privation, he saw many things. He saw the cruel-hearted cougar, dusk-furred, suddenly frolicsome, chasing butterflies in the cool summer air; the strong-looking, serious face looked him straight in the eye. "Brother," he said to the tawny animal as the cougar slipped away into the fissures of the cliff. Then he saw a brown-and-white spotted eagle descending on a cottonwood limb, talons out, hungry of face. Its intrepid hooked beak was open. He said to the great bird from which he had gained his name, "Brother," and the eagle knew him, and it flapped off, gliding through the quaking aspens of autumn.

Then he saw a buffalo herd stranded in the snow, and in the center of the bunched-up females, huddling against a blast of northwest winter wind, there was a magnificent male, white from hoof to horn, as if the Maker had painted him with the clay of heaven. And the knowing old bull looked directly into his eye and shook his beard at him. The buffalo breathed an enfolding cloud of steam, which lifted Eagle Coup into the sky, held him aloft, and bore him to the Sun Father.

He woke, then, stunned, knowing that the eye of Sun Father was round, just like his own, and that the yellow cat, the spotted eagle, and the white buffalo bull were all a part of his own heart and mind and that all of these were his allies and friends, who, when the time came, would give of themselves to protect him. When he came down from the fast, Eagle Coup told his friend, Big Neck, "You know that the Sioux make winter meat along the Musselshell. Let's ride to them and count coup."

Now coup counting, like winter counting, was a way of measuring the days, the good and the bad, the weak and the strong. To prove his courage, a warrior had only to show that he had no fear of his enemy. By touching him with a coup stick, he would thus meet him fully, as an equal or a better.

And so, packing parfleche bags of dried smoked meat, the two boys, barely of coup-counting age, rode off on spirited ponies through the cottonwood night, singing the autumn song of the leaf-falling moon. Then, to pass the time as they rode, they told each other stories. Big Neck said, "Some ways back, I saw a whitish animal with frostlike fur. Do you know the one I mean?"

"Possum," Eagle Coup answered.

"Yes. Do you know why he hangs his tail?"

"No, tell me."

"He hangs his tail because he was once in love with Silver Fox, and she threw him off for another. Now he's so ashamed, he hangs his head upside down."

"But why is his tail so bare?" Eagle Coup asked.

"Because Skunk was jealous of it, and he talked Caterpillar into nibbling off Possum's pretty tail and bringing it to him. That's why Skunk's tail is nice and Possum's is all bony-looking."

The two boys passed their first night on the warrior trail in this way, telling tales as their horses went along on the dry riverbed. As they rode, elbow-to-elbow, their hearts touched, as well, for these two were as brothers. No two boys had ever grown up so close. Thoughts came to them at the same time, and often they had no need to speak, for their feelings were mutually shared. Had they loved the same woman, they would have shared her, too. Nothing could separate the love they felt for each other. They rode now as one, their shadows merging in the moonlight, their hearts beating like the same drum.

By the time the sun was high in the blue next day, they dared not ride farther for fear of being seen by the sharp eyes of enemy wolf scouts. They camped in the loose leaves, making a bed of them, and hobbled their horses nearby, in a place with plenty of grass for them to eat, so they wouldn't make any unnecessary noises. They slept all day and that night ate dried meat under the rising moon. The high hills were cool and dark. An owl called from the smooth-skinned aspen trunks.

All about them, the damp woods were deep and dark. From here on, they would feed their horses aspen bark, because the grassy meadows were gone, having yielded to leaf trees. Farther ahead, as the riverbed wound to its source, there was a pine forest. Now they muffled their horses' feet with deerskin hoof covers, for the crackle of a branch or twig or the crunch of stone would alert a listening scout. This night, their second, they told no idle tales; they rode silently, their ears reaching out for the slightest sound.

By morning, they slept in the mouth of a cave by the riverbed of mottled, leaf-strewn stones. From where they camped, they looked down on the wide valley of the Yellowstone, backed up by the Crazy and Beartooth mountains. Now, deep in enemy country, they peered through rimrock shadows at the level plain below. The winter hunt camps were set up at the valley's edge, and the Sioux were in them, singing and feasting. They expected, and rightly so, no attack. This was their annual buffalo hunt that would keep them through the long winter. Both boys felt the sudden sense of danger rise to their throats.

The far-off singing and the occasional lyric of a coyote, broken off into high staccato notes, furthered the mood of adventure, of seeking glory in enemy country. Here, they knew, they could be killed as easily as seen. Here, they could be tortured to death, torn limb from limb by a four horse-pull team. Here, a rider's mount might plunge into a prairie dog's hole, break a leg, render its rider meat for torture. Here, this night, they were safe in the groves of chill yellow aspen and frosted cottonwood, but down in the dry runs and ravines, in the great rock-ribbed prairie they were easy quarry.

They spoke now in low, whispery tones, making winter smoke breath. Their bodies trembled visibly from the cold. Far from the safety of their own camp, they kept thinking of death, and though, from their first lullaby, they had learned to suffer fear and conquer it, there was now a coldness in the pit of their bellies.

They slept until the hour when the owl makes a final call. Then, rising in silence, they each put a pebble under their tongues to stifle thirst and went down toward the buffalo fields. The two boys ran along smoothly, feeling the forest under the soles of their moccasins.

"We are near," Big Neck whispered, breaking silence and startling Eagle Coup with the sound of his voice. Past stunt pine and gambel oak, they came loping into the gray half-light of the morning. As they neared the open country, they could see the life on the plains begin to stir. "We are near," Big Neck said again softly, his breath coming up short.

At last they came to a dry wash that separated the open valley from the dense hillside. Here, as far as the eye could see, the plains rolled out flat in all directions. Dropping down out of sight, they crouched in an arroyo, wondering what to do next. They had come so long a way. Was it merely to touch their enemy, the Sioux?

But now the earth rumbled with the hooves of the buffalo, and they could hear the cries of hunters, the grunts of buffalo, the whine of arrows sunk deep in neck, hump, and flank, and the wounded bulls roaring, the calves panting, the mothers stumbling. The blood of the hunt had numbed the air with crying and dying. Lying just out of sight, nerves taut as deer thongs, the boys measured their chances, wondering at their brave act of pride. Too late to turn back, each took the long drawn breath that sent them over the edge, tumbling over the arroyo's fringed side.

Suddenly, a half dozen hunters on horseback quirted their mounts and made chase, while the boys split off in two directions, arrows ripping the air all around them. Big Neck, going east, was pursued by three horsemen. Eagle Coup, going west, had the next three, then four more, all of them carrying quirts, bows, and lances. Their only chance was to run like rabbits—several ways at once, feinting and turning, hoping to trick the enemy horses. More moccasined feet joined the chase. Even as he ran for his life, Eagle Coup heard a horrible cry that was so like his own, it stopped him in his tracks. Big Neck had collapsed, riddled with arrows. Then the horsehair whips lashed out. As Eagle Coup tried to fend them off, some fat women came up, waddling and slow, and somewhat absently stuck skinning knives into his ribs, laughing as they did so, the men with whips cheering them on.

Big Neck's coup stick lay in a little lake of his own blood, and he died choking, looking at the sky, an expression of wonder forever etched on his brow. And now there were ankle ropes and wrist ropes binding Eagle Coup, who, head bent, awaited torture, hoping it would—but fearing it would not—be brief.

They took their time staking him out, preparing to wrest him limb from limb. Four horsemen riding toward the four directions were positioned to crack his bone and socket joints, to rip leg from hip, arm from shoulder, to thus quarter him.

He saw what happened now in the same way that he had seen his animal spirits in his dream. What was happening to him seemed to be happening to someone else. The knotted ropes tore at his limbs. A horse danced sunward, another nightward. One went to the bottom of the earth, another to the top of the sun. He heard his ribs crack, his sinews come undone. He felt his body fly apart like rays of light, from everywhere at once, splaying out.

And then the stars exploded in his skull. The wind went through him. He watched the cougar caressing his fingers and wrists; the coyote licking his face; the buffalo breathing warmth into his toes. Overhead in the blue sky, his ally cried with longing, telling him to rise. Then he felt them licking him, breathing into him, singing to him all over again.

At last, he got up, a shadow version of himself. He walked weakly over to his fallen friend. Big Neck was dead. "We are near," was all he could say to him, remembering Big Neck's last words. Then he stumbled on, moving feebly, strangely, as if unalive.

What a homecoming it was! There were barking dogs and big-eyed children reaching out to touch him. There was loud, glad talk, joking, and laughing. There was feasting and moccasin giving. Elk teeth rang on anklets and wrists. Leggings of white antelope decorated with beads and quills were heaped on him. However, when he was given a tomahawk adorned with eagle feathers, he pushed it away, saying that he would henceforth be known as White Buffalo Calf, and that he would fight no more.

Seventy years later, praying again on a mountaintop, White Buffalo Calf heard a familiar but long-lost voice. He turned to see his old friend Big Neck.

"Do not grieve over me any longer," he said. He wore the same buckskins he had worn on the day of his death. "Think no more of the snows that have fallen, only of those still to fall."

White Buffalo Calf looked into the face of his friend and asked, "Are you a spirit?"

Big Neck laughed. His laughter was soft like pines sighing in the wind. "I am what I was," he said. "Nothing is changed."

"Why have you waited so long to tell me this?" White Buffalo Calf asked.

"Why have *you* waited so long to ask?" Big Neck said, and, laughing again, he walked away into the thin mountain air.

In his last years, White Buffalo Calf became a shaman who taught that there is life in death as much as death in life. He told his people to give up fighting. It was he who, giving up his breath, said, "So long we have fought, so little we have loved." And thus he joined the friend he had left on the coup-counting plain one hundred and fourteen winters before.

PART FIVE

MYTHS OF
TWO WORLDS

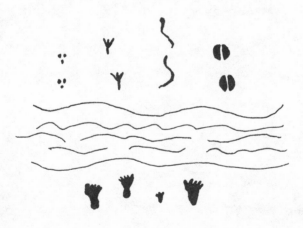

BOOK 14

The Keepers of the Cliff
The Dream of the Man Named No Flesh
The Song of the River Mother
The Story of the White Deer Named Virginia
Dare

The Keepers of the Cliff

OF THE SCOUT WARRIORS OF THE RIVER CROW, WHO
ARE STRUCK DOWN NOT BY ARROWS OR LANCES BUT BY
A STRANGE DISEASE, AND OF THEIR VALOROUS SPIRIT
AND FINAL REDEMPTION AS THEY VANQUISH THE
ILLNESS FOR THEIR PEOPLE

HERE was a clan of the River Crow who were like no men on earth. They stood well over six feet. Their hair fell in shiny rivers upon their backs, and when they let it all the way down, it touched their heels. In battle or hunt, they wore it braided or tied back, but when in camp, they let it fall loose. Now these warriors had no wives and they lived at the edge of the butte known as Sacrifice Cliff, from which, in any direction, they could see from afar the wide plain that lay below them. Their lonely work as scouts was to always stay alert, looking for the approach of their enemy.

They sat, legs folded under them, hair down, eyes sharp as flints, trained on the two notched peaks where the sun bled before the coming of the night, for that was the direction their enemies took in entering the valley. They say these River Crow men, these guardians of the night-watch land, had eyesight to match the white-headed eagle, nerves to dare the buffalo bull, ears to quiet the owl, hearts to soar like hawks. They carried sinew-backed bows of mountain ash, which, when stood on end, were nearly their own height. For as many snows as anyone could remember, they lived their lives under the great blue, guarding all of the Crow villages down in the valley. They say their songs of brotherhood were carried by the cloud people, that on a still night, you might hear them or see their ceremonial fires leaping up, taller than bristlecone pine, tickling the star children and making them laugh. From the valley, the women brought them buffalo tongue, dried elk jerky, and roasted buffalo hump to feast on, so they had no worries, these brothers of the cloud whose stealth eyes could see into the days to come.

The day came, though, when a strange sickness was upon the land, traveling, they say, up the big mountain-parting river called the Missouri. The people of the north, the Blackfeet, had no fear of the sickness, and many of them died. The Sioux had no fear, and they, too, died in heaps of hopelessness. They died in wasted villages, smeared with smoke from the fires of the medicine men, whose efforts came to nought and who also died.

The strange sickness had its beginnings with those visitors from across the great water. They were people of magic—so it was thought. They were pale people who carried black sticks that barked thunder. The sticks made lightning and killed from afar. Yet the River Crow, when they heard such talk, felt no fear. Sun Father watched over them. Mother Earth guided them. The Maker loved his grandchildren, the River Crow. No harm would come to them.

The sap of youth ran in their veins; and, as it is often said, the sapling will bend but does not break. One morning, though, there was a warrior of their clan who could not rise from his bed of buffalo hide. His body, he said, had such weight that it was like an oak trunk grown into the earth. He slept but dreamed nothing. His eyes temporarily caught fire, then the flame died, his spirit weakened, and his face and body broke out in red spots like the poison spores of an evil mushroom. The spots, the dying warrior said, were more painful than snakebite or arrow wound. Then, in his heart, and in all the hearts that saw him, there was a new thing, and it was the look of fear.

Quickly a sweat lodge was built. Stones were heated to white heat, then water was poured on them, making clouds of steam. His brothers carried the dying warrior to the sweat lodge to sweat the evil spirits out of him. When he was wet with sweat, his spotted skin rife with rivers of running salt, they carried him to a creek and let the cold, cleansing water heal him. The fallen one did not seem to know or care what they did, whether medicine feathers brushed smoke across his eyes, whether chilly water ate his bones, because by then he was beyond the beat of the skin drum, beyond the chant of "All Is Well," so that when he died, they bound him, blanketed with the things he loved most in life—his bow and his bonnet—to a leaning pine on the edge of the lookout butte. He had dried meat for his lonely journey on the spirit road. His slain horse waited for him at the foot of the cliff.

Then things worsened. The warriors were stricken; the toadlike spots visited every face. The red death visited all, turning bones weak and feet drunk. With every sleep, more warriors died, their cries echoing in the night. Some went suddenly; others leapt at invisible enemies, ran off the cliff, danced crazily in the air. Some went honorably, battle knives plunged into their own hearts; others went slowly, turning their ill-fallen faces to the sky, asking Sun Father not to abandon such faithful children. And then the weak begged the strong to leave the village, but often it was the strong who died first, dropping in their tracks. However, no brother abandoned his brother; each one slept a last sleep on the ancient sentinel ground of the cloud-covered cliff.

In the end, out of the many, only a few were left, some sixteen men, clinging like the patient fog to the sacred rock; and one night those remaining held a council fire. Heavy-hearted, all but blind from the sickness, they smoked, sharing a last medicine pipe. The eldest of them, a man named Flame Heart, said, "That which took our brothers is also in us. We can neither run nor fight. The only thing we can do is die." Yet there was a youth present, the last to be inducted into their band. His name was Child-of-the-Earth, and he spoke plainly now and with great heart, and the others listened to him well.

"Listen, my brothers," he said, "I believe that our prayers, though we have said them well, have not been heard. We must send Sun Father a message he understands: We must build a fire as big as our camp, so that the flames go all the way up to the House of the Sun. Then, my brothers, our prayers will be heard."

So at dawn, they built a fire that rivaled the coming of the sun; the tongues of flame leapt high into the sky. Then Child-of-the-Earth said, "It is good. He has heard our words." And he gave the finish sign, and all sixteen mounted their horses and, looking toward the sun, rode them off the edge of the cliff. Those horses' hooves, they say, winnowed the empty air but could strike no better footing than the breach of cloud that overhung the cliff. And thus was ended the bravest guardians of their kind—the sheer fall, the shale crash. The splinter-boned tribute is still there, though the sixteen memorial mounds have long since been covered over with loose talus and more fallen shale. Sacrifice Cliff, they call it today, but it is secretly known as Prayer-to-the-Sun, for sometime after the proud sixteen rode the bright clouds to their death, the evil sickness left the land and never came again.

The Dream of the Man Named
No Flesh

IN WHICH THE MEDICINE DREAM OF THE VISIONARY
NO FLESH FORETELLS THE COMING OF A PALE GOD
WITH BLEEDING PALMS WHOSE APPEARANCE IN SPIRIT
HERALDS THE ARRIVAL OF THE FIRST WHITE PEOPLE

ONE day, a long time after the death of those tragic sixteen, a warrior came into the camp of the Crows and said he was from the four directions and that he had had a beautiful life-making dream. He said his name was No Flesh, and his looks proved his words. And this is the story he told when he first came to the Crow country, his face hungry-eyed, hollow-boned, leaning on his buffalo cane.

"You see me; I am alive. My brothers' blankets have worn to bare thread; their moccasins have turned to thin flaps in the time that I have been on the earth. Look at me; I have seen a lot, but I have learned only a little. Wandering through this beautiful land, I have watched a great dream buried in a blizzard of lies. We have with us now a new brother whose skin is the pale bark of the aspen. He sings, you say, a strange song, though most of you, I know, have never heard it—have never met the singer. You have suffered the song but have not met the man. Now I come to you with a small truth. Do not fear what you do not know. You have not drunk from his tin cup, which holds the twin sweetness of coffee and sugar. You have not seen his horse or his gun or heard his heart beat in the word of his tongue. Though his skin is light, as ours is dark, the Maker has put us here together—for why else should we meet?

"Now I will tell you of my great dream, which is also my song.

"I tell of a forerunner, the herald of ghosts, who took me to the land of clouds, where the Maker himself introduced me to one of

223

the white gods who wore clothes of skins like mine but whose face was pale as the dust of a moth's wing. From an opening in the sky, I was shown all the lands of this earth—not just the Turtle Island we live on—and all the hunting grounds of our fathers, since the beginning. Now the Maker told me that all that I looked on was one earth and that all the people on it were one brother, one sister.

"Then the pale god opened his hands, and I saw the wounds in them that made fresh blood. I asked him how it happened that his hands were bleeding, and he answered, 'They bleed for love, as a mother loses blood to have the thing she cherishes most—her child.'

" 'And who is this child who will spring forth from your hands?' I asked the pale man who bled before me, and he answered, 'You, my son, for you I have come.' So now I am come to speak of him, what little I know. Yet what there is, is good, and it can bring only goodness to each one of us."

The Song of the River Mother

HOW THE VISIT OF THE FIRST MISSIONARY IS TOLD BY
THE VISIONARY WOMAN TOUCHING WATER, WHO
LEADS HER PEOPLE BEYOND THE RELIGION OF THE
CROSS BACK TO THE OLD WAY OF THE WATER MOTHER

W O R D got round among the different peoples of the plain, mountain, desert, and sea that the pale-skinned people, visitors from afar, had come to their land and that they wished to have council blankets prepared for them so they might share what they knew of the world.

And always, since the story had first been told, the people looked for the man with the wounded palms. Now, on the banks of the great river that flows to the sea, in the land of mist and moss, there lived the people called the Pascagoula. They were different in color from their kind. Their ancestors, they said, came verily from the sea. They had skin the color of honey. They lived on oysters, and were watched over by the River Mother, who was half woman and half fish. At night, when the moon was clear and full, they gathered around the beautifully carved figure of their goddess, and, shaking rattles, beating drums, and playing flutes, they sang to her.

One day, there appeared in their village a man with light skin. Some said it was the color of the mouth of the water moccasin; others compared it to a cloud suffused with the pink light of the sun. The man wore a black robe, and on his face a beard of moss like that which hangs from the water cypress. His hands were free of wounds, but he carried with him a small silver cross, which, he made the people understand, was a gift of the man with the wounded palms.

He drew from his robe a black box with white leaves in it; and these he kissed with reverence, saying that they contained the words of the Maker. The power of these, he explained, would move the bones of the mountains, would part the hair of the sea. But the people wanted to see these things; and all he offered was the promise that if they were good, one day the man with the wounded palms would visit them.

Among the Pascagoulas, there lived a young woman named Touching Water, who saw the strangeness of the pale man but also his power, which she neither revered nor feared. It is she who tells the tale of how he tried to overcome them, for it was she whose vision put him to rest.

"I, a Pascagoula, have seen many things since the coming of the whites to our land. I have met and talked with the man in black with the long white beard, which our children are so fond of touching. He wears a loose black dress and carries with him at all times a small silver cross. This, he says, is the source of his magic. There is magic in the man. Surely it is so, for he speaks our language, and yet no one has taught him one single word. He came among us with knowledge of it. And this impressed our chiefs. He is solemn, handsome, soft-spoken. When he speaks, we listen. There is much in what he says: He speaks of the Great Flood. We know of it. Our own priests tell of the time of the rains, when the great canoe was prepared and all the animals got into it, except Possum, whose tail dragged in the water and lost all of its fur.

"The man with the small cross knows this story by heart, and his heart is good in telling it. 'The Spirit that moves upon the waters,' he says, so sweetly that we can feel the power of his words, and those of his Lord, the Sky Dweller.

"But I am Pascagoula and I do not know how long the man with the pale skin and the silver cross will be upon this earth, any more than I know how long we Bread Eaters will be upon it. Yet he says he knows this, and more. His kind, the whites, he says, will always be here. They are the chosen children of the Sky Dweller, he says. Such a thing troubles our people. We pray for a vision. We fast and wait for a sign.

"One night, I go out into the bay when the moon is full. I ask our Mother, who resides in the water, what to do. Should we listen to the stranger who has come among us, who shares our bread eaten on the rocks it is cooked on? Suddenly, the water dances in the moonlight, the stirring of fish trembles the small dugout boat, and all at once there is a great commotion of fins. The soft air is full of fish. If I was catching them, my arms would not be strong enough to capture even a few, for the fish are all shapes and sizes, and so many, they cannot be counted. The little boat thrashes in the waves, rises and falls, and the fish overleap it—shark and porpoise, turtle and sea cow, ray and mullet beyond measure. Then the water begins to spin and to go above my head, and the boat goes down into the center of a hole wherein beats the heart of the sea. And there, it is calm.

"I am alone. The moon is full. I can hear the heart of the sea, beating. Then it is our Mother. I hear singing I have never heard before. The waves part. It is our Mother. I have heard stories about her, but I have never seen her with my own eyes. She looks grieved as she looks upon me. She stands upon the water with the tail of a fish and the body of a woman. And her hair spreads out into the moonlit water like lovely waterweed. She does not speak, but a song comes from her lips, and I am given to understand it, for her language is the same as ours.

"She says this: 'Come to me, child of the sea. Do not let your people look upon the bell, book, or cross of the friendly stranger. For what I am, you are also, and together we are stronger than this man and all of his brothers.'

"Then she smiles upon me and drops back into the water of the bay, and her long black seawater hair spreads out upon wet moonlight. Then there is only the watery tangle of her hair, which sinks into the foam. Then even that is gone. When I tell my people what has happened, they listen. But the man with the silver cross grows angry with me, for what I say does not agree with what he says. 'Our Mother would not lie to us,' I say.

"He said, 'You will be damned for talking this; you will burn in Hell.'

"But we know of no such place. Our chiefs say not to listen to him anymore, because when he talks, his voice is like a loud wind that rushes upon us but changes direction often and means nothing. He is not the same after this; I have heard lately that he is sick, that he will die soon. We live on.

"We are Pascagoula, the Bread Eaters."

The Story of the White Deer Named Virginia Dare

IN WHICH THE STORY IS TOLD OF THE LOST COLONY OF
THE FIRST WHITE SETTLERS AND THEIR FIRSTBORN GIRL
CHILD, VIRGINIA DARE, AND IN WHICH THE LEGEND
TELLS OF HER APPEARANCE AS A SNOW WHITE DOE

ALONG the bay islands, where the pale people set up their first permanent settlement, there was born a child, the one known as Virginia Dare. And the people of the islands, the Chesapeake people, called the newborn White Fawn. Around the pine-speckled islands and sea-grass peninsulas, her story was told. It said that upon the child's death, her spirit would assume the form of a frosted fawn whose face, because her race had come from across the sea, would always gaze wistfully in that direction, as if yearning for that faraway shore. The story went on to say that if ever a runner should catch the fawn after she was fully grown into a white deer and shoot her with an arrow whose head was cast of silver, this would restore her to mortal form.

Now, the far banks and islands of coasts, not often met by travelers, were home to the Hatteras people, but the long salt-bitten winters presided over by hungry moons separated them from their pale friends, and in time, they lost touch with one another. One autumn day, a hunter named Little Oak came upon some ruined, abandoned log houses in the saw grass of the settlement of Roanoke. There were no pale people living there anymore; the berry brambles and rose hips had grown up between the cracks of the wind-washed logs. Slow autumn turtles lay by the cold hearthsides of cracked ashen clay. All that the hunter named Little Oak could find was an old baby's rattle, clutched by the claws of a rose thorn. Then he spied a beautiful white doe. By instinct, he drew his bow, but he would not let the arrow loose, holding it in check, the barred turkey feathers itching at his ear.

Time passed and the white doe was well known among the hunters of Roanoke Island. Often she was seen browsing amid the brown herd of deer that lived there. But she always remained apart, turning her head to the east, sad-eyed and dreaming in the direction of the distant sea. Those who were compelled to hunt her said that their arrows, though well-aimed, fell harmless at her hooves—whereupon she would leap with the west wind, swift as milkweed down, bounding the sand hills, driving the quick curlews and iron-winged cranes up into the cold gray, slate-colored sky.

Talk of the white doe flowed like a river tumbling from its source in the clefted rocks; it went various ways. Some of the people had fear of the animal, thinking her spirit was one of desolation. They said none but a spirit deer could travel the high grassy grounds of Croatan and yet the same day be seen in the cranberry bogs of East Lake.

Always sad, head ever turned toward the eastern-glinting sea, always beautiful, always a little apart, the white doe danced in a dream of her own making. Then, early one autumn, the people of the islands decided what to do: They would hold a great deer hunt, and all the finest bow hunters would be invited to join in. Afterward, there would be a feast and celebration. Now the plan, they say, was to hunt the milk white doe. If any runner or hunter—and all the best were gathered there—could bring her down with an arrow, then all would know if she was flesh or spirit; and, thereafter, if she should prevail, then no one would ever go after her again. It was thus decreed, and the hunt and race was on. Some took to the high sunburned mounds above the sound; some went to the low thistle meadows of the flat ocean islands. Hunters and runners alike spread out like a peat fire across good ground, quaking ground, low ground and high; and the bird-swept prairies rang with their chants. The best bows were drawn and the straightest arrows notched. Only one hunter, however, had an arrow with a cast-silver tip that had come over the sea from the island known as England—a silver arrow point given, they say, by the great queen herself. This was a thing that could, it was told, reach the heart of even the most charmed of lives.

And it happened that the swift white doe was chased from the rank grass of the shaky land; a bowstring's angry twang sent her flying on the north wind's breath. Through tangled wood and trailless bog, through morass and highland, she sped. And the myriad bowstrings made the sounds of harmless bees in the wake of her whiteness. She plunged on through the billows of the sound, reaching the sand hills of Roanoke. Here, she stood atop the ruins of the old fort, gray-logged and silvery-splintered, breathing the easternmost breeze from afar, panting, her small tongue flickering like a pink petal. Now, in the deep, wind-blown grass, Little Oak appeared, took aim at the glowing form before him, and let loose the fated bowstring that burned the air and sent the silver-headed arrow on an irretrievable mission. The beautiful sad-eyed doe leapt, heart pierced, into the air and sank desperately to the ground. Then Little Oak threw down his bow, ran to her side, lifted the head of snow, soft as a cloud, looked into the dying eyes, and saw, suddenly, the face of a pretty young woman, who, through dry, heart-spent lips, whispered her name, Virginia Dare, and died.

So goes the story. And the lost Virginia Dare, what of her? Did she die in infancy? Did her child bones mingle with the dust of her legend and blossom in the wild roses of Croatan? Did she ever grow to womanhood? Did she end her life in whatever darkness that still enshrouds the lost pale colony that vanished into the deep mists? Whatever trace is left, the ghost rustle of the white fawn in the eastern light of dawn is here in these fragmentary words, for, as they say, the dead will not give up their dead, and the story will always remain a mystery.

BOOK 15

White Eyebrows, His Run for Life

HOW A WHITE MAN IS CHALLENGED TO RUN AGAINST
THE BEST RUNNERS OF THE NORTHERN PLAINS AND
HOW HIS OWN LEGEND, FORETOLD IN THE TALES OF
THE PEOPLE, BECOMES A SACRED TRIBUTE TO THE
MYTH OF THE WHITE WARRIOR

O U may have heard about the pale-skinned man who could outrun the swiftest warrior. The story is true: He really could outrun them. It would be hard to say, though, whether his speed or his legend traveled faster among the people of the high plains, the craggy mountains. His name was John Colter, but the people called him White Eyebrows. They say he once ran one hundred and fifty miles, half-naked, pursued by a few hundred Blackfeet warriors.

Autumn in the Three Forks was when it happened. He and his friend John Potts were setting beaver traps. Far off in the haze of the firs, they heard a magpie's comic shriek, cut off, suddenly, by something unseen. Neither man paid much attention to it. Then came muffled thunder; the ridge above the treetops rumbled. "Buffalo?" Potts called to his friend, but Colter, listening, did not answer, for the next thing he knew, they were surrounded by a thousand warriors.

Colter stood stock-still, the green water of the Three Forks playing upon his knees. Although four hundred arrow-cocked bows were drawn in their direction, foolish Potts pulled up his long rifle. There came a singing of feathers. Potts sank to his knees, then stumbled forward, saying, "John, I'm dead." He dropped facefirst into the rusty water of the river.

Colter knew what was next: lank feathers dancing on black hair in

235

sunlight, rivers of loose hair, clothes of deerskin and trader's cloth—blanketed, banded, breechclouted men—indeed, more warriors than Colter had ever seen in one place before. He held still as the chief came forward, knife flashing in his hand. Some smooth swipes cut the leather clothes from Colter's back, letting the cold autumn air onto his bare skin. Shorn of clothes, he was left standing, the semblance of a breechclout at his waist, the hacked-off remains of his leggings.

Then he was asked if he could run, and, knowing this might be his only hope, he shook his head, said no. "Now," the chief said, "go now!" And Colter leaned forward and broke into a wild sprint, his speed, even at the outset, surprising him. As he ran along the river, he heard the blankets thudding down, the flap of leggings behind him; then the earth began to tremble with the footfalls of so many men. Opening his stride, he surprised himself again by thrusting forward, but now his feet were furred with prickly pear spines and his chest was on fire. A quick over-the-shoulder glance told the tale: The best were behind him, close behind; the heavier-footed ones were still a cloud of dust back at the fork.

To outrun the lean wolves at his rear, he would have to outlast the pain, press on with an even harder sprint, grind down the pads of his pursuers. Already he felt his fading stamina, the burned metal of his dry mouth, the beating, tolling bell of his heart, the burn rising, boiling up in his chest. He was going too fast, yet any slower and he could not hope to live.

So it is with some men: They fix their eye on a goal, with no hope given, and reach it by sheer will. He, seeing the leafy gold of cottonwoods up ahead, made for them, turned them to a compass, merged his mind with those October leaves, so that, wholly focused, he forged on with renewed speed. The Blackfeet runners saw his restored gait. Their own bodies streamed with sweat as the pale white warrior whom they called Seekheeda began to gain ground. The moment before, the lead runner thought he was going to close the distance; now he was not so sure.

Ahead—but not by much—Colter forged his second or third wind spirit, pulling out even more. The Blackfeet lead runner felt his companions, hanging doggedly at his elbow, start to fade, drop back. No mortal man can run this way for long, thought the runner, his eye trained on Colter's shoulders, which still showed no sag. However, it was not his upper body that would fail him; it was his damaged right leg, where a twice-fractured bone had not fully mended—a result of his last bittersweet encounter with the Blackfeet people. The wound from last winter's musket ball might yet bring him down. However, the gold leaves up ahead had a hold of his mind, and his body, broken thing that it was, wasn't his to abuse or disabuse anymore. His stride, shortened now, turned ragged, began to look troubled. The wolf-gaited man behind him took notice of the limp and increased his speed. A blood song rang loud in his ear: Seekheeda would soon fall to his knife.

Colter, though, had urged his body beyond the boundary of pain, had gone to that sanctuary where time falls flat, where things take on a strange light. A gout of blood came out of his nose, but he did not notice. It fountained down his face, across his chest. An anvil lay on his breast; he hardly felt it. The blood coursed, but so did the man, running mad, trailing rags of red spit on the wind. Soon, soon, thought the Blackfeet behind the staggering white man.

Now Colter felt it coming, a great shadow across the sun. He was in that separate land where the mind knows no master. The gold trees gone, the sun gone, the willows gone, he imagined himself flying purple through the winter trees on the black wings of a hawk. His legs came up under him, tucked into his feathers. The sudden cramp set free, he cried out as he hatcheted the wind with his darkened wings, hooking into a cloud. And then came the settling feeling of the long glide down the golden afternoon.

Then his groping fingers clawed him free of his dream. He was on his hands and knees, dragging himself into the river of the Three Forks. Looking up, he saw a flock of red-winged blackbirds chuckling in the cottonwood leaves. Over his shoulder, one runner was still coming on; in back of him, a brown fog of dust-flung footracers, the numbing race still going on. All right then, Colter said to himself, I'll be a water snake this time, and he slid on his belly down the muddy bank and into the coils of the swift-running river. Thus ended John Colter's race for life. They never caught him, though the chase went on for several more days and nights. He ran, so the people say, out of time and into his own legend, to the sacred place where a man becomes more than a man.

The gods do not favor the color of the skin, but the color of the blood; and all blood, the world over, is red. Once, they say, the people found the huge body of a man preserved in a southern swamp. Long the man had been dead, but you could clearly see who he was from what he had once been. His hands were larger than the largest man alive; his skin, neither dark nor light, was some cross color that shared something of the two. Whoever or whatever he was, his race was run; he was made for legend: "Once a god dropped down out of the sky, a god unmet by mortals—"

So it was with John Colter.

The Day When the Dream Was Done

OF THE TIME OF GRIEF, WHEN ALL THAT IS GREAT IS
COUNTED AS LOST, AND OF THE FIRST PEOPLE OF
TURTLE ISLAND, WHO ARE WITNESS TO THE BEGINNING
OF THE END OF THEIR SUN DREAM OF GREATNESS

THERE came a day when the people learned to fear, rather than revere, the ones they called the whites. In the beginning, the people of the plain, the people of the sea, the people of the lake, the people of the river, the people of the valley, the people of the desert, and the people of the mountain were one people, the first people, the people. They shared their place under the sun with their brothers and sisters of Turtle Island; they fought, as children fight, over the use of a stream or valley, sometimes over the possession of the good land itself. But they did not seek to destroy one another, merely to have what they wanted; and so, having driven off their foes, they let them live. After their claim was made and the battle was won, the winners stayed and the losers left. So it was; so, they said, it would always be.

But now came the time that we speak of: white men, wagon men, horse-and-buggy men, traders, trundlers, settlers, soldiers, gold-gleaners, governors, madmen and sane. They arrived with the absolute faith in their right to go anywhere they wanted to go and to do anything they wanted to do. And there came a time like the Ant Wars. Only now, these two-legged builder ants were followed by blue-coated soldier ants, killers whose purpose was to destroy the enemy, whatever enemy it was. And there was no surrender; there was no pity. These were not ants—for if they had been, Sun Father would have made another flood, and the land would thus have been cleansed of them.

So the first people rose and fought for what was theirs: the sacred flesh of Mother Earth. And her flesh bled, as well as theirs, and no one won in any of these shameful contests, but the dead were piled high and always, with each sun, there came more of what had come the sun before. And the lodges of the pale-skinned people were now more numerous than the holes of the prairie dog, the houses of the beaver, or even the hills of the ant. In nothing were the pale-skinned people more skilled than in the making of lodges—and children. The more lodges there were, the more children they had to fill them. And the lodges got bigger, and so did the children. But the people, the first people, grew fewer and their children decreased in number.

The Vision of Geronimo

IN WHICH THE ONE FOUGHT THE MANY FOR THE FEW,
AND IN WHICH POWER IS GIVEN TO THIS SINGULAR
WARRIOR WHOSE NAME, GERONIMO, IS SYNONYMOUS
WITH COURAGE AND WHOSE UNWILLINGNESS TO GIVE
UP IN SPITE OF THE ODDS AGAINST HIM MAKE HIM,
SOME SAY, THE FINAL WARRIOR

THE sun was bright one spring afternoon when the people of the desert, those known as the Apache, made camp along a narrow stream. Soon the men would return, but now, in the midday sun, there were children playing and women making preparations for the evening meal. Frogs were singing downstream, where the water was slow; on the sandbanks, the women were cooking, calling softly to one another, and the children were splashing in the stream, laughing. Suddenly, the frogs stopped singing.

Along the ridge and up the river came the blue-coated soldiers, their horses making a *plosh* sound as their hooves chunked in the pebbly gravel of the sunlit stream. The shadows off the bluecoats were also blue, though a shade deeper, darker. The frogs and the children stopped singing, and it was as if a cloud had come over the sun and all life had stopped breathing.

What burbling noises burst from the mouths of babes, skewered on the bluecoats' swords? What shrieks were heard as young women, caught bathing downstream, were raped in the reeds? What elders were sabered, throats cut and bellies slit? What unborn children died in the dream of that dying day?

Darkness, darkening blood, the buzz song of flies, the buckskin doll caught up in a tiny dead fist—these were the things that met Geronimo's eye as he returned to camp.

He saw, he wept, and he could not stop the tears that stained his cheeks. The sky was blue, as always; the black hawk sang a song to

241

her young; the kingfisher flashed in the sun. What was wrong? The world was the same. Mothers were caring for their young; there were songs and sunlight. What was wrong?

Standing alone on the ridge, looking down on the dead, Geronimo saw Sun Father, who said to him, "What you look upon is shadow; come out of the shadow world and into the sun so that I may see you."

Geronimo did as he was bidden, and Sun Father stood before him, a man like any other, but his face and body, the edges of him, were cast in shadow, while the core of him, from head to foot, was lit up like the sun itself.

"I see," Sun Father said, "that you possess strong legs and that you have a brave heart for fighting, and that your arms are strong. Yet I wonder if you live in shadow or sun."

Then Geronimo saw the other thing who was standing there beside Sun Father. She, he could not see well at all, for she was of shadows made; her dress and moccasins grew out of the earth, but the upper part of her came from the darkness of the center of mountains, the heart of the earth. She appeared round. She was corn turned in a heavy wind; she was the smoke of twilight settling on the shoulders of a hill; she was the feeling that comes before, and after, the rain.

"She who bore you will bear you up," Sun Father said, "and I who forged you will give you power."

Clear was the voice in his ear, strong the spirit body that grew in him on that lonely death ridge. Thus far, he had learned to love; now he would learn to hate. And the hate he saw all around him became his calling. It would rise, as the spirit of flame rises before the wind. Geronimo, the bonfire that blew across the desert sand, a storm of flame that did not stop until he sang his death song. The words are these: "I am waiting for the change."

The War of the Plains

HOW THE FIGHT BETWEEN WHITE AND RED COMES TO
A CLOSE ON THE PLAINS, THE GREAT PLATED SHELL OF
THE TURTLE, AND HOW THE VOICES OF HONOR RISE
ABOVE THE BATTLEFIELD IN A SONG OF NAMES: RED
CLOUD, CRAZY HORSE, BLACK KETTLE, SPOTTED TAIL,
SITTING BULL

A N D with their singing, the people drew their numbers into a whirl-wind across the tall grass of the four directions. They talked peace; they talked war. Red Cloud of the Sioux said, "We will die where our fathers died." And the bluecoat guns, which spoke twice, talked all night and made a level band of leaden hail. Moving along the skylines, the night parties, warriors, made the cries of wolves. At dawn, a Sioux man-woman, wearing a blanket over his head, rode like black lightning over the low hills, catching, as he said, soldiers in his hands, zigzagging through their camp, counting coups.

However, a commanding officer of the white brigade commented, "With eighty men, I could ride through the Sioux nation." And he tried on Lodge Trail Ridge, under curdled winter clouds, as the cold air turned colder and the people—Sioux, Cheyenne, Arapaho—grew out of the rocks into the fighting shapes of dusk. Blood froze, and the blue-coated men fell like the slant-arrowed snow, and the warriors picked up their dead and rode away into the powdery black night.

But now the forts were ever more prevalent and the buffalo herds ever more scant; and the warriors moved like dark shadows across the canyons and basins, the rough rock country where the guns that once spoke twice were now given to babble. The warriors went down like blades of grass before a great blast of winter wind. The white man's medicine, pouring in from the east, was strong, but only because there was so much of it, an endless supply.

Red Cloud lived to see the white man's words spelled out in his

243

black ink's blood: "From this day forward all war between the parties
to this agreement shall forever cease . . . so long as the grass shall
grow." But the grass, stunted by the thunder of guns, died. Black
Kettle of the Cheyenne heard of the gold-haired longhair, the blue-
coated warrior named Custer, sent by the White Father to protect the
interests of his people. But Black Kettle wanted no part of war, choos-
ing to camp under a great cottonwood by the ice-skinned Washita.
Making pemmican and dressing hides for winter wear, the old chief
was suddenly full of foreboding. A squaw cried on the pony trail
above the narrow river: "Soldiers!" The dark memory of Sand Creek
came to him—his first wife dead from that pitiless massacre. Came
then the trumpet charge, the shrill blasts ripping the morning air,
the muffled drumming of hooves on snow, the silver sabers gleaming
in the sun. Black Kettle, gut-shot, shoulder-shot, helpless, fell into
the icy water, his new wife dead in the drifted snow. And the tepees
were knocked down, all the buffalo meat and hide burned, and the
people's horses put to death, screaming. The gold-haired saber
leader, Custer, went up in rank, and his war promise to make peace
went on, as before, with the drawn saber as his signature.

Now as the necessary trinity of buffalo, water, and grass was less
and less, the people moved about, in hiding. And always, the white
man was in abundance. Red Cloud said, "The white children have
surrounded me and left me nothing but an island. Once we were
strong, but now we are melting like snow on a hillside."

Now Spotted Tail said, "The white man is not content with our
grass, water, and buffalo; now he wants the very earth we stand on."
So the warriors counted fewer coups but made better war. Sitting
Bull of the Sioux said, "You scare all the buffalo away. I want you to
turn back from here. I am your friend." The blue-coated men laughed
at his note and oiled their guns. The Sioux moved up into the Grandmother Land called Canada.

Those who stayed saw the last hunting grounds grow into the dead
path of the iron road, from which the whites could shoot buffalo,
saving only the tongue, while enjoying the comfort of plush velvet
cushion. Crazy Horse of the Sioux knew the time had come, and,
offering his left hand to a blue-coated commander, he said, "Friend,
I shake with this hand because my heart is on this side: I want this
peace to last forever." The man named for the wild horse that dashed

through his camp on the day of his birth was then put into the guardhouse, where he fought to get free one last time. He was held back by one of his own chiefs, Little Big Man. Still, blood gushed from his heart side, and Crazy Horse, the man who defeated Custer, was suddenly dead. And with the death of Crazy Horse, the war of the plains died. From this time on, the people walked the white man's road. Sitting Bull, on that road, sang one last song: "A warrior I have been. Now it is all over. A hard time I have."

BOOK 16

The Story of Messenger

The Prayer of Black Elk

The Story of Messenger

OF A MESSENGER AMONG THE PEOPLE—CALLED
MESSENGER—WHO SPEAKS OF SOMETHING NEW, A
MESSIAH WHO APPEARS OUT OF THE ASHES OF DEFEAT
AND WHO PROMISES TO DELIVER THE PEOPLE TO
GLORY

H E word went round and round that there was a messiah upon the land; it was just as the prophecy had said. The great herds of buffalo were going and the tall grass on which they lived was being taken up by the whites from the east. However, everyone said that a good wind was coming and there was a way to dance back the buffalo. The sacred ground would return again when the messenger from the north brought word of the messiah from the south. This, then, is Messenger's story, a Kiowa whose vision of redemption rivaled that of Sitting Bull.

"That year, the Sioux prophet, Sitting Bull, came down to the grassy plains to talk to us. There was a great gathering from the north. Altogether we were Cheyenne, Arapaho, Sioux, Caddo, Wichita, Kiowa, and Apache. We remained together for about two weeks, dancing every night until the sun rose. I remember one night when we were all gathered together. Sitting Bull said he had something to show us. He stepped into the center of the dancing circle. He walked up to a Sioux woman, passing an eagle feather in front of her face. The moment she saw the feather, she fell to the earth and lay asleep. Then Sitting Bull passed among the people gathered there, and, one by one, he made them fall with his feather. And they lay still on the dancing ground, all of them stretched out, their eyes closed as if asleep.

249

"I was not one of them, so I saw this with my own eyes. Then, many hours later, each one woke up, slowly, stretching as if from a deep sleep. I heard what the people said. They said they had gone on to the Spirit World, where they had met their dear departed families and friends. In the Spirit World, they hunted buffalo, as in other days, and they sported on their ponies and there was plenty to eat for all. After they woke up, they were sorry to have come back. The people made songs to sing about the good remembered days with their families in the Spirit World.

"Sometime after the night Sitting Bull showed his medicine, Left Hand, of the Arapaho, went to him for advice. 'What should we do?' he asked. 'The whites want to buy up all of our land.'

"Sitting Bull answered, 'The people are hungry. Tell them to sell their land to the whites. Soon the messiah will come and return your land to you.'

"The messiah, we learned later, was a Paiute priest named Wovoka. Some of the people had already been to visit him, and they had returned with magpie feathers, which they said were an important part of the Ghost Dance. When the white traders heard about this, they imported crow feathers and sold them to the people. I also heard that some of the people took the grass money paid to them by the cattlemen and bought the sacred red paint from Wovoka's desert country to use in the dances.

"It was around that time that I was given the name Messenger, because of something that happened. Like many other Kiowas, I began to have dreams and visions of the Spirit World. In one of these, I met four young women riding on horseback. I saw that their saddle pouches were full of wild plums. One of the women offered me one, but I was afraid to eat it because I knew that this same woman had died a few years earlier.

"I asked her if she knew any of my family, and she said she did. I was directed to a man who told me that next to his tepee were my relatives. As far as the eye could see, there was tepee after tepee; they had sprung up like blades of grass. When I went into the tepee he pointed to, I saw at once that it was just as he had said: My family was all in there—father, two brothers, and two sisters.

"They were very happy to see me and did not ask how I had come to be there. Instead, they offered me buffalo meat from a large kettle over the fire. They could see that I was afraid to eat it, and they urged me to smell the meat, saying that it was good and I would like it.

"In time, I became known for this vision, and for others that I had. And I was asked by the people to travel to the messiah and hear his words. I traveled by way of the iron road. At the Agency at Pyramid Lake, I got a wagon ride to the upper end of the Mason Valley. Not long after, we came to the small house of Wovoka, but I was told there that I must wait, that he was sleeping. I went away and returned the following day, and this time I was taken in to see him.

"He was lying down on the floor of the cabin, with a blanket covering his face. He was singing to himself. The room was bare and dusty. At last, Wovoka stopped singing and removed the blanket from his head. He was a dark man with small, pinched features. He did not smile or show in any way that he was pleased to see me or seek to know that I had come such a long way to see him. 'What can I do for you?' the messiah asked.

"This I felt was a strange question. Did the messiah not know the reason for the visit? Was he making a joke? His face was most serious.

" 'I would like to travel with you to the Spirit World,' I said.

" 'There is no Spirit World here,' he said.

" 'I would like to see my little child who died,' I told him.

"He stared at me.

" 'There are no spirit children here,' he said. 'Look around; see for yourself.'

"In the small dark room, he looked like a shadow. Hard times were upon the man, I felt. He did not look as happy and wise as my friends the Arapahos had said. He looked tired. And when I looked at his palms, I did not see the marks they had told me about, the scars of what they called the crucifixion. Not seeing the scars, I felt a heaviness in my heart. Even Red Robe, who had gone away, had the scars of his conviction. Wovoka looked empty, like something the wind had run through.

" 'Are you truly the messiah the people are talking about?' I asked.

" 'There is no other,' Wovoka replied crossly. Then he added, 'You tell your people to stop dancing the Ghost Dance. Tell them I say to do this.'

" 'Why should I do this?'

" 'I gave the Sioux the new dance. But they twist things, and make trouble. More trouble will come. Tell your people.'

"Then with a wave of his hand and pulling his blanket over his head, he dismissed me as if I were a white man. I went home and talked to the people and told them of Wovoka's wish. But even before I saw their faces, I knew it was all over for us, and even though the dreams kept coming to me, they were no longer important."

The Ghost Dance began with the Paviotso, a branch of the Paiutes of Nevada. The man imputed to be its founder, Jack Wilson, better known as Wovoka, mixed the prophecy of the wounded palms with the people's rituals. Medicine men like Sitting Bull sought redemption for all native people. But the ghost way of Wovoka frightened the whites. In the end, Sitting Bull himself was killed by his own people; his assassins having been paid by federal officers. After the Battle of Wounded Knee, the Ghost Dance died. And the voices around the camp fire no longer sang:

> I circle around
> The boundaries of the earth,
> Wearing long wing feathers
> As I fly, as I fly

With the death of the Ghost Dance and the leaders who had made it what it was, a dream, a vision, a promise of hope, the people drifted into a time of desolation. Now there was no past and no future. Their gods having deserted them, they resorted to the ills of the poisonous milk called firewater. Living in a present devoid of deities, crowded off their land and onto reservations, the people gave themselves up, turned their hopes in along with the tickets that entitled them to eat the meat of rotten cattle. The last buffalo drives were cattle hunts, and the old stringy steers were let loose to be run after with a whoop and a cry by old men who had grown up in the presence of endless herds of sacred buffalo. It was over, and even the dream of what it once had been was dying.

The Prayer of Black Elk

IN WHICH THE GREAT DREAMER BLACK ELK HAS A
DREAM OF UNITY, WHICH SEEKS TO BRING ALL COLORS
TOGETHER AND TO UNIFY ALL RACES IN A BOND OF
SPIRITUAL BEAUTY, AND OF THE DREAM'S FRAGILITY

THERE was a man, born in the Black Hills, whose thoughts reached far, to the gods of sky, earth, water, and fire, to the Maker himself, they say. And his mind, fired by his strong heart, looked on visions beyond mortal dreaming. All things he studied equally and well, and he brought home what he had learned. He sat among the people, teaching them what was worthy, and they listened in silence, wondering at his wisdom. He said, "If I should speak to you, there should be at least a little thunder and a little rain." And when he spoke, even in the season of drought, which was upon the people then, there came rain and the voice of thunder.

Now one time when he was very old and likewise very wise, he spoke to the Maker so that everyone could hear what he said. "Great Maker," he mourned, "pity us, your two-legged children, for we have suffered much and will do so again. The bluecoats drive us from our ancestral home; their governors give them gold stars for doing so. And who are we—your poor children—to stop them? We have tried, and they have sent thunder and lightning from the mouths of cannons. They have more than we have, for the clever arts are theirs; and ours are only what we know of this earth. Our spirit is strong, but they have things that obey their commands: guns, wagons, sabers, and all manner of weapons we have not even seen. Now you have made the good road and the road of difficulties, and we have crossed each in its proper time, and will again as the need arises.

"My grandfather, I forget nothing that you have made: the stars, the grasses, the two-leggeds, the four-leggeds, the winged ones, and those who crawl on many legs; all these and more, you have made You have given us the living water and the sacred bow, the wind and the herb, the power to heal and the healing, the daybreak star and the stone pipe, the sacred hoop of all nations and the tree soon to bloom. You have shown me and my kind the strangeness of the greening earth, the beauty of the mystery light all around us—but Grandfather, though you have given us so much, there is yet a little that we need, that we must ask you for. Let the buffalo come back Let the tree bloom. Let the bluecoat come no farther. I know in my heart that the heavens and all below them, earth and her creatures, all change, and we, part of creation's great hoop, must also suffer change.

"We are not bodies only, but, like the bird people, winged spirits as well, able to travel, as I have many times, to the cloud world and beyond. Grant that the violent winds of change withdraw that the treeless hills grow again, that the level plain again be furred with buffalo, that the air be free to breathe, that the ground swell with new grass for the calves of spring, that the strange forms that come in the dark of the moon come no more. Grant us the breath of life, as we have once known it—not as we know it not. We know that the stinging bee makes sweet honey, the dying worm turns into a beautiful butterfly, that frogs, once legless, learn at last to jump, that the rotted trunk gives way to seed, that the newborn eaglet, all feather and fluff, one day will seize the great snake by the neck and toss it above the clouds—all these things I know and re spect, and yet the change that comes, unknown and unexpected brings misery upon your children. Grandfather, if you give us noth ing else, give us sight; let us see what is happening to us. Let us no crawl blind like the worm. Give us your sacred sight, oh Grand father."

And thus the holy man's prayer ended, but they say he died un fulfilled, with tears in his eyes and heart. They say that he said a the end, as his eyes dimmed, "When I look back now from this high hill of my old age, I can still see the butchered women and children lying heaped and scattered all along the crooked gulch as plain as when I saw them with eyes still young. And I can see that something else died there in the bloody mud and was buried in the blizzard. A people's dream died there. It was a beautiful dream."

Epilogue

THERE, the work is done, the tale told. Hopefully, some part of it may endure beyond the fire cloud at dusk, the rumble of time's empty belly. The day comes when our life—whatever has blessed it—must suddenly, or slowly, end, the circle complete. But of this work, some echo may yet be heard, even after winter has caught the song maker and filled his heart with frost.

Character Key and Glossary

ABALONE GIRL: a first woman deity who resembles Eve. In her second incarnation, she becomes an earth-and-water deity whose nature is completely selfless.

ANIMAL PEOPLE: This may mean animals as well as insects.

BEAR WOMAN: spirit of the forest, guardian of those who are lost, traveling companion of Mother Earth.

BIRD WOMAN: also called Spruce Grouse, Grouse, Blue Grouse; mythical character of Northwest tribal peoples.

BLACK ELK: the Oglala Sioux visionary whose dream of tribal unity, nonviolent redemption for all Indian people, as well as white and Indian pacification, was destroyed by the Battle of Wounded Knee and the subsequent treatment of reservation-bound Indians.

BLUE RACER: benign serpent deity who marries a deity, Younger Sister, who is a representative of mortal women.

BREAD EATERS: *See* Pascagoula.

BUFFALO: To the Plains people, as well as many other tribes, the buffalo was not only a food source but a sacred being.

BUTTERFLY BOY: a witch, but a lovely, spell-casting one. His presence is both male and female; his beauty is thought to be vanity. The lore of this character comes from the southwestern tribes.

BUTTERFLY DANCER: Southwest canyon deity who symbolizes selfishness and nontribal participation.

COYOTE: trickster, storyteller, First Angry, leader and misleader, bringer of positive change, sexual miscreant, antagonist, and clown. His duties include bringing rain and assisting in childbirth.

CROOKED NOSE: a fictional tribe of the plains; they might, in the context of this book, have been called the Enemy People.

DEER BOY: a mortal who turns into a deer spirit.

259

ECHO: much-respected southwestern deity, one who confers kindness.

ELDER LIGHTNING: powerful deity of the sky; may be dangerous, threatening, and curative at the same time.

ELK BROTHER: For many tribes, Elk is a holy person equal to Bear, or even Eagle. His bugling mating song corresponds to the Pueblo red cedar love flute.

FEATHER: The feather is a metaphor for flight, a messenger to the spirit world.

FEMALE RAIN AND MALE RAIN: water deities. Female Rain is soft; Male Rain is hard.

FIRE SPIRIT: fire god of the northwestern woodlands.

FIRE-IS-GIVEN: a Crow warrioress from the early 1800s. Actual accounts of her prowess exist.

FIRST ANGRY: *See* Coyote.

FIRST HUNTER: a First Man deity who resembles Adam.

FIRST LIGHT AND MORNING GLOW: southwestern Pueblo sister deities.

FIRST MAN AND FIRST WOMAN: divine symbols of the presence of man and woman; also symbols of the first food, corn.

FIRST PEOPLE: guardians of water, air, and earth; insects, animals, and star people.

GILA MONSTER: First Medicine Man; great healer. He can also be a witch.

GREAT SNAKE: serpent deity; also plumed serpent, Quetzalcoatl. Too powerful, spiritually, to be totally benign; carrier of lightning.

GRIZZLY BEAR: a rough and often capricious animal person who, nevertheless, is a sizable leader of all animal people.

HAWK: This includes all hawk presences in the book. They are wise, frugal, watchful, unselfish guardians whose warrior nature is profoundly brave and protective.

HOLY PEOPLE: The deities are creatures (Coyote), men (two-leggeds), and insects (Locust), as well as plants (corn), and phenomena (rainbow).

JACK WILSON: also known as Wovoka. A Paiute from Nevada, he characterized the Native American prophecy of the coming of a "Red Jesus."

JOHN COLTER: also known as Seekheeda or White Eyebrows. He was an Early American trapper mythologized by Native Americans and European-Americans for his celebrated 150-mile run across the country of the Blackfeet in the early 1800s.

KACHINAS: the spirits that protect and guide mortal beings.

KEEPERS OF THE CLIFF: a Crow legend retold from an original tale told by Plenty Coups, the great nineteenth-century Crow chief.

LISTENER: the first tribal person, similar to First Man; like Adam.

MAGPIE: One of the many Native American tricksters, Magpie is an audacious, clever, fun-loving, trick-playing bird. He has been known to hoodwink Coyote by appealing to Coyote's vanity. Some tribes consider the Magpie's white and blue-black feathers sacred and use them in ceremonials.

MAKER: God, also called Great Maker.

MIST WOMAN: feminine deity who represents wetness in all forms: rain, snow, mist, water.

MOON WATER BOY: warrior son of Sun Father; feminine presence; that is, more cautious, essentially wiser, perhaps less "heroic."

MOSQUITO WOMAN: primary woman; like Eve. The legend holds that those mortals who refused to hear the warning of Small Spotted Frog were changed into mosquitoes. This "good" mosquito becomes wife to Listener, the first mortal father.

MOTHER EAGLE AND FATHER EAGLE: the two most powerful spiritual presences on earth, second only to such powers as Sun Father and Mother Earth. Nearly all tribes venerate the eagle as a symbol of holiness and perfection.

MOTHER EARTH: earth deity and feminine presence, mother figure for all living things; wife of Sun Father; mother of Right-Handed Sun and Moon Water Boy.

MOUNTAIN AROUND WHICH MOVING WAS DONE: symbolic center of the earth; the heart of creation of the surface world.

MOUNTAIN OLD MAN: primary mountain deity; spiritual adviser to mortal and deity alike.

MOUNTAIN SINGING: mortal chief who becomes a mountain deity. He is in love with Mist Woman.

MOUNTAIN WING: good mountain spirit; protective of mortals.

OLD WOMAN MOON: comparable to the man in the moon in female form; a Cassandra, a prophetess. Not to be confused with the light-giving moon itself, which is often characterized in Native American mythology as a pale stone, sometimes abalone, pearl, or shell, in general.

OWL BOY: misbegotten child of the marriage of a mortal man and an animal person, Bear Woman. He teaches us propriety, though his presence is almost always fearsome and death-related.

PASCAGOULA: The Pascagoula tribe, once residing at the mouth of Pascagoula Bay, Mississippi, were thought to have been absorbed by the Biloxi Indians.

PIERCED NOSES: the Nez Percé tribe of the northwest.

PLENTY COUPS: the great Crow chief who lived during the 1800s.

POLLEN: The sacred pollen of the corn plant is used by a variety of tribes in their ceremonials.

PORCUPINE: an animal person who has as much wisdom as he has quills.

PUEBLO: The word *pueblo* was first used by the Spanish conquistadores to designate the Indians they found living in villages of mud, sand, and stone.

RAVEN: trickster, shapeshifter, storyteller character similar to Coyote.

RIGHT-HANDED SUN: warrior son of Sun Father, masculine presence; hero twin of much magnitude.

ROCK WATER BOY: brother to Morning Glow/Wood Rat Girl. The misconduct he initiates brings about a great change, creating what are known today as kachinas, the spirits that protect and guide mortal beings.

ROLLING THUNDER: based upon tales told by the great Crow chief Plenty Coups, 1800s.

SEEKHEEDA: *See* John Colter.

SEES-IN-THE-NIGHT: youthful initiate, mortal, southern or northern Plains warrior from the 1800s.

SERPENT MAN: the one who chases Slim Girl; also known as Handsome Young Man; a witch, the evil twin of a dangerous serpent deity.

SHADOW WIFE: ghost of the northwestern woodlands.

SHAPESHIFTER: a selfish deity who can change shape at will. He is reformed by First Man to become Guardian of the Game, Keeper of Animals.

SITTING BULL: The Sioux medicine man and warrior whose spiritual powers and warrior tendencies frightened whites during the last days of the Plains Indian resistance in America in the late 1800s.

SLIM GIRL: mortal woman, southern tribal person.

SMALL SPOTTED FROG: water deity, deliverer of mortals; comparable to Noah.

SPIDER WOMAN: Often thought to be related to Mother Earth, Spider Woman is also a skylike deity because of her web powers. She is both compassionate and, at times, fearsome.

STONE GIANTS, CACTUS MONSTERS, FLYING DEVIL BIRDS, ETC.: All monsters in this book are the offspring of sexual misconduct. Their spilled blood makes the badlands; stone giants, once felled, turn into sacred mountains.

SUN FATHER: sky deity, masculine presence, father figure for all living things; husband to Mother Earth; father of Right-Handed Sun and Moon Water Boy. He has affairs with other beings, as well, and fathers other children.

SUN HORSE: One of five sacred horses belonging to Sun Father; in this text characterized as Dawnway, Noonway, Nightway.

TALKING GOD GRANDFATHER: deity of great beneficence to mortals. He acts as an intermediary for them; he also confers the power of speech upon the people.

THE PEOPLE: This may mean animal, insect, or human. In the beginning, all three were combined; their presences were not separate.

THUNDER OLD MAN: spirit of Thunder.

TOUCHING WATER: an eighteenth-century Pascagoula (Bread Eater) woman who resisted the spirit of the white missionary who came to convert them to the "Religion of the Cross."

TURTLE DANCER: a chief based upon a Cheyenne warrior who distinguished himself in the 1800s.

TURTLE PEOPLE: also Star People. Thought to be "terrapins from the heavens" by certain southern tribes. They are the very essence of wisdom.

TWO-LEGGED PEOPLE: This means only humans; however, in the beginning, four-footed animals were thought to walk on two legs, and so were human, as well as animal, representatives.

VIRGINIA DARE: first known girl child born of white settlers on Roanoke Island in the early seventeenth century.

WATER MONSTER: water deity, both male and female, depending upon the myth; often aggressive and unruly.

WEASEL: untrained, unthinking, unpropitiating mortal character.

WHITE BUFFALO CALF: based upon the life and tributes of Plenty Coups, 1800s.

WIND PEOPLE: many and various, they often give aid to mortals, especially Little Wind, who whispers in people's ears.

WOLF EYES: symbolic of the Apache people.

WOOD RAT GIRL: Morning Glow after Mother Earth changed her into a rodent.

WORLD CHANGE: the millennium; the time foretold in prophecy of Native American resurrection, the coming of an "Indian Christ"; the return of all lands; the dancing back of the buffalo; the appearance on earth of paradise.

WOUNDED KNEE: Most historians agree that the outcome of the massacre of Native Americans at Wounded Knee Creek in the late 1800s drew the final curtain on the drastic events that permanently confined Indians to reservation life.

WOVOKA: *See* Jack Wilson.

ZIGZAG: lightning.

About the Author

GERALD HAUSMAN began his Native American studies nearly thirty years ago at New Mexico Highlands University. There, living with the Navajo, he began to study *The Ways*, a cycle of creation myths that are used in the healing practice of medicine men. Hausman's close association with Navajo friends in the mid-sixties led him to publish his first translation of their myths, *Sitting on the Blue-Eyed Bear: Navajo Myths and Legends* (Lawrence Hill & Co., 1975).

From that time to the present, Gerald Hausman has gathered hundreds of Native American tales from all parts of the country. He has written more than a dozen books about Native American culture and has lectured and told stories at major universities and high schools throughout the United States. Most notably, he has done readings at St. John's College (Santa Fe), Harvard University, Queen's College, the Berkshire Playhouse, the Boston Public Library, the Seattle Academy of the Arts, the Omega Institute, and the Living Desert Museum. In addition, he has done storytelling on National Public Radio and Pacifica Broadcasting.

Mr. Hausman's recently published *Turtle Island Alphabet: A Lexicon of Native American Symbols and Culture* (St. Martin's Press, 1992) was selected by *American Bookseller* as one of the twenty best Native American titles of that year. Highly acclaimed by reviewers, the book has been called a classic study in which "Hausman honors Native American philosophy and spirituality even as he reveals it."

Gerald Hausman's work with children has been honored by a citation from Children's Protective Services and the Massachusetts Society for the Prevention of Cruelty to Children. He is the author of two books for children: *Turtle Island ABC*, illustrated by Barry and Cara

Moser (HarperCollins, 1994), and *Coyote Walks on Two Legs*, illustrated by Floyd Cooper (Philomel, 1994). In addition, he has recorded five audio books of Native American legends for all ages: *Navajo Nights, Stargazer, Native American Animal Stories, Turtle Island Alphabet,* and *Ghost Walk.*